A BREATH OF SUNLIGHT

SYDNEY
WINWARD

A BREATH OF SUNLIGHT

SUNLIGHT AND SHADOWS BOOK 1

A Breath of Sunlight

COPYRIGHT © 2021 Sydney Winward

Cover Designed by MiblArt

Published by Silver Forge Books

Trade Paperback ISBN 978-1-7374854-1-4

Digital ISBN 978-1-7374854-0-7

www.sydneywinward.com

For my husband who has been such a huge support along every step of the way. I couldn't have done this without you!

T oday was the day the king of the fae was to choose his bride.

Sunshine rained down from pink-lined clouds like drops of gold. It glistened and sparkled and beamed, its energy strong on the summer solstice in the Sun Kingdom of Heulwen. Laughter rang out in the castle courtyard as men and women alike from all over the kingdom gathered for the upcoming festivities. Many stood near the large, circular fountain while others conversed on a well-manicured lawn. Golden ribbons stretched from pillar to pillar while flowers of garlands, wreaths, and bouquets littered the large area.

Calle (K-ah-l) Everdon wrung his hands, pacing back and forth beside the window. Sunshine filtered through the glass pane, and while he usually considered it a welcoming companion, it glanced right off his skin as if sensing his anxious energy.

He gazed out at the women below as they entered the castle. Many wore crowns of flowers. Their emotions lay transparent on their faces. Lips twisted with anxiety. Eyebrows furrowed with both worry and determination. Eyes brightened with hope.

Calle ran an anxious hand over the scratchy stubble on his face. All the unmarried women were to attend the celebration.

All of them.

On cue, his sweetheart, Nyana, slipped through the door, a comb placed in a simple blonde bun. Her light blue dress was plain and unadorned—a similar style to a servant's—unlike her usual clothing.

She rushed into his arms, and he clung tightly to her as if she might be yanked out of his life at any moment.

At the thought, he clung tighter.

"Calle," she murmured as she pushed him away to hold him at arm's length. He reluctantly obliged. Her long, gentle fingers smoothed each eyebrow, his high cheekbones, and finally lovingly traced the long points of his fae ears. "Don't fret over this. Everything will turn out fine."

"How do you know?" He searched her blue eyes for a sliver of truth within their depths. "How do you know my brother won't choose you?"

"Because I have taken every precaution possible to avoid his notice. I look plain, don't I?"

She smiled brightly, her aura radiant as she turned in a full circle. A lump formed in his dry throat. "No," he rasped. "You could never look plain."

He grabbed her hand and pulled her closer until their foreheads touched. An ache of longing solidified in his gut. "I beg you, Nyana. Run away with me. Leave all this behind."

The tension in the air thickened, slicing through the excited laughter coming from outside. Unease churned within him, and only increased tenfold at her answer. "You know we cannot run. You are a prince, Calle. You have duties to your people. Running today of all days would mean treason on both our heads."

"But I can't lose you."

"And you won't," she whispered, cradling his face. "I won't stand out amongst hundreds of other women. He won't single me out. He won't pick me."

"*I* would pick you." He squeezed her shoulders and gazed at her with a serious expression. "You know he takes everything I want."

"But he doesn't know about us, and he won't until after he has chosen his bride."

An easier breath filled his lungs, and he let it out slowly. She was right. He was paranoid, and rightly so. He and Nyana had only dared to court in secret—without his brother's knowledge. He couldn't bear to lose her. It would break him.

Her soothing touch moved to his neck-length red-brown hair. Each stroke of her fingers cooled the burning anxiety rising within him.

"I wish I could heal you in here," she said, placing her hand over his heart after a few moments of comfortable silence. "But I am not capable of magic like you."

Not all Sun Fae were capable of magic, like Nyana and Calle's older brother, Liam. Liam overcompensated for his lack of talent with his cruelty and unending jealousy. They were always at odds with one another.

Calle grimaced and rubbed the scar over his gold-tattooed wrist where Liam had sliced him to the bone during a fit of anger. Heulwen's skilled healers had saved his hand, but only just. Perhaps "at odds" was too tame a term for their relationship.

"Is your hand bothering you today?" she asked, a frown on her pretty face.

He shook his head, his eyebrows furrowing at the twelve-pointed Heulwen scar tattoo. It gleamed beneath the sunlight like golden lava. "Just trapped in the past. Promise me, Nyana," he glanced nervously toward the door as if someone in the hallway might overhear their hushed conversation, "stay out of Liam's view. He'll find a way to take you. I know he will."

"I promise." She pressed a lingering kiss to his lips before giving him yet another radiant smile. "And after this is all over, we can court in the open."

Golden streams of magic flowed out of his fingertips like a gentle river. He coaxed the magic until it formed the shape of a flower. He tucked the flower into her hair, knowing she'd take it out before anyone else noticed. "I'm looking forward to the day."

4

Their hands slid out of each other's in farewell. His gaze lingered on her long after she left. The heat slowly left the room as if a cloud blocked out her warm presence. A chill shook him to the bones—one consisting of relentless dread. Deep in his gut, his magic churned with trepidation. Something didn't feel right.

Taking a deep breath calmed his overbearing nerves. He straightened his clothing and exited the small drawing room in the east wing of the castle. Servants bustled past him with food piled high on golden platters for the summer solstice celebrations. The scents of cheese, wild boar, and spiced wine didn't entice him, but rather drew anxiety further out of his core.

He greeted many people by name on his way, until his friend, Joel, fell into step beside him. His brown hair fell across his forehead, his green eyes seeing far more than one expected. He possessed sun magic, but his came in the form of music. He could charm any animal into submission or strike peace in a room with only a few notes. An artist at heart with his head forever in the clouds.

"I've figured it out," Joel said without preamble as he flipped through a book filled with notes in his nearly indecipherable handwriting. "Liam has a very small chance of picking Nyana to become—"

"Shh!" Calle hissed as he pushed his friend into the shadows, only to suck in a pained breath when the action sent a jolt of agony through his wrist. He cradled his hand to his chest as he glanced each way down the hallway, but no one appeared to have heard the comment. "You know you can't say her name. Not yet."

Joel scrunched his eyebrows together, his fingers resting on the flute tied to his belt as if ready to draw it and use it as a weapon. "One song, and I think I can hide her from his view."

With a sigh, Calle shook his head. His entire body was both weary to the bone and fully alert. "Liam has his own disenchanters. It will only draw more notice."

His wrist still throbbed as they continued down the hallway, following hundreds of others into a vast courtyard. The music grew louder with each step, as did the number of guards. Fae guards wore the kingdom's colors—red and gold— on a generic uniform. However, surrounding Liam at the top of the steps...

The royal palace guards stood alert, each harpy wearing gold armor and a red cape over one shoulder with the Heulwen emblem on their breast. Their wings were tucked neatly behind their backs, but Calle had seen those wings unfurl faster than one could blink. Harpies were dangerous, but he counted himself lucky they served the royal family. On the day of a harpy's birth, they were sworn into a blood oath to protect the royal family of the Sun Kingdom to their very last breath.

Each of the harpies—both men and women—bowed to him as he approached and created a path for him to join Liam's side. Joel found a place on the other side of the courtyard near the musicians.

Calle straightened his crown and smoothed his clothing as he looked over the crowd. Laughter and radiant, excited smiles had joined the music. He marveled at how many women were in attendance, each competing to stand out from the crowd. Some wore their hair down around their shoulders. Others wore crowns of flowers or sunlight. But none were as beautiful as the woman who held his heart.

Releasing a deep breath of relief, his shoulders relaxed. There were far too many choices for Liam to notice Nyana.

He quickly spotted her small frame in a group of five other women. Her gentle features were pulled into an anxious strain, her mouth pinched. They made eye contact across the courtyard but glanced away just as fast.

"You seem nervous, Calle," Liam chuckled beside him, and he jumped at the sudden, unwelcome intrusion. It took all his self-control not to glance back in Nyana's direction.

"I'm simply curious about which one of these lovely women you will choose for your wife," he replied in a steady voice. His mouth twitched as he feigned amusement. "I can't help but wonder who will be left for me."

Liam clapped him on the back a bit harder than a friendly pat. "You will get your turn when you turn twenty-one next year. But the question is...will you choose beauty or an advantageous match?"

The vein in his neck pulsed with every pounding heartbeat even as he gave a nonchalant shrug. The Everdon royal family had chosen their spouses this way for many generations, and even though their parents had both passed, he and Liam continued the tradition. In the past, women already a part of the court had been chosen, but every once in a while, a beauty from an outlying village would turn an eye.

"I suppose I will find out when the time comes."

Relax, he ordered his body. It refused to cooperate.

He eyed the sword, which had been directed at him more than once, tied to Liam's belt. At one time, he'd wielded a greatsword himself, but since the "accident", magic was his only weapon.

It churned within him, begging to be released.

He reined it in.

"I'll get straight to the point," Liam said as he turned slowly, a dark glint in his cobalt-green eyes. "Today is an important day. If you so much as step out of line once, I will show no mercy."

A harpy guard beside him, Avonia, shifted her unique white wings with a golden shimmer, but otherwise kept her eyes forward and a hand on her sword. She and her husband, Typheal, were good friends of his. They'd had a daughter once named Scarlett, but she had been abducted on her first birthday fourteen years ago. He remembered the panic and absolute terror of the event. Her parents still grieved the loss to this day.

Calle flexed his injured hand as he nodded half-heartedly. He would die before he let Liam anywhere near Nyana. He hoped it wouldn't escalate to blows between him and his brother.

As if appeased, Liam's smile returned as he scanned the crowd. His gaze stopped on...

No...

But the look had been so fleeting, and it could have been anyone in Nyana's group.

Uneasiness knocked the breath out of him. He sucked in a gulp of air, wishing to hold onto something to steady himself.

Liam's grin grew wide as he spotted someone in the crowd. He jogged down the stone steps to greet them, leaving him with half the harpy warriors while the other half followed. Avonia and Typheal moved to stand on either side of him. Their presence helped calm the storm raging within him.

"We won't let him lay a finger on you," Avonia murmured, her eyes hard. Typheal nodded in agreement.

"You must." His throat bobbed up and down as he swallowed. Finally, he tore his gaze away from his brother's back to look at the two people who had been like family for as long as he remembered. "I know something bad is going to happen. I can feel it in my gut. I couldn't live with myself if something happened to you two."

Typheal answered this time, the natural golden strands in his brown hair glimmering beneath the afternoon rays. "We may be blood bound to both you and the king, but we are loyal to you. Whatever happens…we are with you."

He swallowed again, grateful for their undying loyalty.

He cast another glance in Nyana's direction. She turned as if feeling his gaze on her and placed her hand against her heart. *I love you*, the gesture said. He raised a hand to do the same, but someone clamped their fingers around his wrist.

Pain shot up his arm and through his hand, enough to nearly buckle his knees. He sucked in a breath and barely held in a cry.

"Come," Liam said as he tugged him down the steps. "There are several people I want to introduce you to."

Pain pulsed through Calle's wrist with each beat of his heart. The day passed agonizingly slowly as young ladies captured every moment of Liam's attention. Music and laughter made a mockery of the rainclouds in his soul. On more than one occasion, he nearly grabbed Nyana's hand and pulled her away from the festivities to the freedom that awaited outside the kingdom. But she was right. They would be hunted. Running was no way to live.

Afternoon transitioned to dusk. Torches burst to life in the courtyard, illuminating everyone's animated expressions. Shallow breaths entered Calle's lungs as he stood at the top of the steps, several feet behind his brother.

Liam held out his arms, and the entire courtyard quieted to hear his words. "My loyal subjects! I am pleased to have met many new faces today, and rekindled relationships with some old as we celebrate the summer solstice. As is tradition on one's twenty-first birthday, I am to choose a bride tonight. If you are not picked, do not be discouraged. You might have a chance with Prince Calle next year."

The crowd rumbled with excited chatter, even as Liam cast Calle a mocking grin as if he were leftovers and not the main course.

He clenched his right fist as hard as he could while his left remained limp at his side. He could not do much with his non-dominant hand other than hold light objects.

"Without further ado..." Liam strode down the steps in Nyana's direction. Dread pounded into him like a relentless rainstorm, at least until his brother glanced over his shoulder and cast him a wicked grin. His blood flooded with a river of ice.

Liam knew.

He'd always known.

Calle dashed down the steps with panic nipping at his heels. He shoved his brother aside right as he reached for Nyana's hand and stood protectively in front of her with outstretched arms.

The courtyard fell into a shocked hush as he stared back into Liam's furious eyes.

"Touch her," Calle hissed, not caring who heard him speak, "and I will kill you."

It was not an empty threat.

Nyana's gentle fingers gripped the back of his shirt, and although he didn't turn to see her expression, he felt fear emanating from her. He could only imagine what awful things Liam would do to her if they married. He'd beaten a couple women he'd courted, one of them nearly to the brink of death. Nyana's sweet, tender spirit couldn't survive a husband like Liam. Likely everyone in the kingdom knew—or at least suspected—Liam was capable of abuse and cruelty. But he was the king. Who could stop him?

"Step aside," Liam growled.

"Never."

"I warned you if you stepped out of line, I would show no mercy. Come here, little chit."

"No," she answered in a quivering tone.

When Liam began to reach out again, Calle hit his hand aside. Foreboding silence echoed around them as everyone watched. Guards stood on the tips of their toes as if ready to jump in at a moment's notice.

"You can have anyone you want—just not her," he begged.

Nyana's fingers trembled against his back when anger smoldered hotter in Liam's eyes. Color climbed his brother's neck, wounded pride rising with it. Calle's own hands shook. Whenever he'd hurt Liam's pride in the past, the next few minutes usually ended in bloodshed.

"Please," he begged again. He would have collapsed to his knees and kissed his brother's feet if it would have made a difference, but he didn't dare leave Nyana unprotected.

Liam ground his teeth together, his fingers now resting on the sword on his belt. "Step. Aside. Your king has spoken."

Instead of succumbing to Liam's unspoken threat, Nyana wrapped her arms around Calle's waist from behind, making her choice. He attempted to swallow his fear, but it remained lodged in his throat. They should have escaped the city when they'd still had the chance. Now he'd have to fight, and he wasn't sure he could win.

He eyed Liam's sword, the harpies standing at his back, and the hundreds of spectators standing between him and the nearest exit.

Before he had another second to evaluate his surroundings, Liam drew his sword with frightening speed and swung it toward him. A surge of magic rippled through him, and he raised his arms in time to block the attack with a sturdy rod created from ribbons of magic. A *clang* echoed through the courtyard. His hand protested at the effort to keep his brother's weapon at bay. Liam pressed harder, and his fingers slipped. He slammed his magic into Liam's chest. His brother flew several feet before he smashed into the fountain. Water splashed around him, the cherub's bow breaking in half against the blow.

"Go!" he cried as he pushed Nyana into the chaotic crowd. People screamed as they fled the scene. "Don't look back. You know where to meet me."

"Calle," she sobbed, her blue eyes wide. "I can't leave you."

He pulled her against him and crushed her lips with his own. "Go," he said again in a husky whisper. "I'll be right behind you."

He turned just in time to block the next attack from his enraged brother. Liam's eyes were bloodshot, sticky ribbons of blood dripping from his hairline. Liam smashed his sword against his magic rod once, twice, three times, until his weapon shattered into golden dust. He rolled out of the way of the next swing, but he wasn't fast enough to avoid the tip of the sword slicing his left shoulder.

A cry of pain escaped him. His arm refused to lift when Liam swiped at him again. He ducked the attack and kicked him in the knee, producing a loud *crack*. His brother's howl stirred the harpies loyal to Liam into action. Three harpies tackled Calle to the ground. Someone held an arm against his throat, choking the air from him. Black dots fizzled into the edges of his vision as he clawed and kicked and punched. Magic heated his hand, and the moment he touched it against the arm on his throat, the harpy hissed and flinched away. He gasped in a breath of air, only for his windpipe to get blocked by another arm.

Just when his vision threatened to fade completely, the weight on top of him disappeared.

He gasped in breath after breath as he sat up in a daze. Avonia and Typheal were fighting to protect him.

Sunlight fueled him as he charged forward and locked himself in battle once again with Liam—rod against sword. He struggled to keep up with Liam's strength when one arm still hung uselessly at his side, even as his brother limped and favored one leg. But he didn't need to win. He only needed to distract him long enough for Nyana to escape.

Calle dodged Liam's lunge and managed to disarm him with a lucky hit to his hand. Calle tackled his brother to the ground, and they traded blows with fists. Magic stirred within him as he punched him in the jaw. Heat blasted out from his fist and seared one side of Liam's face. Liam screamed and clutched the burn that stretched from his forehead to his jaw.

Not daring to stay a single moment longer, he pushed up from the ground and sprinted toward an exit. But in a blindingly fast movement, a harpy dropped down in front of him and kicked him in the chest.

The air *whooshed* from his lungs as he stumbled backward, and he couldn't right himself before he was pinned to the ground again, two sets of brown wings blocking his view of the sky.

One of the harpies turned him around and smashed his face into the ground, arms pinned on either side of him.

But then his entire world froze as if encased in a block of ice. He ceased struggling, his eyes wide. Liam's scarred face contorted with anger as he held a fistful of blonde hair in one hand, and his sword in the other. The weapon protruded from Nyana's creamy skin. Her face twisted with pain as blood soaked the front of her gown.

Calle screamed her name and struggled against his captors with every ounce of strength and magic he possessed. But just as he escaped, another couple of harpies pinned him again.

Tears streamed down his face as he watched Nyana slump to the ground. Her chin trembled. Her fingers shook. And then her body became still as the life left her eyes.

"No," he sobbed. "No!"

Again, he screamed her name, but she didn't respond. He attempted to free himself from the weight on top of him to get to her, but he only cried out when Liam stepped on his left wrist and ground his boot until only a fiery trail of agony remained.

"You have defied me for the last time," Liam spat, his words stilted by the burn tugging on his lip. "I will make sure you never again see the light of day."

"Go to h—"

Something heavy smashed against the back of his head, and darkness quickly shrouded his vision. The last thing he was aware of was heat searing into his forearm before his consciousness became as black as the midnight sky.

CHAPTER
1

Six years later

A tusk horn blew out a deep, melancholy note to signal the start of another day. The note echoed in the deep ravine long after the noise ceased, followed by the sound of stirring men and women.

Calle opened his eyes to dim surroundings, only a couple shades lighter than absolute darkness. He stared at the rocky wall of his nook—a small shelf lodged into a steep, rocky ravine, just large enough for one man to sleep.

His body refused to move. It lay still as the last of his spirit melted away like hot candle wax. He breathed in and out slowly, willing himself to succumb to his endless fatigue.

But he kept breathing.

And he kept living.

Minutes passed before the second horn blew—a warning. If he didn't reach the bottom of the ravine before the third horn, he would be whipped.

He winced as he finally moved. The newest lashes on his back split open and burned as he pulled himself to standing. He swayed on unsteady feet and closed his eyes when he leaned a shoulder against the cold, rocky wall. A chill seeped through his threadbare tunic, adding to the unending layers of frigid misery.

A foggy breath escaped him on a sigh. As he did every day, he held out a hand and willed his magic to form a ball of light between his fingers.

But no light formed.

The brand on his forearm not only marked him as a slave, but it suppressed his magic.

His entire body ached from head to toe as he grabbed onto the rope dangling outside his nook and hefted himself over the ledge. One arm dangled at his side, his hand now more useless than ever after Liam had injured it further all those years ago. He descended into the deep, inky ravine. He only wished his good hand would slip and he would fall to his death, but self-preservation forced him to hold on to the dirtied rope with his fingers and legs.

Feet covered in holey leather touched the bottom of the ravine just as the third horn sounded. One of the slave masters scowled at him, but otherwise made no move to whip him.

At least not today.

He kept his head down, not bothering to greet the other slaves just as they kept to themselves. Life was too short to make friends in the Pits. No one had any desire to make the effort anyway.

A slave master pushed a dark-skinned woman forward. Judging by the untried smirk growing on her face, she was likely their newest recruit. The slight downward slant of her long, pointed ears indicated she was a Forest Fae. Her black hair poked out from a red headband, her ears standing out in the dim light of the cavern. She held herself tall and proud as a slave master shoved mining tools into her hands and pointed her in the right direction.

The fae woman held Calle's gaze as she walked by, but as she passed, she ran a hand through his hair. Her smirk grew wider. "Love your locks, fae boy. I'm going to remember you."

Confusion seeped through his numb walls as he watched her disappear around the bend. She wouldn't be smirking for long. The women were usually some of the first to die from mistreatment and horrible living conditions.

He touched his hair, his now-usual frown deepening. It had grown long and ratty, along with his dirt-stained beard. If Nyana saw him now...

An invisible hand squeezed his heart as he pushed thoughts of her away. Remembering her only hurt and added to the many injuries inflicted upon his soul.

A well-dressed man shoved mining tools into Calle's arms, eyeing him carefully. He'd killed three slave masters with a pickaxe only six months ago in a desperate attempt to escape.

It had earned him twenty lashes and no food for two weeks. He couldn't believe he'd survived it.

He wished he hadn't.

Lanterns lit his way down the dark, chilly path. Slave masters watched him, whips in their hands, as he passed. Rough blue and gold streaks sparsely coated the cavern walls, becoming thicker and more prominent the further he traveled into the belly of the Pits. The temperature decreased, his body shivering. His feet expertly traversed the loose rock on the ground, while newer recruits slipped, some even falling occasionally.

A rough slab of blue caught his attention, and he took up position beside it. He released a weary sigh as he tightened his grip on the pickaxe with one hand. His fingers trembled, every inch of his muscles famished with fatigue.

Please. No more.

But no one answered his silent, monotonous prayer.

His gaze traveled upward, at the several hundred feet of slick, gray rock rising toward the unknown. He hadn't seen sunlight in six years. Memories of sunshine faded in his mind, leaving far too much room for dull, gray nothingness.

"Get to work," a man behind him growled before giving him a rough shove to the shoulder. He stumbled on weak feet and smacked his head against the rock. The impact left him dazed, but he still forced himself to lift his pickaxe and slam it against the vein of dalium.

Clink. Clink. Clink.

Minutes passed. Or perhaps hours. He couldn't be sure without the position of the sun to guide him.

The fae woman from earlier sidled up to him and mined only feet away.

He ignored her.

"You can't fool me," she said after a few minutes. "I bet those locks are beautiful beneath the right lighting. A simple wash will have it shimmering in no time."

He turned his shoulder and continued to ignore her. And what was with her fixation on his hair?

He made the mistake of glancing in her direction, only to find her gazing hungrily at his unruly mane of dirty red-brown hair. Eyebrows furrowed in annoyance, he opened his mouth to tell her off when he spotted a tattoo peeking out from her left shoulder. A blizzard swept through his body, chilling him to his core.

The purple design swirled from her shoulder to her collar bone. He'd seen it before. Many years ago. Just before one of his friends—*male* friends—was found face down in the courtyard fountain. Dead.

A valkyrie.

A shudder ran through him as he snapped his attention back to the ore, pretending to not notice the tattoo. Valkyries were fierce warriors, all women, who took pleasure in killing men. How had one been caught? And why was she in the Pits?

She scooted closer, and his body tensed. His grip tightened on his pickaxe, ready to lodge it into the woman's neck if she attacked. Without his magic, he knew he couldn't best a valkyrie. Especially with the use of only one hand.

When the supper horn echoed loudly in the ravine, he sighed in relief, the tension melting from his shoulders. It took several trips to return his gear and the ore he'd mined before he joined the other slaves at a long table. He kept his head down and slowly ate his portion of stale bread and moldy cheese.

As always, he tore off a chunk of bread and passed it to one of the women, the one who looked like she needed it the most. She softly thanked him, though he only nodded in reply.

A half dozen slavers conversed as they stood guard, but otherwise paid little attention to them. Little by little, conversation around the table picked up. Calle didn't join in. He did, however, keep a wary eye on the valkyrie woman. She kept glancing his way. Six years ago, the attention might have flattered him. But he was concerned that he may be her next target, slave or not.

"I heard a bit of interesting gossip from the slavers," a woman said. Her haunted eyes lit up when many turned their attention to her. He kept his gaze glued to the unappetizing food in front of him.

She continued, "A shaman from the Sun Kingdom predicted King Liam's wife was carrying a girl. He must have beaten her hard because she lost the child only days later."

Calle sucked in a surprised breath, only to choke on a small piece of bread. He coughed it up, his eyes watering as he stared at the woman in horror. "He did what?"

Everyone snapped their surprised stares in his direction as if shocked to hear him speak. The sound of his own voice shocked him as well. He couldn't remember the last time he'd heard it.

The woman's eyes became even more animated as she continued her tale. "The queen has born two daughters, and the king has yet to have an heir. Some say he is cursed for killing his brother, Prince Calle, and his sweetheart."

I'm not dead.

But he might as well be.

"What happened to his wife?" he asked. "Is she still alive?"

The woman shrugged and stared at his ears, likely noticing they came to a long, straight point nearly flat against his head. "You're Sun Fae, aren't you? Was he your king?"

Not wanting to answer, he returned his gaze to the moldy cheese on the table. If he wasn't in the Pits, he might be able to stop Liam from hurting his wife. Not for the first time, he cursed his brother for sending him here. If he ever got out, he was certain the next time he saw Liam, one of them would end up dead.

The cheese crumbled to pieces in his clenched fist. That woman could have been Nyana. But was it better to live a life of maltreatment and abuse or die for love?

His soul deflated, and he closed his eyes as he tried to picture her face. The image was hazy, becoming more so with each passing year. Not a day passed when he thought about what he could have done differently to save her life. Somehow, Liam had found out about their romantic trysts. Only two other people had known about their relationship—Nyana's cousin and his friend, Joel. Either they were betrayed, or Liam had them followed.

No matter what Calle's actions had been, he would have lost Nyana.

22

I'm sorry, he said silently. *Forgive me, Nyana.*

Another slow, laborious breath left his lungs. Six years... How much longer would he remain in the Pits? How much more could he endure before his soul gave up completely and his body died?

A chuckle pulled him out of his thoughts, and he opened his eyes to find the fae woman staring at him as she pulled apart chunks of bread. The corner of her mouth turned upward in a smirk. Her gaze was once again fixed on his hair.

The woman may be a valkyrie, but like everyone else, she had no means of escaping nor weapons to fight.

Regardless, he planned to sleep with one eye open tonight.

CHAPTER
2

Skaja crouched low in the shadows, her white-gold wings tucked behind her back. Sometimes she wished her wings were plain—perhaps black or brown feathers—as she often drew too much attention to herself. But when sunlight hit her wings at the right angle, it created a dazzling effect. She liked to use it to her advantage.

She eyed the two dozen men hauling dalium ore from the Pits and loading them into carts, and then shifted her attention to the descending sun. Just a few minutes more.

Her leader, Paula, joined her in the shadows of a gnarled black bush. Twenty years her senior, Paula sported new lines on her forehead and around her eyes, but the light of the thrill still lived in her expression.

"Inari should be in position in the Pits about now," Paula said, her gaze on the dry, rocky plain between them and the ravine. "I trust she will be creative with her lack of weapons."

"Oh, Inari will enjoy this far too much." Her mouth lifted on one side. "How much hair do you think she will accumulate?"

Paula rolled her eyes at Inari's quirky interest. "Remember, we're not trying to annihilate the operation, only wound them. Liberate as many women as you can. Kill the men."

The amount of male blood on Skaja's hands was innumerable. But like all her valkyrie sisters, she believed men were cruel and heartless. They deserved nothing but death and suffering.

A rush of nervous excitement pulsed through her blood, and her wings ruffled at the flaring emotion. She rested each hand on the daggers strapped to the back of her shoulder blades, making sure they were still there for the dozenth time.

"This entire undertaking relies on you," Paula said, her tone urgent as the sun sank a bit lower in the sky. Skaja was the only harpy among her valkyrie sisters and had the best advantage to create a distraction. "You must be ready."

"I am."

A breeze lifted a strand of her straight, dark brown hair. She pushed it out of her face and watched for the perfect opportunity. Several men exited the Pits, and she knew at least a dozen more still remained within its dark depths. She counted three men wielding bows and arrows—those were her biggest concern, as they were the most likely to strike her down.

A nervous thrumming pulsed in Skaja's throat as she crouched, ready to spring forward. At last, the sun moved into a position to give her the best angle. She leaped upward, her wings unfurling on either side of her. The wind caught beneath her and lifted her into the sky. Sunlight brushed her wings, her feathers shimmering in an array of color. Men turned their awed stares to the skies.

In their momentary distraction, the valkyries began firing.

Two men received an arrow to the throat before the others leaped into action. Valkyries riding on the backs of griffins joined her in the sky and together, they dove downward. Several of her sisters entered the ravine while she dove for a man wielding a bow. She reached for her daggers, snapped them open from their folded position, and stabbed him before swooping into the sky.

Skaja wasn't moving fast enough, and an arrow shot straight through the bottom feathers of her wing, narrowly missing her.

One more time, she swooped down and twisted to kick the archer in the chest with both her feet. He cried out as he flew backward and straight into the ravine.

He wouldn't survive the fall.

As more of her sisters fought above ground, she dove with nimble grace into the Pits.

Sunlight vanished instantaneously, and it took several long moments for her eyes to adjust to the darkness. Lantern light guided her downward, barely illuminating the dim space.

Men cried out below as one by one, valkyries picked them off. Griffins carried both valkyries and rescued women. They may not be able to save every female, but they could certainly try.

Skaja rammed a dagger into a male slaver's chest as she landed on a rocky ledge. She spun around and slit the throat of a slave before she leaped off the ledge and spiraled downward.

The echo of clamoring weapons and battle cries filled the ravine. The noise disoriented her. A cry from in front of her echoed from behind. She blinked through the confusion as she attempted to orient herself.

She squinted in the darkness, and when flying became too hazardous, she landed on the ground and folded her wings behind her.

Bodies littered the ravine—slave masters and slaves.

Movement on one side of the ravine caught her eye, and with daggers drawn, she raced toward it. She wove through a small maze of rocky walls in pursuit and stopped short when she lost sight of her target, her breathing ragged. Unlike the echoes in the larger cavern, the maze was eerily silent.

Darkness continued to attack her vision, giving her a disadvantage. Even then, she spotted no more movement, even as her eyes continued to adjust to the dim light. She could have sworn she'd seen someone run in this direction. Had she spotted an animal instead? Or was it simply a trick of the light?

The air shifted behind her. Her throat squeezed in surprise as she spun around, and she dodged out of the way as the sharp end of a pickaxe swung in her direction. But she wasn't fast enough to dodge the momentum of the attacker.

His shoulder hit her. The air was knocked from her lungs moments before her back smashed into a rough, rocky wall.

He swung his mining weapon again, aiming for her head. She ducked and it struck rock. Small pebbles scattered across the ground, and as Skaja attempted to put distance between them, her foot slipped, and she crashed to the floor.

The man charged at her, skidding across the rocks with well-practiced feet. She scrambled for a weapon, but found her daggers lying at the base of the wall. Both her wings pinned beneath her, she lifted her legs at the last second, expecting to knock the air from him enough to deter him.

However, what she didn't expect was how little he weighed. Instead of blocking his advance, she lifted him from the ground with her feet. The sudden weight on her legs collapsed them, and he landed directly on top of her in a shocked heap.

They both grappled for the pickaxe, and although he only used one hand, he managed to pry it from her fingers.

Skaja rolled out from beneath him as he struck again with the weapon. She scooped her daggers from the ground, and now using his weakness against him, she spread her wings and knocked him off balance. His underweight body stumbled into the wall, and as he turned around, she held the tip of her dagger against his throat.

Both of them breathed heavily in the darkness, neither saying a word. His throat bobbed up and down as he swallowed, but he never took his eyes off her.

Her grip tightened on her dagger, loosened, and tightened again.

Do it! she screamed at herself, but it was as if an invisible hand clamped around her wrist, preventing her from finishing him.

Although his features were too difficult to make out in the dim light, she noticed the almond shape of his eyes and the furrow of concerned eyebrows. They were...familiar. As if she'd seen them before. A long time ago.

She shook herself out of it and once again attempted to stab him, but her hand refused. Instead, her fingers trembled like they'd done during her first kill many years prior. What was different about this man? Why was she reacting this way?

"What are you waiting for?" he growled, and the sound of his voice shocked her out of her daze. It was deep but young, one belonging to a man in his twenties. Despite his ragged appearance, he likely wasn't much older than her.

Surprising even herself, she dropped her arm, her dagger falling limp at her side. She shook her head and backed up several steps. He held her gaze with an intense stare of his own, but he didn't raise his pickaxe again.

"Skaja!"

They both jumped as her name echoed through the small, cavernous maze. She rushed toward the entrance in time to intercept Inari. She flared her wings to make them bigger, and to prevent her friend from seeing the man behind her whose life she'd just spared.

"Inari," Skaja breathed, noting the bloodstains on her clothing and the locks of hair fisted in her palm. "Let's go. We're done here."

"Not quite. I'm looking for someone. He's not among the living or dead. Beautiful red-brown hair. I need to end his life so I can add a lock to my collection."

"I haven't seen someone with that description," she lied. "Come on."

Inari lifted an eyebrow and stood on her toes to peer over her wings. "What are you hiding?"

"Only the aftermath of a good gutting. But he had black hair."

"Drat," Inari growled as she kicked the wall. "I was watching him closely, and he disappeared from beneath my nose. I haven't been this disappointed since Adderwall."

While her friend complained, Skaja glanced behind her only to spot the man's silhouette hiding in the shadows. A brick dropped in her stomach. How would Paula punish her if she learned of her indiscretion? Sparing a man's life?

Inari climbed onto a griffin with another valkyrie while Skaja followed close behind. They leaped into the skies in their escape. A trail of blood followed their progress to the exit of the Pits, and she couldn't help but wonder about the blood she hadn't spilled.

Who was the man? And why hadn't she been able to kill him?

CHAPTER
3

Calle watched the valkyrie woman leave, his gut churning with both relief and dread. She'd spared his life and protected him from getting killed.

The moldy cheese threatened to come back up, so he leaned against the cool, rocky wall, closed his eyes, and focused on taking several deep breaths. He touched a strand of his ratty hair, a shudder racing down his spine.

Now he understood.

The Forest Fae valkyrie had wanted to add his hair to the collection of lives she'd taken. Until now, death had been a welcoming idea. But facing it a few minutes earlier...

It was terrifying.

He leaned against the wall until his heart slowed and his breathing came easier. The Pits were uncomfortably silent— the aftermath of a killing spree. He didn't dare step foot into the main cavern lest any valkyries remain. Nor did he want to see bodies strewn about. In fact, he felt sure any living slavers would conveniently find a punishment for him if he showed his face at all.

Valkyries…

What business did they have here?

His thoughts turned to the pretty harpy who'd fought with fierce brutality. Although she hadn't been able to see in the dark—judging by her faltering mishaps—his eyes had adjusted to the dark years ago. He'd never seen a harpy outside the Sun Kingdom, as they all served the royal family.

The recollection of her bubbled up happy memories long forgotten, and a foreign smile lifted his lips. For the first time in six years, something sparked happiness. And it was the violent tussle with a man-killing valkyrie.

But the thought circled him back to a bout of confusion. Why had she spared his life? He likely looked like a homeless monkey, so it couldn't have been his looks. Valkyries had no compassion for men, so that couldn't be it either.

He frowned as he considered the option of her being under a blood oath to him as a harpy, and unable to kill him because of it, but he quickly brushed the idea aside. She was a valkyrie, not a guard from the Sun Kingdom.

Calle shook his head and cut her from his thoughts. His grip tightened around the handle of his pickaxe, and his gaze traveled upward to the top of the endless ravine. If he didn't escape now, he would lose his chance.

Having waited for this day for a long time, he already knew his next course of action. He crept through the bloody and body-strewn maze, grimacing at the faces of slaves, but rejoicing at those of slave masters. The valkyries had provided a path of escape. If he ever saw the sunlight again, he swore to himself he'd kiss the daylights out of the next valkyrie he found and worship the very ground she walked on.

If she didn't kill him first.

His pulse thrummed alive within his chest. Blood rushed through his ears, and hope blossomed like a flower tasting the sunlight for the first time.

A surge of heat rushed through his body and melted the damp chill set deep in his bones when he reached two parallel rock faces that climbed upward as far as the eye could see. He located a cart filled with a pile of empty sacks and surreptitiously rolled it to the base of the wall.

"In case I fall," he whispered to himself.

The sound of his voice once again alarmed him. He'd spoken more today than he had in several years.

Tucking the pickaxe into the waistband of his pants, he placed his back against one side of the parallel wall and quickly kicked up his feet so they pressed against the other wall. Terror shuddered in his breath as he began the awkward climb. Foot. Foot. Shoulder. Back. Foot. Foot. Shoulder. Back.

Perspiration dripped from his forehead and soaked the front of his tunic. His limbs ached with fatigue. His legs shook with the effort of keeping himself from slipping. He made the mistake of looking down.

The safety of the ground rested far below him, the cart a miniature version of itself this far up. His legs shook even more, his weak muscles threatening to collapse.

He blew out a long breath before continuing the strenuous trek upward, but then froze when he heard a voice echo beneath him.

"What the hell happened here?" someone shouted.

Icy fear traveled through his blood. He recognized the voice. It belonged to the slave masters' employer. Arlo Stokes.

He held his breath and didn't move a muscle as a group of slavers passed by beneath him. No one looked up. If they did, he would be a dead man. Or worse—a slave for the rest of his likely short life.

"How many?" Arlo thundered, followed by a low murmur from another man.

Quicker than he thought possible, Arlo swung his fist and smashed it into the man's face. The man stumbled backward, but otherwise remained upright.

"You were supposed to have a means of defense!" Another punch.

Calle's legs shook more with each moment of stillness while the arguing ensued below. He focused on taking several deep breaths, but no matter what distractions he tried to employ in his mind, his fatigued body trembled with exertion. Moving his head slowly, he glanced upward at the many remaining feet above him.

His heart gave a start when he spotted a sliver of sky, a dark blanket dotted with several stars. The sight renewed his hope, and he caught a second wind, finding reserves of energy he never knew he had.

As soon as the voices disappeared around the bend, he resumed his climb—faster this time. He could almost taste freedom.

The rock crumbled beneath one of his feet, and his heart jumped to his throat as he slipped. He fell several feet, knees and elbows smashing against rock, before he managed to wedge himself between the walls once again.

His back screamed in agony, rock pressed against open lashes. Tears of pain leaked from his eyes and blurred the patch of sky above him. He couldn't do it. He couldn't keep going.

But still, he tried.

Every muscle in his body ached. Every scrape and sore on his skin begged for him to stop. He didn't listen, but rather gave every ounce of strength he possessed.

Desperation clung to his every pore. Hope provided him energy.

His foot slipped again, and in an attempt to catch himself, his left hand flew out to cling to the wall. An intense pain clutched his wrist and ran up his arm. Mingled with his weary muscles, his body gave out completely.

Wind whipped his hair and beard as he fell, until he crashed into the cart below. The sacks inside broke most of his fall, but the sound of splintering wood echoed across every inch of the ravine.

He urged his body to move, but it refused. Even as footsteps echoed in his direction, he couldn't bring himself to flee.

Several people rounded the corner. Arlo himself grabbed him by the front of the shirt, yanked him to his feet, and snarled in his face. "Well, well, well. What do we have here?"

****

Their group stopped to rest in the forest for the night, mostly for the sake of the couple dozen female slaves they'd rescued. The women were dirty, ragged, and far skinnier than they should have been. Just looking at them boiled her blood.

Skaja clenched her fists as her gaze traveled down one of the freed slaves. She was bone thin, her hair a ratted mess, and the shadows beneath her eyes spoke volumes of the horrors she'd endured in the Pits. Skaja's hatred for the men in charge of overseeing the Pits' operations boiled her blood hotter. She'd seen this time and again, but different times and different places. This mistreatment angered the valkyries and drove them to kill men and protect women.

Paula's voice lifted into the night sky as she spoke to all of them. "You see? This is why men do not deserve to live! They've taken freedom, virtue, and basic rights. All men are evil. They—"

"Not all of them," one of the slaves interrupted.

The valkyrie leader lifted an eyebrow, annoyance passing across her face. She was not used to being challenged. "Pardon?"

"Not all men are evil," the woman answered. "The slave masters, yes. But many of the slaves I labored beside were kind. One of the men offered to take a whipping in my stead. He shared his rations of food. He killed one of the slavers to protect my virtue. I am saddened that you may have struck him down."

Low murmurs passed between valkyries, some surprised, others disbelieving. Skaja only crossed her arms and watched.

"You are vouching for this man?" Paula asked with a hint of anger in her tone. "After everything you endured?"

"I would have endured far worse if it hadn't been for him. He never said much, but he watched out for the women, nonetheless. I want to know who killed him. He had auburn hair. Amber eyes. He was a Sun Fae."

Skaja's pulse thrummed in her throat as another frenzy of voices argued one against another. Inari's voice rang loudest as she, too, demanded to know what had happened to him.

A lump formed in her throat, and she swallowed it as she remembered the man from the Pits, whose life she had spared. In the dark, she hadn't been able to make out his features very well, but she wondered if the man the woman spoke of was him.

Could he have done all those things?

She ruffled her feathers as she glanced back in the direction of the Pits, a strange new desire growing stronger with each passing second. She didn't want to return. She knew she shouldn't. But the desire boiled in her blood and she couldn't stop it.

With a shake of her head, she ignored the pull to return.

Paula held up a hand, and all conversation ceased immediately. "What's done is done. We can only move forward. Come. Let us enjoy supper and rest for the night. In the morning, we shall return home."

At the thought of flying many more miles away from the human lands, another shudder ruffled her wings.

Once again, she fought hard against the overwhelming desire to fly back to the Pits.

As everyone sat around a fire to enjoy their food, Skaja found a quiet place to sit on top of a rock. The moon shone bright overhead, lighting patches of green leaves in the boughs of trees. Stars twinkled like peaceful candles. Yet, even in the serene atmosphere, her gut churned with discomfort. She couldn't expel the feeling that she'd made a mistake in leaving the man doomed to more suffering.

The feeling pricked at her like the unforgiving teeth of a garguaran. The gnawing urge pricked her again and again until she felt sure a pool of blood surrounded her feet.

She ran her fingers through her hair as she once again glanced in the direction of the Pits, a sense of urgency growing louder and louder until it screamed in her mind.

Not able to stand it any longer, she jumped to her feet. A couple dozen valkyries and freed women turned their attention to her.

"Everything all right, Skaja?" Paula asked.

Schooling her expression, she nodded. "I'm a bit pent up after today's excitement. I'm going to go for a fly. I'll be back soon."

"I'll go with you," Inari volunteered.

"No," she said quickly. "I mean, perhaps next time. I just want solitude for a bit." When Paula tried to protest, she beat her to the chase, "I won't go far."

Before anyone could argue, she jumped into the skies and spread her wings. They glimmered in the moonlight like flakes of sparkling snow. But instead of the leisurely fly she'd promised, she flew as fast as her wings could carry her. The sense of urgency in her bones grew stronger and stronger. She wasn't sure what the feeling was. Intuition. Gut instinct, perhaps. All she knew was she needed to get the fae slave out of the Pits.

And fast.

I am such an idiot, she said in her mind. Infiltrating the Pits by herself was a stupid idea. All for a man?

She wondered what punishment Paula would give her should she learn of her actions tonight. Rescuing—let alone sparing a man's life—was one of the biggest infractions a valkyrie could make.

Yet, she urged her wings faster until wind tore through her hair.

If she made it out of the Pits alive, she would get in so much trouble for doing this.

CHAPTER
4

Calle's legs shook as he attempted to keep his feet underneath him. The effort became too much, and he collapsed. Arlo dragged him like a rag doll. Veins bulged out of the brawny muscles in his arms and his neck. The fury painted on the man's face rivaled Liam's.

Arlo hauled him into a cavern filled with lanterns. Calle blinked against the sudden brightness. The man shoved him onto the ground. He barely had enough strength to push himself to his hands and knees, but not enough to reach for the pickaxe tucked into his waistband to defend himself with. Other men followed and watched with caution as if awaiting orders from their superior.

"Why is it…" Arlo started as he crossed the cavern and grabbed several whips off a shelf, "…that you are the only male slave still alive?"

He shook his head in desperation. No sound escaped his mouth as he stared at the whips. *Save me from this fate. Please.*

But the man kept advancing, the end of one whip trailing on the ground. In a sudden movement, Arlo cracked the whip against Calle's back. A blinding pain shot through him, followed by his own scream.

He clenched his fists to endure the pain, but it never ceased.

"S-s-sir," another man stuttered. "He must have hidden. The valkyries attacked during supper."

"Quiet!" Arlo roared. "Unless you want to join him."

When no one else protested, the slave master proceeded to hand out the remaining whips. "The Sun King has instructed us to keep him alive as long as possible. I think it's been long enough. I want you to whip him until he dies. But make it slow. I want him to feel every lash."

He only barely recovered from the crashing wave of the first lash when the second cracked across his back. Another cry left his lips. Black dots swirled on the edges of his vision. He wished the valkyrie woman had killed him. He couldn't endure this again.

Another flash of pain struck him like a bolt of lightning, followed by another, until both his arms and legs gave out.

Please, he silently begged for the pain to end.

But he still lived.

And he still breathed.

The next whip snapped through the air, but instead of cracking against his back, it wrapped around a metal arm bracer. His dazed eyes attempted to focus on the figure in front of him. Long brown boots. A skirt longer in the back than in the front, and an armor-plated bodice that revealed two bare shoulders, a purple tattoo standing out on one of them.

The white wings stood out in the dark cavern, and he couldn't help but feel relief. The valkyries had returned to finish the job. Perhaps his pain and suffering would finally end.

But instead of killing him, the valkyrie unraveled the whip around her bracer and whipped one of the slavers across the cheek. The next few moments were a blur of haze and wings as he struggled to stay conscious. She fought with ferocious speed, stabbing one man through the chest and slicing another across the throat.

"Get up," she ordered Calle.

A blinding pain ripped through his back as he attempted to move. He only managed to push himself onto his hands and knees, but right when his body collapsed again, someone caught him under his arms.

Angry shouts echoed behind him, and then his feet left the floor.

Through his semi-conscious daze, he managed to creak his eyes open, only for a jolt of surprise to flash through him. The winged valkyrie held him in her arms as they flew through a maze of rock, weaved in and out of ravines, and then burst out of the Pits in a single, fluid movement.

A rush of cool air hit his face, but as hard as he tried to keep his eyes open, his focus continued to melt into black.

"I need you to hold onto me," she said, her voice like honey trapping him in a warm embrace. The sound coaxed him a little further from the darkness. "You're slipping."

His head rolled back as he tried to lift it, but finally, he opened his eyes enough to find her face inches from his. She gazed back at him with worried brown eyes. For a moment, he contemplated allowing her to drop him so he could fall to his quick and sudden death. Living was too hard. He didn't want to suffer anymore.

But somehow, he found the strength to lift one arm and wrap it around her slender shoulders. Her skin was soft, the surprise jolting him further into consciousness.

And then his gaze drifted to the large wings spread out on either side of her.

His eyes shot open, and he gasped when he noticed the golden sheen on white feathers. The color was unique—too unique to mistake.

The shock caused his arm to slip, and they dipped several feet in her attempt to regain her hold of him. When they flew straight again, his mouth opened in disbelief. "Scarlett?"

However, she only gave him a look of both confusion and distrust. "How many times did they whip you, fae slave?"

He shook his head and scrutinized her once more. Golden strands lay in her dark brown hair, shimmering the same way as the gold on her wings. The brown eyes were familiar, as were her playful red lips.

But as he opened his mouth to say more, he closed it again when she cast him yet another distrustful look.

"Are you going to kill me?" he murmured.

"No."

"Why?"

Her intense gaze shifted to stare ahead as she flew. "I don't know."

Finally, he followed her gaze and inhaled sharply. The night sky spread out on either side of him, dark blue and filled with thousands of stars. A large forest lay on one side of the canvas, while a rocky plain lay on the other. They flew swiftly away from the horrors of the last six years of his life, and toward something completely foreign and beautiful.

For a moment, he forgot his pain, his suffering, the many horrors he'd experienced. And he inhaled a breath of peace.

He'd forgotten how beautiful the world could be.

They flew for about fifteen minutes before she descended toward a series of high green cliffs. But the moment her feet touched the ground, it was as if she could no longer bear his weight and they collapsed together. He hissed when he landed on his side, but unlike before, the pain hardly deterred him.

He was free.

Oh, bless all valkyriekind. He was free.

Once again, his gaze roamed to her wings as she tucked them behind her back. A harpy. Just like from the palace. He had to know... "Do you know my name?" he ventured, both terrified and hopeful at the same time.

A dark cloud passed over her expression as her lips turned downward. She glared at him with fury in her eyes. "I don't know, and I don't care. *This* is your fault!" she shouted as she gestured to her arm.

Blood smeared her forearm, seeping from a wound. She must have gotten hurt in their escape.

"My fault?" He stood on shaky feet and pointed at her face. "I didn't make you come back for me. That was your choice."

His throat felt raw from not using his voice for so long.

Skaja, if he remembered correctly, paced back and forth across a long stretch of green grass before she stopped and ripped a piece of fabric from her underskirts. She tied it around her arm using one hand and her teeth.

"Now they're going to know I went back," she growled, once again directing her glare at him. "Do you know what happens to valkyries who spare a man's life?" She didn't wait for his answer. "They're thrown in the Cage. With a wild beast. I must once again prove myself as a loyal companion worthy of a position among my sisters."

"Why *did* you go back?"

"I don't know!" she shouted in reply. "I should have left your dirty carcass to the mercy of the slavers."

For what seemed like the dozent time, he glanced at her wings. The gold shimmered beneath the moonlight. He'd known only two people with such wings—Avonia Svera...and her abducted daughter.

He would move mountains for his dear friends who had tried to save him and Nyana from Liam. He would even risk his own life to find out the truth.

"Try to kill me," he goaded through his dry throat. "I bet you can't do it even if I don't lift a finger."

A frustrated war cry escaped her moments before she tackled him to the ground and raised a dagger. Pain flared in his back. His heart beat fast, but he stayed still as he stared into her eyes, daring her to take his life. Her hand shook as if fighting against an invisible barrier, until finally she dropped her dagger.

I knew it, he thought to himself as he watched her curiously. *She's blood bound.*

And by the looks of it, she didn't even know.

"What did you do?" she snarled. "Using some kind of magic?"

He wearily pulled the sleeve of his tattered tunic up to his elbow to reveal the magic brand on his forearm—the brand that blocked him from using magic. "It's not *my* magic."

"Then whose?"

Instead of answering, he sat up and continued to watch her. She paced back and forth, but never turned her back to him. The gold in her hair glinted in the moonlight, adding a dazzling effect to her disgruntled exterior.

"How long have you been a valkyrie?"

Not only was she blood bound, but he had a good idea of exactly who she might be. He knew her name. Her *real* name.

She stopped pacing and turned to him with furrowed brows. "I've been a valkyrie all my life. Paula found me abandoned and took me in."

"I doubt that," he murmured.

"What did you say?" But when he didn't reply, she snapped open her dagger and tipped his chin upward with the point, so he looked into her eyes. "You doubt my words?"

"Yes." Despite the threat of the blade, he wasn't afraid of her. At least not anymore. "I have a hard time believing your parents would have sworn you to a blood oath, only to abandon you. I would sooner believe you were taken by force."

The firelight drew angry shadows across her face. Her eyes became twin pools of fiery amber. "I have taken no blood oath," she spat. "You know nothing of me, fae slave."

"Then kill me," he dared. "Prove me wrong."

A furious screech escaped her as she withdrew her second dagger as if the first wasn't enough to do a thorough job of the deed. His gaze remained steady on her, and he didn't even flinch as she sliced both her blades at him. However, they sliced the air only an inch from his nose.

She screeched again, even angrier than before as she attacked and sliced and stabbed.

Each assault missed.

Finally, she threw down her weapons, her eyes still blazing while she glared. She took deep, heavy breaths. He couldn't help but admire her beneath the moonlight. Breathtaking wings. Lively eyes. A pert mouth. Although his heart belonged to Nyana even in death, it had been a long time since he'd seen a beautiful woman.

At last, he blinked. Despite his pain and fatigue, the warmth from her mere presence returned like it had earlier in the Pits. A lazy smile spread across his face. "You're beautiful when you're angry—"

Her foot lashed out and struck him in the chest faster than he thought possible. The air *whooshed* from his lungs, and he found himself sprawled on his back once again, staring up at twinkling stars. He grunted when she pinned him down with a foot crushing his ribs. He grabbed onto her boot with one hand in an attempt to shove her off, but his body was no longer strong. Not without sunlight to fuel him.

His other hand lay useless at his side. There was no point in trying to use it.

Strands of brown and gold fell into his face as she glowered at him, only inches away. "What magic is this? Who gives you this protection?"

He remained quiet, not certain she would believe him if he told her.

"Who are you?" she asked.

"Nobody." At least not anymore.

Another snarl twisted the features of her face into anger.

"I want nothing to do with you." She spat to the side. "Go on. Scram. You're free. I owe you nothing more."

When he didn't move, she shoved him once more with her boot, spread her long wings, and jumped off the cliff. Her beautiful wings lifted her effortlessly across the sky. He watched her silhouette grow smaller with each passing second until she disappeared entirely.

A small grin tugged on his lips. She'd be back. And he found himself looking forward to their next encounter.

"Thank you," he whispered to the darkness in the direction she'd flown. He was free. And he didn't plan to waste the opportunity.

CHAPTER
5

Skaja moodily landed back in the forest, quickly throwing a three-paneled cloak over herself to hide the cut on her arm. The chilly night warranted the extra protection against the elements, so no one would question it.

She frowned as she weaved around sleeping figures on the ground. All her life, she'd been taught that men were horrible creatures. Awful, selfish, cruel, unkind. The fae slave was anything but those things. Annoying, yes. Confusing, yes. But not terrible.

The only interactions she'd had with men were when fighting or killing them. Her first conversation with a man was...strange...and yielded no answers, only more questions. What magic protected him from her daggers? If he wielded such magic, why had he been stuck in the Pits? How had those men been able to whip him?

And why had he called her Scarlett?

"You look pensive tonight," a voice said behind her, and she spun around to find Inari sitting beside a fire. She trimmed the end hair off either side of her prized locks, tied the strands of hair together with a leather cord, and attached it to her staff. Dozens of hair bundles hung from the wood in a wide array of colors.

Her friend carried the staff with her wherever she went.

Glancing around to find only two other valkyries awake and engaged in conversation opposite the fire, she sat beside Inari and gazed into the flames. "I have a lot on my mind."

"Would you like to share?"

Did she?

But as she gave a sideways glance in Inari's direction, she wasn't sure if she could trust her closest friend with a dangerous secret. Besides, an insistent, desperate need to protect the fae man tugged on her relentlessly.

Ridiculous.

Instead of speaking of the man, she confided in another confusing topic. "Do you ever wonder about your family? Your birth family?"

Inari paused in her task long enough to glance up. Streaks of white paint were smeared across her dark face in celebration of their latest victory. "The thought crosses my mind occasionally. Your family must be heavy on your mind tonight. You have not smiled once since the raid. And you were gone on your flight for a long time."

"I suppose so," she murmured to the ground. The fae man's words tugged on her soul, and she couldn't help but repeat them. "Do you think my parents truly had the heart to abandon me?"

"Many of us were abandoned. Paula is good and kind to have taken us in."

"But...doesn't it hurt? To know your parents hadn't wanted you?"

Her friend sighed as she finished tying one cluster of hair only to start on the next. "You know dwelling on the past doesn't help anything. You are wanted here. You, especially. Paula loves that you are a harpy. What I wouldn't give to have a pair of wings too."

"They are burdensome at times," she replied with a chuckle. "I'm always stepping on my feathers. And don't get me started on finding a comfortable sleeping position."

Inari pointed a cluster of hair at her, an exasperated look on her face. "Your idea of a comfortable sleeping position includes taking up all the space. I see no logical reason why your wings need so much room."

The two of them laughed, releasing some of the pent-up anxiety in Skaja's heart. The fae man was just that—a man. Devious. Manipulative. Confusing. He seemed kind, but perhaps it was simply an act. All her life, she'd been led to believe they were heartless beasts. Just because he seemed different, didn't mean he was.

"There," Inari said as she latched her final hair cluster to her staff and turned it in a full circle as she admired her work. Her mouth turned downward with disappointment. "The one who got away... That one is smart, I'll give him that much. He likely planned for this day well in advance to have slipped away so soundly. Surprising, too."

"Surprising?" Skaja opened her wings a little more to feel the heat of the fire on her feathers.

"He mined using only one hand. The other must be lame. I can't imagine where he could have gone with only one working hand."

Lame?

A frown puckered her mouth. When she'd fought him in the Pits, he'd attacked with surprising strength. But then she recalled how he couldn't hold on very well when she'd transported him out of the ravine.

"You are obsessing over this man," she said quickly to cover up her contemplative thoughts.

"And? Have you seen his hair? I'm dying to know what it looks like without dirt in it and a good brushing."

She rolled her eyes. Unfortunately, Inari wasn't the only valkyrie with a strange habit. Another enjoyed sleeping with men before she killed them. And one collected the pinky fingernail of each of her victims.

On the other hand, she only killed men out of necessity, especially where the safety of women was concerned.

Closing her wings to keep the gathered heat closer to her body, she stood and bid her friend goodnight before finding an empty patch of grass to lie on. A sudden weariness washed over her, and her eyes drifted closed. Hours of fitful sleep passed.

But then suddenly her eyes flew open and she swore under her breath in the darkness of early morning. She'd left the fae man on top of a cliff. How was he supposed to get down?

Slumbering breaths greeted her, indicating no one had heard her cursing her own stupidity. Quietly, she climbed to her feet and tiptoed through the camp. Before she managed to talk herself out of her decision, she leaped into the air and flew back in the direction of the high, grassy cliffs.

By the time the blush of dawn filled the sky, the cliffs came into view.

As well as the man she'd thought about far more than she was willing to admit.

****

Calle woke at the crack of dawn, eagerly starting the day despite the weariness dragging on his body. The sky lightened little by little, until the world around him became visible.

He stood at the edge of the cliff, gazing down at a long, winding river below. His gaze traveled from an expansive forest to the faint silhouette of a city. A familiar city. Oddwaran.

Many different people lived in the city, from human to fae to forest dwellers. One such person was a family friend named Jarvis, a human he could trust. And another one- or two-day's journey into the forest was where the man he desperately needed to visit resided. Cian.

His fingers absently trailed over the golden tattoo on his wrist, tracing each of the twelve points of the sun star. The man could work miracles. Getting out of the Pits was already a miracle, and he didn't dare hope for more. But he needed help and protection, at least until he could figure out the path ahead.

The skies grew lighter with each passing minute, and he watched the mountain range with hopeful anticipation. His heart quickened. His body thrummed alive. He leaned forward. And then the first ray of sunlight broke over the mountain.

Warmth bathed his face with agonizing relief. He was powerless against the tears trailing from his eyes and soaking his cheeks as a rush of energy entered his worn and weary body. The horizon lit up like a brilliant fire, chasing away the darkness, the pain, the cold, and the hopelessness.

It was beautiful.

****

Skaja's heart gave a start as she stood a little way behind the fae man, watching him stand as still as a windless night. Tears trailed down his face as he gazed at the horizon. He closed his eyes and breathed in deeply.

The pale pallor of his skin faded ever so slightly. The dark circles beneath his eyes vanished. His previous ill appearance changed into vibrancy and good health.

She swallowed the lump in her throat as her gaze raked across the whipping scars on his back. His bloodied shirt hung from him in tatters, and the brown of his trousers was faint as if he'd worn them for a long time. How much had he suffered in the Pits?

Not able to handle the emotions stirring within her, she spoke. "What are you doing?"

The man jumped at the sound of her voice and quickly swiped his tears away, but he kept his gaze on the mountain range before them. "I haven't seen sunlight in six years. It's beautiful."

Six years?

She gawked at him. That was a long time to never see the light of day. "What awful thing did you do to deserve the Pits?"

At last, he turned to face her and gave her a pained smile. "I loved a woman."

She searched his face for any trace of a jest but found none. "I'm serious. What did you do?"

A deep, burdened breath left him as he turned his head to face the rising sun once again. "I was born with magic, and my older brother was not."

He had mentioned his magic the previous night, and her gaze traveled to the sleeve of his shirt, which hid the magic-hindering brand on his forearm.

"What happened to the woman?"

"She's dead. My brother killed her."

Her feathers ruffled on their own accord as she stared back at him. An aching pain lingered in his eyes as if he were remembering the incident. The thought of his brother killing this woman set her blood ablaze. "So, you're innocent?"

He nodded, then shrugged. "I burned his face a good deal when I tried to save her. And I embarrassed him in front of many people. But I don't believe I deserved the Pits for my actions."

"You were enslaved unjustly. You gave your portion of food away to other slaves. You protected the virtue of women. You took whippings for others." She shook her head as she pierced him with a stare. "You are supposed to be a man."

"I *am* a man. Have you met no decent men in your life?"

"I haven't met any men at all." Her voice took on a warning, dangerous tone. "It's hard to get to know someone when I'm slitting their throat."

He looked her up and down, but no fear lived in his expression. "Just how much male blood is on your hands?"

"Quite a bit."

"And female blood?"

"None."

His gaze lingered on the swirling purple tattoo on her left shoulder, the one that claimed her as a valkyrie in her clan. Her bare shoulders not only proudly displayed her identity, but it was an easy outfit to work around her wings.

For a moment, when he opened his mouth, she thought he might ask about the tattoo. Instead, he said, "You stranded me on a cliff."

"Why do you think I returned?"

An annoying, secretive smile spread across his face, nearly hidden beneath his mountain of facial hair. "That must be why." His eyes glimmered with amusement. "How do you propose I get down? The cliff is quite steep, and I have no rope to propel me to the bottom."

When his gaze shifted to her wings, she turned a shoulder to him. She had not thought this far ahead, but she refused to carry him like a pack mule. "No."

His eyes flickered with contemplation as he edged closer to the drop-off and peered over the side. "The cliffside is quite steep, but I think I can manage the climb down if—"

The ground crumbled beneath his feet, and he yelped before disappearing completely.

Panic raced through her at his sudden disappearance. Real, terrifying panic. She wasted no time as she ran toward the edge of the cliff and jumped off after him. She tucked her wings close to her, spiraling downward faster than he fell. The ground came closer and closer until she managed to hook her arms beneath his.

Her wings unfurled on either side of her, catching wind beneath her feathers and slowing their descent. Terror still seized her pulse as she glided past the walls of cliffs, over the river, and finally dropped them into a field of knee-high grass.

Breathing heavily, her anger as her guide, she lifted her hand and slapped him across the face. The noise reverberated in the field, mingling with the soft whistle of wind in the long blades of grass.

He stared back at her with a shocked expression, a red imprint growing redder on his cheek. Several moments of silence passed between them as they stared at the other. "You slapped me."

"Your magic may not allow me to kill you, but I can still slap you." And kick him, it seemed. Ridiculous magic ward.

"You care." His smile grew wider as his fingertips trailed across the small wound. "It's been a long time since anyone has cared."

Her eyes shot open in surprise before furrowing into a glare. "Now wait one moment... I don't care one speck about you."

"Then me falling wouldn't have made you angry."

"You inconvenienced me is all."

Still, he smiled as he turned his back to her, touching his face with his fingertips. The sight of the sentiment caused her to ball her hands into fists. Was he asking to get slapped again? Because she wanted to, if only to teach him a lesson or two.

But she refrained.

"Thank you for saving my life," he said suddenly, now gazing toward Oddwaran. "Just now and in the Pits. I never thought I'd see daylight again."

Barbed words died on her tongue as she stared at him. The man before her was...perplexing. Nothing like her valkyrie sisters.

Before she thought of a reply, he said, "I can manage on my own now, I think. I don't have any coin, but there must be some way I can repay you for what you have done for me."

She blinked several times, his words catching her off guard. Repay? But...but...men were supposed to be selfish and uncaring.

To hide her growing discomfort, she ruffled her wings and turned her gaze toward the forest to give a standoffish appearance. "There is nothing you can possibly give that I want. However...you'll likely be eaten by wolves or chupacabras before you reach your destination. I can at least see you that far."

"Won't your valkyrie friends miss you?"

She shrugged and risked a glance in his direction to find him watching her curiously. "Most likely. But they are used to me disappearing on a whim."

The fae man grinned, setting a torch to her annoyance.

"Don't look so smug." She shoved him in the shoulder, only to misjudge her strength against the weakness in his body. He stumbled and barely managed to catch himself before falling flat on his face. "Let's get you something to eat first and then we'll continue."

The heavens knew the fae man needed sustenance in his belly.

CHAPTER
6

The first real, edible meal after six years of slavery consisted of smoked fish, elderberries, and golden newt eggs. Calle couldn't remember eating anything so delicious in his life. But when he reached for a third egg, Skaja smacked his hand.

"I've known people who ate too much after starvation," she said as she kicked dirt over the fire. "You know what happens? They die."

"What a great way to die."

She paused moments before she kicked him next. "You sure are a lot of trouble for a fae slave. Nearly getting whipped to death. Falling off cliffs. Eating your way to your grave. We have been acquainted for less than a day, and I have saved your life three times."

"Four," he corrected as they continued their journey to the city, though keeping him from eating anything more hardly counted as saving his life. "You almost stabbed me in the Pits, but you didn't. If I had been at full strength, you would have been the one on the other end of the knife."

She tapped a finger against her chin. "I'll remember you said that when you fail miserably to stoke the flames of your ego."

A full-blown laugh escaped him, startling him even more than the sound of his voice had. Even after it faded, his smile remained. How couldn't he be happy? He was free. "I like you."

"I don't return the sentiment."

"I don't believe you. Admit it. You like me back."

Skaja gave him a sideways glance, her expression wary and guarded. She didn't refute him this time, but she also didn't agree. "You are a pain in my arse, that's what you are."

"A *royal* pain in your arse," he amended before he thought twice. He cringed at his words, but she didn't seem to notice. If people knew his true identity, it was a sure way to get killed before he found his feet. Better to lie low until he regained his strength.

Long grass brushed his knees as they continued toward Oddwaran while making light conversation. When they reached the bridge arching over a long, slow river leading to the city, they stopped.

Uncertainty flickered across him as he glanced down at his ragged clothes. He'd no sooner be tossed out of the city than be allowed to wander the streets. He looked awful, and his bloodied and tattered clothing would draw more attention than he wanted.

"Why are you stopping?" Skaja asked, but then she clamped her mouth shut as a cart wheeled past them. The passengers stared at them, as odd of a pair they were—a beautiful harpy and a disheveled man.

"I need to reach the center of the city. I fear I won't make it looking like I slept like a mole in a dirt mound for six years."

She scanned him up and down. "You mean you don't always look like this?"

His mouth twitched at her jest, and he jested right back. "I could catch the eye of beautiful ladies once upon a time."

"Oh? I wasn't aware that moles could catch anything at all."

Instead of reacting to her amusing insult, he watched as several more groups entered and exited the city. Too many stares lingered on him, and he shifted with discomfort. Did anyone recognize him?

He nearly snorted. Unlikely.

What he needed was a change of clothes. And glancing down at the dirtied, blistered toes sticking out from massive holes in his footwear, he needed new shoes as well.

Money, clothes, shoes, food, shelter. The list of needs went on and on until Calle's situation became hopeless. But he'd made it this far. He hadn't survived so long for nothing.

As he started to formulate a plan, Skaja shoved something into his arms. He glanced down in surprise to find her cloak, the same shade of blue as the midnight sky. His wide eyes darted to her to find her arms crossed as she looked anywhere but at him.

"I will let you borrow it, but the moment you're done, I want it back immediately. I'm not going in there. Too many...men."

Discomfort lingered in the hunch in her shoulders, in the angle of her wings. How could she hate men so much? He truly didn't understand valkyries.

But still, he nodded and threw it over his shoulders to cover his tattered clothing. The cloak only reached his knees, and he felt as if he were a grown man wearing child's clothing. An approximate seven-inch height difference between him and Skaja was suddenly much more noticeable.

"Thank you," he said with a dip of his head. "I will hurry back as quickly as I can."

He threw the hood of the cloak over his head and hunched his shoulders in an attempt to make himself stand out less. He walked quickly until he fell behind a group entering the city with their wagonload of crops.

Little by little, they inched forward, closer to the front of the line. A single guard stood at the foot of the bridge admitting travelers or inspecting wagons. When his group reached the front, he kept his head down and prayed no one would notice him.

A sigh of relief escaped him as the group was admitted into the city. He followed closely behind, took one step on the stone bridge, but stopped suddenly when an arm shot out to hinder his progress.

"Halt," the guard said.

Calle regretted looking the man in the eye, only to find disgust in his expression as he looked him over.

"Please, sir," Calle murmured. "I need to get inside. I won't cause any trouble. You have my word."

However, his words fell on deaf ears. The guard forcefully grabbed his arm, twisted it to face the other way, and pulled up his sleeve to reveal the brand on his forearm. He gasped. "You're a slave."

Before he could inspect the brand closer to find out *whose* slave he was, Calle snatched his arm back and tried hard not to wince against the pain shooting through his wrist.

"We do not tolerate escapees," the other man said, his hand tightening on his spear. "You are hereby arrested to be detained until—"

"He's my slave," Skaja interrupted as she appeared at his side and grabbed his arm, a relaxed expression on her face. How she could appear so relaxed when his heart thundered in his chest was beyond him. "Yes, he looks a bit scroungy, but there's no point in upkeeping his appearance when he's going to die soon anyway."

She shifted to better reveal the tattoo on her shoulder. The man's face turned ghostly pale as he looked from her, to him, and back to her before taking a large step back. His spear shook in his trembling hand. He opened his mouth, but no sound emerged.

Continuing, Skaja said, "Now forget we were ever here, and you and I won't have a problem. Understand?"

The guard nodded quickly. He dropped his spear and hastily scooped it up, his eyes wide with fear. He didn't stop them as they crossed the bridge together, arm in arm.

The moment they cleared the bridge, he pulled her beneath the shade of a nearby tree and released a shuddering breath. He wasn't a free man. Not entirely. Not until this brand disappeared from his arm. He could have been sent back to the Pits.

Far too easily too.

"Skaja," he said, a world of emotion in his eyes that he wasn't quite sure how to express. Warmth filled his soul as if brushed with a shower of sunshine. He gazed into her deep brown eyes and felt a stirring of something different. Something new.

Her hand flew seemingly out of nowhere before striking his cheek. Heat spread across his face as he gazed back at the anger in her expression. "What did I do this time?"

"For making me enter the city. I told you I was not comfortable."

"And you had to strike me to express yourself?"

"Sorry." She ruffled her wings and glanced nervously over her shoulder. "I've never dealt with a man before. I'm doing my best."

He opened his mouth to continue the argument, but one look at the anxiety in her eyes convinced him to change the topic to something with more levity. Wrapping his arm around her shoulders, he led her forward. "You think I look scroungy?"

She ducked beneath his arm and glared. "Touch me again, and I will kill you."

"Uh huh."

As they walked down a busy street full of peddlers, wagons, horses, and other travelers, Calle watched her out of the corner of his eye. She tugged on a metal circlet on her upper arm, and it pulled upward in a coiled design to attach to a golden necklace near her throat. The piece of jewelry hid her entire tattoo, leaving nothing poking out.

Smart.

He assumed people—men especially—wouldn't be too keen to have a valkyrie within their walls.

Nervousness tumbled around in his heart as they neared their destination with no further incidents. Finally, they stood in front of a barber shop. A sign hung from a post with two pairs of scissors crossed to form an X.

"Looking to get a trim?" Skaja rolled her eyes. "Don't look at me. I'm not lending you any money."

"Although a trim wouldn't hurt... I'm looking for the owner. He's a friend. Would you like to come inside?"

The way she ruffled her feathers gave him her answer before she even opened her mouth. "No. I'll stay out here. But the moment you come back out I'm leaving. Understand?"

"You don't have to stay."

"I said I'll wait," she growled.

He didn't dare argue, especially when her blood bond likely enticed her to stay. He wouldn't say no to the security her protection offered. If Liam had found out he escaped and was alive...

He shuddered. He would be hunted if he weren't already.

With a quick nod of his head, Calle ducked inside the building. A bell tinkled on the door overhead, and he winced as the sound alerted others to his entrance. However, no one was in the main room. Not even the owner.

Silence continued to greet him, and his heart calmed a fraction. He stepped further into the room and glanced about. Three empty chairs were tucked neatly behind three tables, with mirrors attached to the wall in front of each station. No one stood behind the wooden counter. Was anyone even home?

Wooden boards creaked beneath him as he walked into the center of the room, but the moment he turned, another image turned with him.

"Gah!" he shouted in fright at the awful sight staring back at him in the mirror. His eyes widened as he approached and lightly touched the reflective surface to make sure the image was real. Bushy beard. Long, ratty hair. Dirt-stained clothing. "By the gods above... I'm hideous."

Someone behind him gasped, followed by a crash. He spun around, only to find himself facing a man he hadn't seen in many years, a large crate at his feet.

"Only one man has that tattoo on his wrist," he said before scrambling to both knees. "Your Highness."

"Jarvis," he sighed in relief before he reached out and grasped the man's hand, using far too much strength to pull him to his feet. Not only was the man large, standing six inches taller than him, but he was heavy. Good. It meant he had plenty of work to put food on the table.

Except for today, it seemed. But it was still morning.

"I haven't opened yet," Jarvis said as if in answer to his silent question. "But I'm glad. Prince Calle...I thought you were dead. Everyone thinks you are dead."

Calle gave him a brief explanation of being sent to the Pits and only having escaped the day before. "I wasn't sure who else to turn to on such short notice. I hate begging, but—"

"Whatever is mine is yours. Do you need a place to stay? Some money? Food?"

"I can't stay, but I hoped you might provide a small amount of money and provisions. I swear to you I will pay back every coin double what you give me."

Jarvis dipped into a bow, and Calle glanced toward the window of the shop. Although Skaja lingered on the opposite side of the street, her attention was occupied with watching each passerby suspiciously.

"Don't bow. I can't have anyone know of my identity. It will only make matters more dangerous for me."

With a nod of his head, the other man gestured for him to follow him to the back of the shop and upstairs to his own living quarters. "I can do better than what you ask for. While you take a bath, I'll dig through my son's belongings. I think he has some clothing that might fit you."

Calle entered the washroom and gratefully shed his disgusting clothing. A sigh escaped him as he sank into the cold water of the bath. But he grimaced at how quickly the water turned brown. Not wanting to linger, he used nearly an entire bar of soap until every inch of dirt disappeared from his skin and hair. When Jarvis entered, he took one look at the bath water, and his eyebrows shot into his hairline.

"I thought I put water in there and not mud, but I must be mistaken."

The jest nearly made Calle crack a smile, but he frowned as he held up the bar of soap. "I'm not sure I want to brave my back. Can you...?"

Without a word, Jarvis took the soap, but he paused when he caught sight of his back, covered in whipping scars and open cuts. A deep frown settled on his face, but still, Jarvis helped clean the cuts.

Calle hissed through his teeth the moment the soap touched his open sores. Red mingled with the brown of the water. Tears stung his eyes. His entire back throbbed with pain, and he was grateful when Jarvis helped dry him off and dress him. It was as if all his exhaustion piled on him at once, and when they made their way downstairs, he sank into the nearest chair.

His legs refused to go any further.

Once again, Jarvis attended to him without a word by grabbing a pair of scissors and a razor.

"You don't have to," he started to protest, but the man spoke over him.

"Yes, I do. Don't think I haven't noticed the two dozen times your gaze has darted to the window." The scissors snipped off clump after clump of his hair and beard. He didn't dare look at himself in the mirror again. "Is the harpy your guard?"

"No. She's...a friend."

The man's devious smile grew across his face. "A friend, you say? A special lady friend?"

"No," he said firmly, but he couldn't help but glance at her again. Skaja was a beautiful woman. There was no denying it. And he felt the stirrings of warmth near her. But she would sooner gut him than court him. Besides, Nyana still weighed on his heart.

He'd also lost a bit of weight in the Pits. He couldn't imagine himself in a place where women would find him attractive. At least not yet.

The cold blade of the razor felt foreign against his face, and even stranger was the mass of weight gone from his head.

"I remember how you like your hair," Jarvis chuckled as he started plaiting a small strand of hair on either side of his face. "I think your lady friend would agree with your change in appearance. Take a look."

"No, I don't dare." When he shook his head, the ends of his hair brushed against his shoulders.

"Your Highness, I really think you should."

Slowly, Calle turned his head, his body tense. But as he made eye contact with himself in the mirror, a sigh of relief escaped his mouth. "That's not as bad as I was expecting. Not as gaunt and hollow."

Jarvis grinned from ear to ear and clapped him on the shoulder before handing him a pack of provisions and a sack of coins. "Good luck."

"Thank you," he breathed, careful to keep the pack from touching his back injuries. "It's going to be a rough journey ahead."

"I meant good luck with your lady friend."

Calle rolled his eyes when Jarvis winked. "Don't you have a shop to open?"

"That I do."

CHAPTER
7

With each passing moment, Skaja's wings slanted further with anxiety. She'd never entered a city crawling with men. Especially not with at least a few valkyries at her back.

For a moment, she cursed her own fear. She could dive into a ravine filled with evil men and not even bat an eye, but without those men at the tip of her blade, she wasn't entirely sure of herself.

It didn't help that people kept staring at her.

A man leaned against the wall beside her as if he thought himself charming. His greasy blond hair fell over blue eyes, and he pushed it out of his face. "Did the gods send you to me from heaven?" he asked as he twiddled a piece of his long locks between his teeth. "Because you look like an angel."

She was torn between making a scene as she beat the man to a bloody pulp and keeping herself out of notice as much as possible. "Your white shirt is about to turn red if you don't get out of my face."

The man scampered off, much to her relief.

Her wings fluttered nervously. When would the fae man exit the establishment? He'd been in there for far too long.

Yet another man approached her, and she growled while turning her face away. Unfortunately, he didn't get the hint.

"I swear I will put a knife between your shoulder blades if you men don't scram!"

"But I thought you wanted your cloak back."

When the man placed a familiar blue cloak in her arms, her eyes widened and she snapped her gaze to him. Her mouth dried as she found familiar amber eyes, but everything else was completely different.

His red-brown hair neatly brushed the top of his shoulders, his long ears more prominent than before. His clean-shaven face revealed a strong jaw and an attractive mouth.

Her gaze ran down the length of him, noticing he wore different clothes and shoes without holes.

Words refused to grace her tongue when she made eye contact yet again. The fae man was...handsome. Very handsome. To think he'd been hiding it behind five layers of dirt, tattered clothing, and mountains of hair.

A flush crept up her neck and gathered in her cheeks.

"I suppose this is where we part," he said, breaking her from her trance.

Skaja blinked several times as she tried to catch her bearings—and her breath. An embarrassed flush further heated her face when she realized her wings had grown larger to show her attraction to the man. She snapped her wings back to her body, her pulse fast as she stared at him. He hadn't seemed to notice her reaction.

"Where are you headed?" her voice squeaked, and she cleared her throat to dispel the sudden frog in there.

"To someone I can stay with for a while. I need somewhere to recuperate and lay low."

"She will likely be surprised when you show up."

"*He*," he corrected, but not without an amused twitch of his mouth, "is like family to me. I've known him my whole life."

"And how far is this place?" A group of men walked past, a couple of them casting her lewd stares. She stepped closer to the fae man, realizing with a start that she felt comfortable by his side.

"A two-day journey by foot. Then again…the roads can be dangerous. I might get eaten by wolves…or worse…*chupacabras.*"

She crossed her arms over her chest and glared at him when she recognized her own words thrown right back at her. "Is this your way of trying to get me to accompany you?"

A smile grew across his face, melting her scowl as if she were a block of ice and he were warm sunlight. "Is it working? I would very much enjoy your company."

"Mine?" She thought back to the times she'd slapped him, attempted to kill him, goaded him, and insulted him. Besides, valkyries weren't supposed to travel with men. Rather, they were supposed to slit their throats.

Stepping even closer until they almost touched, she whispered menacingly, "If my sisters find out I spared your life, I will be punished, and Inari will probably kill you. If they find out I've been traveling with you..." She shuddered. "Imagine a ten times worse punishment. You hear?"

"Loud and clear." When he started walking, she followed several steps behind. "We'll travel west and take another road south."

"Didn't you hear me? I'm not traveling with you."

"Oh." However, his twitching lips gave his amusement away. "Then may we meet again in hopefully peaceful circumstances."

Although he continued forward without looking back, she stopped and lifted her head to the skies. A groan of exasperation escaped her mouth, followed by a heaving sigh. The need to protect the infuriating man pulsed strongly in her blood, though she couldn't understand why for the life of her. He was far too reckless. He wouldn't survive the night.

When another man wormed his way in her direction, she picked up her pace and joined the fae man's side. "Fine. But if Inari comes calling, don't come crying to me. She wants your hair. Badly."

"I know."

As they walked through the streets, she cast another sideways glance at him. When the sunlight hit his hair, a bronze shimmer rippled through the auburn strands. Inari was right. His hair truly was spectacular, a color she had never quite seen before.

A serious look took residence on his face as he continuously scanned the path ahead. A shudder ran down the length of her spine. This was the man she had fought in the Pits, the one clinging desperately to life. He would no sooner fight with every ounce of his strength than allow someone to drag him back there.

She swallowed and brushed her fingers against her neck where he'd nearly impaled her with his pickaxe, the one he currently wore on his belt. The man was terrifying when he wanted to be. All happy, optimistic appearances aside.

A man like that...what had it taken to defeat him when he was at full strength and still possessed his magic?

He was a survivor. And survivors were the most dangerous kinds of people.

Her gaze drifted to his left hand where it hung by his side. His fingers curled into a fist and uncurled. Despite what Inari had mentioned, she didn't think his hand was lame. But something certainly was wrong with it.

Several people stared in their direction with shocked expressions. But they didn't stare at her. Rather, they watched the fae man as he passed. Whispers followed.

As if uncomfortable with the attention, he produced a cloak from his pack and threw it over his head and shoulders.

"Wait here," he instructed. "There is one more thing I need to do."

She stared after him as he disappeared into another building, one not marked with a sign. Was she idiotic for accompanying him further? Absolutely.

Not wanting to stay still lest more men risked their lives by approaching her, Skaja maneuvered down the street a little way and leaned against the railing of a dress shop. Several ladies gossiped behind gloved hands. At least until another young woman ran toward them, lifting the bottom of her skirts while stumbling across the road.

"Did you see?" she gasped before she threw herself against the railing only feet away. "I saw him. I tell you I did. I'm not lying."

"Saw who?" another woman asked.

Skaja turned away, uninterested in whatever gossip lay on the tips of their tongues.

The young woman released an airy breath, her eyes wide. "Prince Calle Everdon. Don't believe me? Others saw him too."

The gossip circle murmured their surprise, all while Skaja's feathers rippled with shock. The fae prince? Although she didn't care for men, his story was horribly tragic. All her valkyrie sisters had heard about the incident too. Dozens of people had witnessed the cold-blooded murder of the prince's sweetheart, and soon after, him. By his own brother's hand.

Her eyebrows furrowed. She'd heard a similar story, but she couldn't remember where.

"But he's dead," she interrupted, inserting herself into the conversation against her better judgment.

As if they thrived on spreading gossip, they opened their circle wider to include her.

"But what if he's not?" The woman giggled and smoothed down her hair. "We danced together once. At the king's coronation ball. I wonder if he'd remember me."

The downward slant of her eyebrows deepened. If dozens of people had witnessed the murder, then the young woman must be mistaken. Besides, she wasn't supposed to care about the affairs of kingdoms.

The need to help and protect pulsed in her blood at the thought of the prince. Ridiculous. Something was wrong with her. It all started when she met the fae slave. Whatever this magic was, she planned to put an end to it.

The fae man made an appearance only several moments later, his hood drawn over his head. They made eye contact before he walked quickly in the opposite direction with a deep frown on his face.

Abandoning the circle, she hurried after and fell into step beside him. Neither of them spoke until they left the city altogether and strayed off the beaten path.

"What's going on?" she asked as they entered the nearby forest. "I'm not used to you wearing a frown."

"Then you clearly haven't seen me in the past six years. I've been nothing but surly."

An itch tugged on the back of her neck, but when she glanced behind her, she found nothing but dark trees and a quiet forest. She spread her wings and flew to the boughs above, watching for anything abnormal.

Nothing.

And so very like him, the fae man trudged forward without a care in the world for his own safety. So far, men weren't cruel and vicious—they were careless and stupid.

She watched for a minute more before gliding downward. She tucked her wings in as her feet touched the ground. "What happened in that building? I've never seen you so...angry."

At last, he ran a hand down his face and slowed his pace. He sighed. "I don't mean to be. I just...I was looking for information." He glanced sideways at her as if to gauge her reaction. "About two of my friends. Avonia and Typheal Svera."

"You sure do have a lot of friends, fae slave."

He ignored her comment. "Do you know them?"

"Svera...Svera...Svera..." She glanced up toward the sunlight flickering through the trees as she tried to recall the name. "I don't believe so. Did you find anything?"

"No."

His shoulders slumped as if a hundred pounds of burdens had crashed into him. "I'm worried I've failed them."

Skaja didn't know what to say, so she said nothing. Instead, she watched the trees carefully for looming threats. Once again, she cursed her stupidity for accompanying the man beside her to who knew where, unable to sever the invisible rope tied between them.

A man...

A sigh left her lips. What was she doing?

The further they traveled, the slower he became. Exhaustion dragged his feet. The wounds on his back clearly pained him, as he winced several times when he tripped over his own feet. But he never complained. Not once.

As if the pack on his back weighed too much, he shifted it to one hand but breathed in sharply and dropped it to the ground.

She eyed his limp hand while he picked the pack up with the other. If he didn't start using his weak hand, he would likely get killed out here.

"Stop here for a moment," she said, gesturing to the nearby river.

He didn't protest, but rather slumped onto a large rock with a sigh. He lay on his back, his eyes closed as sunlight touched his face. No, he wasn't lying down but *basking*.

She rolled her eyes. Was he fae or a cat?

The breath fled from her when he shifted, and a shimmer of bronze rippled through his hair. She couldn't help but stare as her heart picked up its rhythm. Her pulse raced faster as she approached and perched on the edge of the rock, only inches from him. Fresh water, pine, and damp earth teased her nostrils as she stared down at him curiously.

Never in her life had she come across a man who would dare close his eyes in her presence.

A strange warmth stirred within her, but she assumed it to be curiosity. Men were strange creatures, she decided.

"I can't decide if you are foolish or brave to close your eyes when I could just as well plunge a dagger into your chest," she said casually, eyeing the small bit of chest hair poking out from the top of his shirt.

The smile returned to his previously serious face, but he still didn't open his eyes. A cat, indeed. No matter how tempting the idea, she refused to stroke his hair to see if he would arch his back at her touch.

"I trust you."

"Foolish then." Skaja drew her dagger, snapped it open, and placed the tip over his heart. His entire body stiffened, but his eyes remained closed. Only feet away, the gushing river flooded the momentary silence between them. "Never trust a valkyrie."

Slowly, he swallowed as if aware any type of movement might get him pricked by the tip of the blade. "I never said I trusted valkyries. I said I trusted *you*."

"Why?"

He opened his eyes, and she found a pool of amber gazing back at her. His mouth opened and closed as if contemplating his next words, but then finally he said, "Because you have shown me kindness."

"Kindness means nothing in a cruel world."

"It means everything."

They gazed at each other for a few moments before she withdrew her dagger and returned it to the sheath on the back of her shoulder. How could he possibly be so sanguine after everything he'd endured? Why wasn't he angry? Vengeful? Sought out to destroy those who cut up the pieces of his life and lit them on fire?

She lifted her hand and held it palm up. "Take my hand."

"Pardon?" Suspicion deepened the furrow in his eyebrows.

"Just do it."

Tentatively, he placed his right hand in hers. Warmth sparked through her fingertips, traveled up her arm, and spread across her cheeks. "No, I meant your other hand."

Even more cautiously, he lifted his left hand and threaded his fingers through hers. A drove of butterflies fluttered in her stomach at the touch. She curiously studied their intertwined fingers, their hands palm to palm. A flicker of gold caught her attention as she noticed the tattoo on his wrist. It was a beautiful design, and for a moment, she wondered what it symbolized.

And then her gaze traveled to his face. Surprise jolted through their shared eye contact and to her wings. Her feathers ruffled, and she was powerless against their reaction as her wings grew larger with interest. Something in his expression changed. The amber in his eyes softened. His lips turned upward the slightest bit.

This was not all right. It was one thing to save a man from death. It was something else entirely to feel a stirring of emotions for one.

Panic shot through her like an arrow to the heart, and she twisted his hand.

He cried out in pain and attempted to jerk out of her grip, but she held on tight. His eyes watered. His expression contorted with both confusion and agony.

"You have a lot of weaknesses, Mr. Sunshine," she said with a growl in the undertones of her voice. "Squeeze my hand."

"N-n-no." He sat up and attempted to tug free from her, but she held on tighter.

"Squeeze it," she repeated, now glaring. "As hard as you can."

"L-l-let go." The fingers of his other hand inched toward the pickaxe on his belt. Although he touched the handle, he didn't draw the weapon.

"Not until you do as I say."

Several more pained tears gathered behind his eyes as he complied. He hissed through his teeth despite the small amount of pressure he applied to her hand. His fingers trembled, and as if the strength suddenly left them, the pressure died completely. He gasped, and only then did she release him.

He turned his back to her and cradled his hand to his chest. She hopped down from the rock and gave him space to nurse the wound as well as his injured pride. Finally, she understood what the tattoo on his wrist was. Although she didn't know what it symbolized, she realized it covered a scar. A deep scar.

"Who hurt you?" she asked as she studied the forest surrounding them, not meeting his gaze. Pine trees stretched tall and wide. Long grass nearly hid the path they traveled. The dark woods lingered behind them as if waiting to reach out and drag them into their depths. "Or did you do it yourself?"

"N-n-no." She heard him take a deep breath before his voice steadied. "My brother..." His words trailed off as if trying to hide the deep ache within himself. However, she still detected it. "He is a prideful, angry man. I was learning the healing art from several elder healers when it happened. Like I mentioned before, he was jealous of my ability to use magic."

83

He winced as if remembering the incident. "It was only a year after our parents died in an accident. He'd been drinking. We got into an argument. It came to blows. I didn't come out as the victor."

"Your brother sounds like an awful bastard."

He didn't reply, and she turned to find him gazing at the river, his eyes far away. A spark of heat flashed through her when she wondered if he was thinking about the woman he'd lost. The one he'd loved.

Envy.

She squeezed her eyes shut and ran a hand through her hair. What the devil was going on with her?

"Let's keep going," she suggested, glancing back at the dark boughs of forest behind them. "I was serious about those chupacabras."

CHAPTER 8

Calle's hand pulsed with continuous agony, and to try to keep the valkyrie from witnessing his pain, he took the lead on the path ahead. What had that been about? One moment, she seemed to be warming up to him, and the next she exploited his greatest weakness. How did she know about it?

A wide stretch of muddied water slithered across the road ahead, and he released a weary sigh. His body wanted to collapse and sleep for a few years rather than finish the journey to meet his trusted family friend. His determination and need for survival were the only things that fueled him and kept him going forward.

But he wasn't sure how much more he could endure.

He took one careful step and used a rock as a foothold, and then another step on a patch of muddy grass. On the next step, his foot slipped, and instead of catching himself with his left hand, he shifted his body at the last second, so his shoulder took the brunt of the fall.

Half his body lay soaked and muddied, and he wanted to lie there and rest despite the fast-approaching evening and the dangers lurking within the woods. He cursed his weak body. Six years ago, he would have made this journey easily. But now it felt as if he were crossing oceans rather than journeying to a nearby town.

"Get up." Skaja's voice broke through his haze of exhaustion.

The long stretch of clouds above shifted to allow the sunlight to break through. The rays stroked his skin, but it wasn't enough to give him the energy he needed to continue forward. If he just had his magic...

She grabbed his chin, and he wearily opened his eyes to meet her brown gaze. Pretty eyes. Brown with flecks of gold to match her hair and wings.

"We'll make camp just up the ridge and off the path. Keep going a little further."

Somehow, he found the energy to push himself onto his hands and knees, and then he stood on shaky legs. His head pounded. His shoulder throbbed. His back ached. And his soul wilted.

How pathetic he must look to Skaja.

Still, gratitude swelled within him. He never would have traveled this far without her.

He was hardly aware of following her off the beaten path and into a small clearing before he slumped onto the ground, his back against a log. Sleep immediately dragged him into the darkness, and he slept like the sun on a particularly wintry day, at least until something *thunked* beside him.

His head shot up, and he blinked back confusion to find a campfire flickering across the space between him and Skaja. The sky had grown dark, stars now twinkling across the deep blue blanket.

Turning his head to find what had woken him, he spotted a smooth black stone lying only a foot away.

"You missed," he said as he picked it up.

"I wasn't aiming for you," Skaja scoffed, though he didn't miss the tender note in her voice. "It's for your hand. Squeeze it in your palm. For hours. Every day. It will strengthen the weak muscles."

Warmth cascaded into him at the thoughtful gesture. He brushed a thumb along the smooth surface. "It's a hopeless cause. Even a renowned healer couldn't fix it."

"Fix it? No. You will probably have an injured hand for the rest of your life. But strengthening it is another story altogether. You can't hold a simple bag, but you can change that. Your hand still works. Now use it."

Although the last thing he wanted to do was hurt himself while attempting to strengthen his hand, he pocketed the stone anyway.

When he opened his mouth to speak, she interrupted by handing him something straight off the fire. Smoke billowed off the surface, emitting a mouthwatering aroma. He didn't question what it was and devoured it. It could have been roasted dung and he still would have eaten it. Maybe.

And when she handed him a waterskin, he thirstily consumed its contents. "Sorry," he coughed as he wiped his mouth on the back of his sleeve. "I don't have manners anymore."

Judging by her twitching mouth, she found it more amusing than insulting.

"If you did, I would assume your captors had taken better care of you."

A shudder ran through him at the thought of his time in the Pits. He blankly stared at the fire as he recalled the backbreaking work, the frequent punishments, the despair and hopelessness.

Six years...

Where would he be now if he hadn't endured slavery? Where would he be if Liam had chosen another bride other than Nyana? Would the two of them be married? With children? Or would they have taken different paths?

A pit of guilt formed in his stomach. He was a completely different person now compared to six years ago. Would he still choose her if she had survived? Would she have chosen him?

He wasn't sure anymore, and the confusion ate at him.

"Will you tell me about her?" Skaja asked, breaking him out of his horrifying memories.

"About who?"

"You know exactly who I'm talking about."

He blew out a long breath as he gazed into the fire. Speaking of her was difficult, but recalling her happy, smiling face wasn't. "Nyana was kind. Gentle. Beautiful. A pure soul full of light and sunshine. She deserved the world." He paused as a frown formed on his face. "I'm not sure she'd like the person I have become. The things I have done since becoming a slave."

"Like what?"

His shoulder lifted in a shrug. "I killed several slave masters. I wished to end my own suffering on multiple occasions. I have become angry and bitter and…empty. I am a hollow shell of what I once was." He covered his face with his hand when a tumult of emotions churned within him. "I'm not sure where to begin looking to find myself again."

With his eyes still covered, he heard her stand, pebbles scraping beneath her boots. For a moment, he thought she began to leave, but then the log beside him dipped with sudden weight. A gentle hand rested on his shoulder. His body stilled with shock. A valkyrie was comforting a man?

He dared to lift his free hand and placed it on top of hers. Warmth settled into the aches of his fingers and wrist. She didn't pull away.

"I can't begin to imagine the horrors you experienced," she said quietly. "I understand a small portion only from what the female slaves we rescued have said. Some of them didn't speak at all. Others looked like haunted shells of themselves."

A few moments of silence passed between them, though their contact remained.

She continued, "I assumed you weren't angry or bitter. You hide it well."

"It doesn't do anyone any good to focus on it. I can't change what happened. I can only move forward."

"What are you going to do? Return home? Challenge your brother? Kill him? I can help if you want."

At the moment, he had no plans other than simply surviving and escaping his brother's imminent fury. But for now...he didn't plan on returning to Heulwen. It would put him in grave danger.

Calle chuckled and envisioned her enjoying herself as she fought a small army of men. But there were far too many for a lone valkyrie. She'd have to fight through soldiers, guards, and perhaps even harpies like herself.

At the reminder, his attention shifted to her wings. He'd waited long enough. He needed to have this conversation with her.

She dropped her hand from his shoulder and asked, "Why do you keep looking at my wings? I've caught you several times now."

His heart pounded as he tried to find the words on his tongue. To give him a few more moments to formulate an answer, he grabbed a nearby stick and drew absently in the dirt. "I apologize. I don't mean to. I just..." He swallowed and concentrated on adding sharp edges to the sun star drawing. "Your wings are a unique color."

Too unique to mistake.

She nodded warily. "I'm the only harpy with these wings."

He paused the drawing, this time braving to look into her eyes. Despite what danger might come his way from this, Skaja deserved to know the truth. "No, you're not."

The feathers of her wings ruffled as if in tune with her emotions. A flicker of fear flashed across her eyes and disappeared just as quickly. "What are you saying?"

"I'm saying I know who you are. Or who you were. I know your real name. And I know who your mother is." And her father. But she'd inherited her wings from her mother.

This time, her feathers remained still as she stared at him. He imagined the shock she must feel. How would she react to the news that she had been abducted at a young age?

Anger flashed across her face, and she snarled at him, baring her teeth as she leaped to her feet. "You know nothing, fae slave. Keep your mouth shut, or I will shut it for you."

Curious. She didn't want to know...

But it was something she needed to know. Even if he risked scaring her away or angering her further.

Continuing in spite of her threat, he said, "You are twenty-one years old, born on the day before the winter solstice." She began arguing over him, but he raised his voice. "You have a birthmark by your belly button. In the winter, the gold in your hair likely fades to bronze, like your father's. Your name is—"

Her scream cut off his sentence as if she tried to prevent herself from hearing. Her hand clamped around his mouth, but he persisted, his next words muffled.

"—Scarlett Svera."

Skaja shoved his face away. She avoided eye contact, and instead of anger, a deep melancholy entered her expression. Her wings drooped, her longest feathers touching the ground where she stood.

"You are wrong," she murmured. "I am just Skaja."

When he cupped her hand between both of his, she remained still. "You are much, much more." The way she held her body away from him told him she itched to leave...and he would let her go. "When you are ready to learn, come and find me."

She pulled her hand out of his grip and said nothing, not even bidding him farewell, before she spread her wings and leaped into the sky. A brick dropped into his stomach at the thought of never seeing her again. What if she never came back?

Feelings of confusion tightened in his gut as he placed his head in his hands. Nyana was supposed to be his one true love. Then why did he feel a fond warmth for the valkyrie?

He doused the warmth with a bucket of ice. He refused to care for another whom he could easily lose. Not again. He could not endure such pain a second time. And allowing himself to fall for Skaja would only burn him. He had to try to stop these feelings before they found root in fertile soil.

His head shot out of his hands, and he cursed his stupidity. She didn't even know his name.

He fought past the fatigue in his body and climbed to his feet, gazing up at the skies above. But he found no sign of Skaja, not even a glimpse of golden-white wings. If she would only give him another few minutes, he could explain everything and where she fit into his world.

However, she didn't return.

After witnessing her expression, he feared she never would.

Guilt churned within his core. Avonia and Typheal might be dead, all because they had fought to save his life. What if Skaja never got to meet them?

A flicker of light caught his attention in the corner of his eye, and he turned to find one of her daggers lying on the ground beside the fire.

Carefully, he scooped it up and inspected it before searching the vicinity for its pair.

Nothing.

He squeezed his eyes shut and held the folded weapon against his aching chest. Although he had only known Skaja for a short time, she had done so much for him. Words simply could not express his feelings of gratitude and fondness.

The valkyrie had saved his life, rescued him from the worst kind of existence, and wormed her way into his heart. He wasn't ready to say goodbye.

CHAPTER
9

Tears fell from Skaja's eyes like silent raindrops as she flew across the darkened skies. The fae man had been correct. About her birthday. Her age. Her hair in the winter. And her birthmark—she was positive she had never undressed in front of him... How could he have known all those things?

She wiped the tears from her cheeks, but they kept coming.

Earlier he had mentioned looking for information about a couple named Avonia and Typheal Svera. Who were they? Her parents?

And why had they abandoned her?

Knowing their names only solidified her heartache. Why hadn't they wanted her? Had she done something wrong, even as a baby? What was the fae man's connection to her parents? Had she really been abducted as a child? Or could it be possible the man was somehow mistaken?

With a start, she realized she had headed in the direction of home. An unfamiliar pain echoed in her heart, but she pressed forward. She didn't want to be near the man again. His presence only created confusion and uncomfortable, unfamiliar feelings. Besides, she feared what he might say.

The pain in her chest continued when she realized she didn't plan on going back. She'd done enough, and she had no further duty to him. Besides, she was a valkyrie. Men were not a factor in her life. Not even him.

She flew across the dark skies, not stopping once. Blessedly, her thoughts eventually transitioned into an empty numbness. A cool wind whipped her hair back, and the sweet taste of midnight lingered around the corner.

Soon, the valkyrie city of Crowbeak came into view. Bright blue water surrounded the island, nestled against a tall, steep cliff. Numerous trees blocked her view until she flew closer, over dozens of valkyrie huts situated in trees or made of rocks, mud, or straw on the ground. A waterfall cascaded off the steep cliff and crashed into the river below. The arena lay near the slowest section of the river, surrounded by griffin stalls, fields, and recreational buildings.

Three towers stretched high above the trees, billowing torches lighting each sentry standing on top. One of them nodded her head in greeting as she flew past, and she nodded back.

Crowbeak was whisper-silent, hushed after long days of planning the attack on the Pits and seeing it to fruition. No one wandered about at the late hour, and she glided toward the cliff without incident.

Nestled against the cliff, high above Crowbeak, lay her own abode. The sight of the circular structure with a thatched roof helped calm the storm brewing within her.

The silence of the night deafened her as her feet touched down on the wooden porch that wrapped around her circular hut. The whisper of her wings and light footfalls seemed amplified in the darkness as she unlatched her door, stepped inside the structure, and closed the door behind her. All her belongings stared back at her in the dim moonlight entering the windows. A stove tucked in the corner. A table in the middle of the room. A fireplace to keep her warm during chilly nights.

Several stairs creaked as she climbed to the second story, her fingers trailing over the railing winding upward.

Her bedroom remained the same as always, despite the week of her absence. A bed lay in the middle of the room with a large window on one side. The drapes fluttered in the light breeze to reveal the beautiful moon gleaming in the night sky. Weapons lined nearly every inch of one of the walls. Mostly beautiful jeweled daggers and magical artifacts she'd found over the years.

She slipped her boots off, and her bare feet padded softly across the room to her vanity. The woman in the mirror shocked her for a moment. She was different. Softer.

Reaching for the dagger strapped to her shoulder, she slammed it down on the wooden surface of the vanity and closed her eyes. Her knuckles strained against her strong grip on the weapon.

Far too many emotions tumbled inside her heart. Anger. Sadness. Shock. Disbelief. And above all, confusion.

Finally, she opened her eyes to stare at the lone dagger beneath her hand. Its pair remained with the fae man, because even after everything, she couldn't help but leave behind some form of protection. A simple pickaxe wouldn't be enough for the dangers ahead.

She reached behind her neck and unclasped the necklace portion of her outfit before unfastening several buttons. Her dress fell to the floor, leaving her in only her undergarments.

The birthmark beside her bellybutton stared back at her.

"How did you know?" she murmured, running a finger over the small mark.

His revelation couldn't possibly be true. She was Skaja. Nothing more.

Tears pricked her eyes as she turned her gaze toward the window, watching as a torch flickered in the distance at the sentry tower. She couldn't handle the idea that her entire life may have been a lie. It was easier to believe the lie than handle what may be the truth.

So, she climbed into the bed, tucked her wings close to her body, and allowed the confusion of the past few days to melt away like ice beneath the fire's glow. The truth could stay buried. She didn't want to dig it up.

"I am a valkyrie," she whispered in the darkness. But her wings contradicted her as they ruffled with uncertainty. A part of her wasn't sure what being a valkyrie meant anymore.

****

Skaja rose early, intent to start the day with as little distraction as possible. She bathed, dressed in clean clothing, donned her weapons, and just as the sun lifted into the sky, stretching its arms to welcome a new day, she jumped off her balcony and reveled in the feel of the wind against her face.

The ground came at her fast, but before she met it with a harsh impact, she spread her wings and swooped low over a field of wildflowers. The crisp, morning breeze sifted through her feathers and playfully tugged at her hair. She took a deep breath and let it out slowly as she glided over the river.

Her reflection followed her path through the air, and when she lightly touched the water directly beneath her, her image distorted on its surface.

Griffins flew above her with valkyries on their backs. They commanded the skies with ease, and she couldn't help but join them in their flight. Freedom touched the tips of her wings, wiping away all traces of lingering uncertainty from the past few days. She was a valkyrie. In heart, mind, body, and soul. They lived for freedom. They valued and celebrated women of all walks of life.

A burst of joy shot through her. A smile spread across her face, and she spun several times through the air. All her worries disappeared like the gray clouds after a rainstorm.

"There you are!" Inari called out, startling her out of her carefree flight. Moments later, her friend glided beside her on a griffin, wings almost touching. "I thought I would have to patrol without you."

Inari gave her a knowing look, which she batted away with a roll of her eyes. "I wouldn't have missed it."

"Liar. You always disappear. I ought to nail your wings to the ground."

"Touch my wings and die."

With a smirk, Inari spurred her griffin ahead, and she followed. The sun crested above the distant mountains as they made their rounds from the south end of the island, all the way to the north. The island wasn't large, taking less than an hour to circle it in the skies. They dipped lower to patrol the rocky cliffs, and later the forests.

As always, the patrol proved futile. Anyone stupid enough to pay a visit to the valkyrie stronghold, if not a woman, would lose their life faster than they could blink.

"Where do you go when you disappear?" Inari asked with a smirk and a side glance. The wind swept her black locks over her mischievous eyes. "Taken an interest in some of the nearby village boys lately?"

"No!" she gasped. Heat climbed her neck and scorched her cheeks, only to grow hotter when her friend burst into laughter. "I've never been there before."

Inari's laughter died down, but her grin remained as they continued flying over the forest. "You're great at killing men, but nothing more. I bet you have never spoken to one."

Her blush refused to disperse as she recalled the fae man's face. What would Inari do if she told her the truth about where she'd spent the last couple of days?

She couldn't risk the information reaching Paula, so she said nothing.

"Look over there," Skaja said suddenly when a silver glint caught her eye for a mere second. They circled around, searching the boughs below until they caught sight of the glint again.

Danger pricked the back of her neck, and instinctively, she reached for the daggers at her shoulders. However, her fingers clasped around only one. She held it tight in her hand, her gaze scanning the trees.

The two of them landed on soft forest earth. A stream trickled nearby. The wind howled as it weaved through the foliage. But birds and other forest critters alike remained silent. The back of her neck pricked again as she turned in a full circle. No sign of anything suspicious, but she trusted her gut. It had never failed her.

Inari inhaled deeply. Her long, curved ears twitched as if listening closely to the area around them. She dropped to one knee and placed a hand against the earth, her listening ears still twitching.

As a Forest Fae, she possessed an uncanny connection to the forest.

"Something's not right," Inari frowned, standing. "The forest isn't happy."

"What is—"

A battle cry from behind interrupted her sentence, followed by the tromping of feet and singing weapons.

Skaja reacted on instinct as she snapped her dagger open and spun around. A grunt escaped her as she blocked a sword, surprised by the sheer strength behind the attack. She kicked the attacker in the stomach. When he stumbled backward, she sliced the man across the gut and ducked to dodge the swing of another sword. She stabbed her dagger into the man's chest and spun around again, her senses now on high alert.

But all was still.

The final attacker lay on the ground, bleeding from a wound Inari had dealt.

She breathed heavily, her eyes wide as her gaze darted back and forth to each of the three dead men.

"Are there anymore?" she gasped, briefly glancing her friend's way.

Inari's grip remained tight on her staff as her ears twitched, but finally, she shook her head. "The forest is appeased." She nudged one of the bodies with the end of her staff, more specifically, the man's ears. "Bloody crows. Look at this."

Skaja stepped over several small puddles of river water mixed with blood and stood next to her friend. The man's ears were long and flat against his head. "He's from the Sun Kingdom."

With a nod, Inari checked the other two lying lifeless on the ground. Sure enough, each of them had similar ears. "Any idea why they're here? I don't know anyone foolish enough to come to our island, especially as a small group of three."

"Me neither," she murmured. She knelt and checked each of their pockets, only to come up empty. A glint caught her eye, and she turned one of the men's hands over to reveal a gold ring with the sun star emblem sitting on his pinky.

Her heart shot to her throat, and she nearly dropped the hand in her shock. "These aren't any regular Heulwen men. These are royal guards."

Inari swore under her breath and kicked one of the dead men in the ribs. As if unsatisfied that he didn't grunt, she kicked him again.

"How did we gain the attention of the Sun King?" Skaja asked as she placed her hands on her hips and surveyed the surrounding area. But no other men rushed out of the trees. They were alone. "You don't think it was the attack on the Pits, do you? The ravine isn't even in his kingdom."

Her friend ran both hands through her hair. "Good question."

She stooped once more, slid the ring off the man, and closed her fingers around it. "This one is mine."

"Really?" Inari raised both eyebrows high. "But you don't take trophies."

"No, but I want this." The symbol resembled the tattoo of the fae man from the Sun Kingdom, the ring a reminder of him. Her heart wasn't keen on letting him go completely. She could almost see his face inside the sun star.

"We'll take another to show Paula." Inari secured her own ring as well. "She should know what happened here."

They both took to the skies, and as they made their way across the expanse of blue, she gazed down at the ring in her hand. She twisted the piece of jewelry every which way to inspect the symbol before sliding it onto her middle finger. A part of her worried the attack might be a message. Whatever followed couldn't possibly be good.

CHAPTER
10

Something poked Calle in the shoulder. He groaned and attempted to bat it away, but then it poked him again. He opened his eyes but squinted against the blinding backdrop of the afternoon sun.

When the object poked him once more, followed by a chorus of laughter, his eyes shot open. A man stood over him, holding a stick.

He scrambled backward to more guffawing, only for his back to scrape against a boulder. He hissed through his teeth but fought through the blinding pain for one of his weapons. His fingers clasped around his pickaxe.

"Whoa there," another man said, and Calle blinked his eyes into focus. Three men stood within several yards of him, and on the road...

Emotion clogged his throat at the sight of a wagon pulled by an aged horse. Eight children and a couple of pregnant women sat squished inside, with several other men and women standing close. They appeared dirty, tired, and hungry. His breath caught at the sight of their ears. Long and flat. One of the women proudly displayed the sun star tattooed on her forehead in a beautiful bronze color by wearing her hair back.

Gold. Silver. Bronze. They were all revered colors in his culture.

"We apologize," the man spoke again with his hands held up placatingly, pulling his attention away from the wagon. "We thought you were like us. Someone escaping Heulwen."

"Escaping?" he rasped, his eyes wide. "But Heulwen is a safe place to live."

The men exchanged glances. "Have you been hiding under a rock?"

"Between two rocks, actually. What's happening in Heulwen? Why are you fleeing?"

One of the men gestured to the others in the wagon and lowered his voice. "We grow crops. When Liam's army takes most of our food, we are losing profits, we can't feed our families, and we can't afford the high tax. It's either flee or watch as my family hangs by a noose."

Bile churned in Calle's stomach as he peered closer at the women and children. They were bone thin. What else had happened in Heulwen in his absence?

Stepping closer, the man peered at him. His fingers tightened around the handle of the pickaxe. He didn't know who he could trust anymore.

"I've seen you before," the man said slowly as his gaze traveled from his hair, to his ears, and then lingered on his eyes. You look like..." He shook his head and exhaled. "Never mind. Where are you headed?"

Realizing he still sat on the ground, he cautiously climbed to his feet, not taking his eyes off any of the strangers. Prince Calle was supposed to be dead, so even if they noticed similarities between him and his past self, they likely wouldn't come to the correct conclusion.

His gaze briefly roamed the area around him, and a part of his spirit fell with disappointment when he didn't spot Skaja. She'd really left...

It was a good thing, though. She likely would have either killed all these men or melted with discomfort.

With caution in mind, he answered, "I'm headed to see a friend."

The man nodded toward his group. "Need companions? We always have room for one more." He eyed the pickaxe in his hand, and then Skaja's dagger several feet away.

Calle wasn't sure if the other man wanted the weapons or extra protection. Guilt ate at him as he shook his head. He couldn't help anyone until he helped himself. Besides, he wasn't sure how much protection he could give in his state. "Thank you for your offer, but I'm headed in another direction. I wish you safe travels."

They spoke their farewells, and despite the hunger pains in his belly and the fatigue resting on his shoulders, he made haste down the road. Something was happening in Heulwen, and he needed to know what.

He stopped for a quick meal consisting of the bread and dried meat from his pack before continuing on. He lightly gripped Skaja's stone in his injured hand, wincing at the pain shooting up his arm. He didn't dare squeeze, fearing the accompanying pain.

Little by little, shadows grew in the forest. The trees seemed to stretch longer and wider. The forest floor threatened to swallow him whole.

Something screeched above him, and he cried out in alarm as he spun around.

Only to face darkness.

Shadows slithered across damp earth like a living, breathing thing. They crawled and reached and clawed, obscuring the path behind him. A chill raked its long claws across the skies as if shredding the sunlight canvas to reveal the inky black sky resting behind it. Shivers danced along his skin as if he once again found himself in the freezing Pits.

His heart pounded against his ribcage as if begging for release from its terrified prison. A lump of fear lodged in his throat, and he turned slowly in a full circle as he attempted to find the way forward.

In only a few moments, he managed to find himself lost in the vast forest, with nothing to act as his guide.

He tipped his head back to stare at the boughs above, but all signs of daylight had long since disappeared. The only person who he could call on for help was likely far, far away.

A wave of dread crashed into him when he brought his attention back to the creeping shadows...

...and the red eyes blinking in the darkness.

Calle's pulse raced as he snatched the pickaxe from his belt and waved it menacingly in front of him in an attempt to ward off the threat. However, three chupacabras edged forward, lips drawn back in a snarl to show sharp, yellow fangs. The blood-sucking canines growled while staring him down with unblinking eyes.

Skaja, I hate you for being right.

Sweat licked his brow as his gaze darted from one beast to the next. He would sooner collapse from exhaustion than outrun them. Taming them into submission might have been possible if he'd had his magic and his friend Joel's gift with animals. But he had neither. Fighting was the only option.

Without warning, the first one jumped at him. He dodged to the side while at the same time striking downward with his pickaxe. His reflexes were much too slow to keep the sharp claws from raking across his arm, and he yelped at the same time the beast did.

He yanked the pickaxe out of the injured chupacabra as the next one attacked. The swing missed, and the momentum spun him to face the opposite direction. Something sharp dug into the back of his leg. He released a scream of agony as the beast began sucking large mouthfuls of his blood.

He twisted and used the momentum to drive the pickaxe into its ribs. The beast yelped, but it only latched on tighter to his leg. No matter how hard he attempted to yank his weapon out, it remained stuck.

Another growl announced the third chupacabra, and even through the blinding agony in his leg, he reached for Skaja's dagger and snapped it open as the beast pounced. He embedded the blade into its neck, severing the tendon and killing it instantly. Its body fell to the ground in an unmoving heap.

The only living chupacabra released its hold on his leg and pounced, knocking him flat on his back. Snarling teeth snapped in his face, and he only barely managed to keep it from tearing him apart.

Strength faded quickly, and every few seconds spent holding the beast at bay was another inch it gained.

Fear slicked his entire body with perspiration. This couldn't be the end. Not after he'd only just escaped hell.

When his body threatened to give out, the end of a wooden club smashed the chupacabra on the top of its head and cracked its skull. It slumped over dead. The darkness in the forest transitioned into something lighter and much less foreboding.

Calle struggled to his feet, favoring his injured leg, and reached for the dagger in the instance of a second threat. But he froze when he stared back at light blue eyes, a wrinkled face, and hair and a beard of wiry gray strands. Tears streamed from the man's shocked eyes, and his hands trembled as he dropped the club.

"Calle," he rasped, stumbling forward.

Despite the pain in his leg, Calle caught him in an embrace, each hugging the other tightly. "Cian."

His dear friend sobbed as he held him at arm's length and grasped his face between his hands. "But you're dead. How...how..."

A wave of fatigue crawled up his leg and filled his mind with woozy fog. His head spun, and he blinked heavily as he tried to keep himself upright. "The chupacabra bit me," he said, clinging to his friend.

The shock on Cian's face transitioned into gravity. "We are not far from my home. You better not keel over because I'm not certain my old bones can drag your unconscious body more than a few inches."

Calle's mouth twitched at the jest, though his head continued to swim as the chupacabra's venom climbed through his bloodstream. He was vaguely aware of his feet limping forward with Cian at his side. He hardly registered walking through the small town he'd sought these past couple of days and into a cottage. By the time Cian laid him face down on a table, perspiration covered him from head to toe.

Something hot stung his leg where the chupacabra had bitten him, and he cried out through the fog in his mind. Cian placed the rim of a cup to his lips and ordered him to drink. He coughed and sputtered on a foul liquid that tasted like something between earwax and fungus. He wasn't entirely sure if he drank it all as he flickered in and out of consciousness.

At last, the fire ebbed in his body, making way for cool relief. Cracking his eyes open, he found Cian busy rubbing healing ointment into the whipping wounds on his back. Although the man was not capable of magic, his knowledge and skills with herbs often surpassed magic healers in Heulwen. The open wounds began closing.

Cian frowned through his administration. "Where did you get these?"

The bitter taste of the foul drink still coated his mouth as he answered, his voice muffled by exhaustion, "In the Pits."

As awareness slowly returned to him, he told Cian every event between the summer solstice six years earlier and the chupacabra attack, leaving out no details.

Emotion clogged his throat halfway through the story when small needles pricked his back. A tattoo... As one of Heulwen's esteemed elders, it was an honor to receive a tattoo from Cian. However, he wasn't sure he deserved it.

Pushing through, he finished his story only to be met by stony silence. The wrinkles around Cian's eyes and mouth deepened as he continued the long and arduous process of tattooing the scars on his back. The pain of each prick paled in comparison to what he'd endured in the past six years.

"Your parents' legacy has been tainted," Cian replied finally.

Shame pricked his conscience. He'd been sixteen when they'd died, hardly a man. "I have not lived up to their expectations."

The old man paused his work and huffed before continuing. "I was not talking about you, Calle. Your brother is hungry for power. He is not a kind ruler. A lot has happened in your absence."

His thoughts flickered to the group he'd met on the road, fleeing from Heulwen. "Tell me."

After several more pricks, Cian answered, "Many people have been forced to swear a blood oath to Liam. His army has grown. He has enforced strict laws and harsh punishments. Those who cannot afford to pay the high tax are either thrown in prison or put to death. Food is becoming scarce because of the need to feed a large army. The rivers have slowed to a trickle as if the very earth is sick from Liam's wicked deeds."

"How awful." Calle's heart broke for his people. For his friends. For those who he considered family, like Cian. "I fail to understand how he has fallen so far. I heard a rumor in the Pits. About him beating his wife."

He turned his head to find Cian's frown deepening. "You do not seem...sad."

"I *am* sad. And horrified. Disgusted."

The bone needle froze above his skin as Cian studied him. "You do not know who the queen is."

It wasn't a question but a statement. He shook his head. "By the time rumors hit the Pits, they often get skewed in one way or another. Who is she?"

Cian returned his concentration to his task. "A very unlucky woman, that's who. They have two children now. Both girls. She protects them fiercely."

Calle couldn't possibly fathom how Liam could be so cruel. To his own wife. And he dared hope not to his children. "He wants an heir."

Cian nodded, his gaze intense. "I understand now why he's so desperate. You're alive. And he knows it."

"But why not kill me?"

"I know your relationship with him has always been rocky. I assume he wanted you to suffer."

"Sounds about right," he muttered.

Another long stretch passed in silence. The pain in his leg had lessened considerably now that the venom no longer touched his bloodstream. The wound had likely healed over by now, similar to how his back didn't hurt quite so much. Six years ago, he had planned to learn more about herbs after he eventually mastered healing by magic. His knowledge was basic at best. But he wondered if he should have focused more on training to fight.

Would the outcome of that day have been different if he'd been a better fighter?

"What is your plan to defeat your brother?" Cian asked suddenly, shocking Calle from his thoughts.

His mouth fell open, and he turned sharply to stare at the old man. "There is no plan. There is nothing I can do."

"There is always something you can do. And I encourage you to do it soon. Before Liam conceives an heir. You're next in line for the throne."

"I can't just..." A shuddering breath escaped him as he returned to lying on his stomach. He shook his head. "I can't just strut into Heulwen and demand the throne. There is nothing I can do, Cian. He defeated me once as if I were a mere nuisance of an insect. I think I will be even less successful next time. I don't have my magic anymore."

"Perhaps not. But you are so much more than just your magic. The people of Heulwen either need another kingdom to overthrow Heulwen, or they need you." The old man squeezed his shoulder with brittle fingers. "You give me reason to hope again, Your Highness. I know plenty of others who would feel the same way. They would fight alongside you."

Fight...

Others...

Considering the pathetic amount of strength he currently possessed, there would be no fighting. Not for a while. Maybe not ever.

He reached into his pocket and pulled out Skaja's warm, round stone. He turned it over in his fingers and ran his thumb across the smooth surface. Dread entered him like a freezing river as he considered his next question. He didn't want to know, but he needed to.

"What happened to Avonia and Typheal? Are they..." he swallowed his rising fear, "...dead?"

"No."

However, he didn't expand.

Please, no...

His voice trembled as he spoke. "They lost their wings."

Prick. Prick. Prick.

The bone needle made the faintest of sounds to fill the terrifying tension in the room. Finally, Cian answered, "You know the punishments for harpies when they break a blood oath."

"They didn't break the oath!" he cried. "They were protecting *me*!"

"It matters little to the king. To him, their actions were those of betrayal. Only Typheal lost his wings. He managed to convince Liam he'd forced Avonia to act as she had. He was marked as a traitor and banished from the kingdom. Avonia is still blood bound and works in the palace. Her wings are intact."

Calle buried his face in his hands. They'd sacrificed so much. And for what? Nyana had been murdered. He had been

113

forced into slavery and now everyone thought him dead. The kingdom was a dangerous place. This was his fault.

Cian placed a comforting hand on his shoulder. "They knew the risks."

With a shake of his head, he said, "They must regret their loyalty to me."

"They don't."

"How do you know?"

"Because they've started a rebellion group in your name."

His head shot up in surprise, but as he scanned the old man's face for any trace of a jest, he found none. "Rebellion group? What are they hoping to achieve?"

The older man paused to dip the bone needle into ink, but he couldn't see the color from this angle. He wouldn't doubt it was gray or black to reflect the horror of the last several years, and all the people he'd failed with his absence.

"They are thwarting Liam's efforts in many ways. Robbing caravans filled with riches. Smuggling people out of the city. Gaining intelligence from inside the palace. Freeing prisoners in the dungeon."

"It's a hopeless cause," he argued. "You know Liam as well as I do. Once his pride is damaged, he'll go to the ends of the earth to restore it."

"Is it hopeless?" A slight sting touched his shoulder blades beneath Cian's hand. "They've been waiting for the right opportunity. Once they learn you are alive, you will give them hope."

The weight of such a hefty responsibility pressed down on him, anchoring him firmly to the table. It wasn't so much hopeless as impossible. If only Cian understood the limitations of his body and magic.

"I cannot be the person you want me to be," he replied quietly.

"And why not?"

Memories of the Pits flashed across his mind. He shuddered as he recalled the many whippings he'd received. The darkness. The cold. The hunger. Pain. Cruelty. A fate worse than death.

And then he remembered his brother. The injuries he'd sustained at Liam's hand. The rage. The hatred. The power. He was nothing. Just a mouse locked in battle with a lion.

He admitted the truth, "I am afraid."

"Understandably so. You are in no shape to do anything. Rest a while." He chuckled. "A long while. It looks like you haven't slept well in six years."

Calle's mouth twitched at the truth of his statement. Before he knew it, even the light pricks on his skin couldn't keep him awake, and his eyes drifted closed. Every once in a while, the pricks would stop, only for him to wake partially when they resumed.

Someone shook his shoulder, and he shot up to a sitting position, bleary eyed. Cian's face filled his vision, and he relaxed. Shock jolted him awake at the tears running down the man's face and toward the large, proud smile on his lips.

"It's done. Come and take a look."

Hesitation gave him pause. He didn't want to see what he assumed would be shameful black designs on his skin, forever etched into his soul. But still, he slid off the table, wincing at the new ache in his back. Not an ache from his whippings, but from the tattoo.

His heart raced with dread as he followed Cian across the meager room serving as a living area, kitchen, and bedroom at the same time. In the corner of the room stood a full-length mirror, nestled between the bed and a couple of shelves filled with herbs.

The dark circles beneath his eyes had disappeared, as well as the pallor in his face. His skin appeared to glow with health. Given a few more months, he reckoned he'd start looking the way he last remembered himself.

Taking a deep breath, he slowly turned so his back faced the mirror, and when he glanced over his shoulder, his eyes widened in surprise. His back was angry and red.

And *gold*.

He blinked back the rising emotion gathering behind his eyes as his gaze trailed over the beautiful golden designs etched into the skin on his back. The design was bold, covering each of his scars, while forming words in the sun language.

Courage. Strength. Bravery. Endurance. Honor. Love.

His wide eyes met Cian's as he turned to face him. "I don't deserve gold. I let everyone down."

Cian shook his head, his eyes sparkling with unshed tears as he smiled. "You did what was right. It's not your fault you did not succeed. You are more deserving of gold than anyone I know."

He ran his thumb over the tattoo on his wrist. The word *sacrifice* repeated over and over to form the sun star. The gold matched the tattoo on his back. He thought of all the people Liam had hurt, of all the people he had wronged.

Anger and determination sparked within him, fanning hotter and hotter until it became a billowing wildfire.

No more.

Liam would not hurt another soul if he could do something about it. He knew what to do next. It would be hard. Impossible, even. But escaping the Pits had been impossible, and yet he'd done it. Though, not without help.

"Go to them," Calle said, his eyebrows set with resolve. "Tell them I'm alive, and I will lead them to victory."

Cian moved past him to grab an empty sack as if he planned to leave immediately. But he halted at Calle's next words.

"And tell Avonia and Typheal…" he clutched the smooth stone in his hand, "I've found their daughter."

CHAPTER
11

A vonia's steely gaze swept over the rebels gathered in the room—one of many inside the hidden underground, impenetrable fortress. For years, King Liam had chased them down, tortured those he had captured, and sent troops to trample the forest to find out where they were hiding. But with the spellcaster changing the location of the entrance often, they were difficult to find.

The blood oath to Liam thickened in her veins the longer she remained away from him and her duties to protect him. He didn't know about her involvement with the rebellion, and she planned to keep it that way.

Typheal climbed the three steps to the top of the dais, kissed her cheek, and stood by her side. Someday, they could be together completely, rather than the occasional visits in the dead of night.

Oh, how she longed for happiness and normalcy.

A murmur started at the very end of the gathering, and the crowd parted like fish swimming around a rock to make a path for someone approaching. Her eyebrows shot up in surprise to find Cian limping in her direction with a staff in his hand, faster than an old man his age ought to move. Typheal rushed down the stairs to help him, and Cian nodded his thanks.

He huffed and puffed before catching his breath at the top. The crowd hushed, waiting for their elder to speak.

Avonia started, "Cian, it has been many months since last we've seen you. How are you faring?"

"Perfectly well," he answered as he wheezed one more time before facing the crowd. Everyone stared at him expectantly, even herself. Instead of waiting until he fully caught his breath, he addressed the rebellion, "Prince Calle," he wheezed, "is alive."

Avonia's heart squeezed hard enough for her mind to become dizzy. She swayed on her feet, disbelief coursing through her blood. Shouts of exclamation echoed off the tall stone ceilings, further causing her head to spin. Typheal steadied her, and his calming presence helped her manage a breathy question.

"He's alive? What? How?"

Surely, Cian was mistaken. She'd seen Calle's limp body being carried away. She'd attended his funeral. She'd mourned him for a long time.

When the room quieted again, Cian said, "King Liam lied about his death and sent him to the Pits to spend the rest of his life as a slave. But he escaped with the aid of a very brave valkyrie named Skaja." The elder turned to face her and Typheal, a sheen of happiness in his eyes. "Otherwise known as Scarlett Svera."

This time, Avonia's knees buckled and she fell to the ground. Sobs of disbelief escaped her, and she was powerless to stop them. Her baby? She was alive? A valkyrie? No wonder they had never been able to find her. They'd never ventured far enough in their search.

With Typheal's steady hands on her shoulders, he lifted his head to stare at Cian. "You are certain?"

"I have not seen her myself, but Calle says there is no mistake. He confirmed she is under a blood oath to him, and Avonia..." The elder smiled, and she barely spotted it through her tears. "She has your wings. An exact replica."

"My baby," she sobbed again. Her entire world shattered around her and rebuilt itself into something fragile and all too easy to break. "We have to go after her. Where is she? With Calle?"

Cian eyed the crowd with a suspicious frown. He motioned with his head toward another door, and she and Typheal followed on unsteady feet into a small room with gray stone walls and a musty odor.

The moment the door closed behind them, the old man's face crinkled as he explained, "As far as I understand, Skaja has left and doesn't plan to return, but at least now we know where she is—with the valkyries. Calle is recuperating at my home. He's..." The lines around his mouth deepened as he frowned. "He's in bad shape. Very bad shape. But given a few months...he will recover."

The prince had been like a son to her all his life, but before she opened her mouth, Typheal demanded, "We must bring him here. He'll be safe with us."

Cian shook his head and leaned heavily against his staff. "He can't regain his strength without sunlight. He needs to remain above ground."

"Then we must send protection to him. I will take several trusted guards."

"And then what? You will risk Liam following you and bringing him right to Calle's door. My property has a ward around it. As long as he stays within its boundaries, he should be safe and hidden."

"That's not good enough!" Typheal struck out at the wall with his fist. "We cannot risk his life."

"No, we cannot. Which is why no one will go. Unless you know an illusionist who will aid our cause, one not already working for Liam."

Avonia's wings flared as hope stretched across her feathers. "I know one. He left Heulwen a couple years ago when his family fled the city. If we track him down, we can send him to retrieve Calle."

"And how can we trust this man?" Cian asked.

"His name is Joel Harrington. He used to be Calle's best friend. They grew up together."

After pondering her suggestion for a few moments, he finally nodded. Relief burst through her, not only at the hope of reuniting with Calle, but also at meeting her daughter. She would see Scarlett again. She had to believe that.

Cian motioned his staff toward the closed door. "Then go find this man and ask him to bring Calle home."

Skaja stood on top of one of the watchtowers with a spyglass against her eye. She breathed in and out slowly, not daring to joggle its position lest she lose sight of the horizon. Gray storm clouds rolled across the blue expanse of ocean that stretched from one side of the island to the other. After they sank the ship from Heulwen yesterday and killed every single man on board, she almost expected a second ship to come in its place.

It didn't.

Not yet at least.

She set down the spyglass and twisted the ring on her finger. The piece of jewelry glinted beneath the sunset, giving an almost magical sparkle to the simple gold band. Two months had passed since she'd seen the fae man.

She had never expected an ache to form in her chest at his absence. Their brief encounter had filled her with sunlight, and now every day felt as if it were cloudy and bleak.

A part of her wanted to take the ring off and throw it from her perch. But she instead found herself cradling her hand to her heart.

A fire burst to life at the first watchtower, followed by the second. Skaja lit her own fire in the open, circular hearth. She watched as the flames danced like two lovers spinning in each other's arms, one dipping the other and about to bestow a kiss—

"Skaja, now that your shift is over, Paula wants to see you."

She jumped when someone touched her elbow, and she twisted to find one of her valkyrie sisters standing on the platform with her. Her heart raced with anxiety, and as if she'd been caught doing something bad, she hid her hand behind her back.

Had Paula found out about what she'd done?

"Where is she?"

The other woman moved past her and picked up the spyglass she'd set down earlier. "The arena. Best be quick. She's angry."

A cold bucket of dread dumped over her head. At least she thought as much until she realized the dark clouds above released its rain in earnest. She jumped off the tower and spread her wings in an attempt to avoid the worst of it, but spatters of rain still fell on her. It soaked her hair and clothing. Droplets of water ran across her wings and rolled off the tips of her feathers.

By the time she landed at the arena, a shiver ran through her body, and she doubted any amount of fire could warm the dread in her frigid limbs.

High-pitched screeches and booming roars drowned her ears from the creatures they kept in cages within a slab of hollowed-out rock at the base of the cliff. Tall, thick walls arced outward from the cliff to form a semi-circle.

The outer door was cracked open, and she slipped through, only to be met by a small door made of steel bars. She cranked open the door and closed it behind her before climbing up tunneled steps to the spectator stands.

A gust of cold, wet air hit her face when she once again faced the elements. She placed her hands on the railing and peered below to find several newbies years younger than her battling against demon toads. Though the size of a person's head, the saliva on their tongues contained poison. One lick would cause paralysis that lasted for several hours.

She shuddered as she remembered her younger years spent training in the arena, and the many scars she'd received.

Tearing her attention away from the girls who weren't more than twelve years old, she scanned the stands. Only a few people remained outside, and Paula, in particular, gripped the railing with tight fists as she intensely watched the training below.

"Lift your weapon!" Paula barked. "It won't do you any good for it to sit in your hand."

Paula muttered a few profanities before she shouted again. After a few moments, she noticed Skaja's presence.

"You're finally here," Paula said as she pushed away from the railing. Anger rolled in her eyes like thunder. "The patrol returned with a severed man's head. Another fool to step foot on our home. Someone recognized him from the Pits. A slave master who made it out alive."

Skaja forced her expression to remain blank, and despite her sudden desire to cradle her hand to her heart, she kept it at her side.

Paula continued. "I expected Arlo and his cronies to send men to attack us. But Heulwen too? They have to be working together. Tell me, Skaja. How do these two places connect?"

Her heart pounded as she answered honestly. "I don't know. Perhaps they have formed an alliance."

"Perhaps..." The valkyrie leader's attention returned to the arena, though her mind seemed miles away. "We could handle Arlo. But I don't want Heulwen's army on our doorstep. Who did we kill? Or did King Liam have profits to be made in the Pits? You have sharp eyes, Skaja. What did you see? What can you tell me?"

A dam of relief burst in her, and her shoulders relaxed as she released a breath. Paula didn't know. Her secret was safe.

"Men, women, slaves."

"Did you see Arlo?"

The question caught her off guard. Another wave of unease turned in her stomach. If she admitted the truth to it, Paula would likely be able to connect the missing pieces together.

Heat tumbled in her blood, the need to protect, no matter the cost. She didn't know why she opened her mouth, or why a lie spewed out. "Arlo wasn't there. At least not as far as I could tell."

Paula gave her a side glance as if searching for the lie, but to her relief, she said nothing more on the subject. Instead, she gestured below. "Those girls will grow up together. They will form a strong bond. Strength and loyalty and trust. These are our valkyrie values."

She cringed inwardly when she realized Paula might suspect something after all. Skaja was plenty strong. But loyal and trustworthy?

Her jaw clenched when she realized she had not adhered to their values. "Anything else you need of me?"

With a shake of her head, Paula gestured to the skies. "No. You may go."

She took a couple steps, but then halted in her tracks. Trust… Could it be that Paula had not adhered to their values either? It couldn't be true, what the fae man had told her. She needed to know the truth.

No matter how much it might hurt.

"I met someone," she murmured, turning slowly to find Paula's attention focused on her. She tried her best to not give away that he was a man. "This person thought they knew me. They said…they said my name is—was—Scarlett."

Paula inhaled sharply, her eyes wide. "Who did you meet?"

"Then is it true?" Her chin quivered despite trying to rein in her emotions. But it was as if the last two months of suppression had come tumbling out. "My parents abandoned me."

The other valkyrie grimaced, but not apologetically. She swiped a strand of her damp, short brown hair out of her eyes. "I have not been completely honest. Your parents did not abandon you. I stole you from them. I saved you from a life of servitude and gave you freedom instead."

Shock punched her in the gut and knocked the breath from her lungs. She reached out to steady herself against the railing. "What do you mean, servitude?"

"Harpies in the Sun Kingdom find pride in serving. At birth, the parents of the child force them into a blood oath to serve the royal family. To protect them with their lives, even against their will."

"Royal family?" she coughed. Her head spun. She might have lost her balance if not for her grip on the railing. "I would have served King Liam?"

What a horrible, sickening thought.

Paula nodded gravely. "And Prince Calle."

Her eyes widened, her heart stuttering with the revelation. Her mind spun as she recalled all the similarities, all the familiar stories, and the fact that she could hardly harm a hair on the fae man's head. Prince Calle's sweetheart had been killed by King Liam, and then Calle soon after. But what if the prince never died? What if he was covertly forced to a life of slavery in the Pits? A life of pain and suffering?

The fae man was Prince Calle.

Stupid, stupid, stupid! She hadn't even bothered to ask for his name because she hadn't cared. And he hadn't bothered to tell her. She wasn't sure if she was more angry, shocked, or confused. And she wasn't sure if her emotions were directed at Paula or the prince. Her parents hadn't abandoned her. Her entire life had been a lie.

But...

But...

But...

What was the entire truth then? Who was she?

She wasn't positive if the fae man really was Prince Calle, but she needed to know for certain. And only one person could give her the answers she sought.

"I need some space," she gasped, and before Paula uttered another word, she scrambled away and took off in flight. If she flew quickly, she could reach his location by sunrise.

CHAPTER
13

No excuses.
    None whatsoever.
    Especially not the rain.

Calle gritted his teeth as his perspiration mingled with the heavy sheets of rain falling from gray skies. It obscured the view of the village like a thick fog. Yet, he inhaled its cleansing mist and lifted his head to further drench his face and bare chest.

His arms shook with the strain of keeping the stack of crates from crashing to the ground. A rope wound around the crates, which then stretched around a pulley secured to a high branch of a tree, and finally the ends of the rope rested in his hands.

He released a labored breath as he lowered the stack and then pulled on the rope again to raise them. His entire body wanted to give out, but he'd been pushing himself harder and harder these past couple of months.

Courage. Strength. Bravery. Endurance. Honor. Love. Sacrifice.

These words were forever etched onto his skin, and he wanted more than anything to live up to them.

Releasing one last breath, he carefully lowered the crates, not stopping to catch his breath as he backed up several paces. The sun may have been hidden behind clouds, but he still felt its power flickering beneath his skin.

Concentration rested on his brow as he dug deep within himself to find the sun's elusive power. But the magic shied away from him as if it were held prisoner in its own cell of darkness.

Nonetheless, he continued reaching for it. He widened his stance and lifted his hands to point at the nearby tree. Minutes passed. Nothing happened.

He planted his feet more firmly and imagined an explosion of searing sunlight bursting from his fingertips. Still nothing.

After standing still while having a staring contest with the tree, he finally dropped his hands in a wave of frustration. The red, scarred brand on his forearm taunted him, reminding him he was still a slave as long as it marked his arm. Even Cian hadn't been able to remove it.

The frustration tore at him until he could stand it no longer. He picked up Skaja's dagger from the base of the cottage and attacked the scarecrow dummy he'd created. Head. Neck. Heart. Bits and pieces of straw flew in all directions.

He traded the dagger for Cian's precious sword. Instead of unnecessarily blunting the weapon by using it against the target, he practiced his footwork. Still sloppy. He'd never been good at fighting with a one-handed sword. He used to fight with a greatsword, and unfortunately, trading it for a lighter weapon wasn't easy without a teacher.

His wrist burned with pain as he held the sword in both hands. But at least this time, he didn't drop it. The muscles in his hand and wrist were growing stronger.

Almost too slowly.

Spattering rain drowned out all noise, making him feel as if he were in his own private cloud. So, when he heard a *scuff* behind him, he spun around.

The pounding fear in his heart quickly turned into shock when he found himself gazing back at a beautiful harpy. Skaja's golden-white wings drooped, soaked with rain. Her brown hair clung to her face and shoulders. Fatigue rested beneath her eyes. But the pain in her expression gave him pause. When he wanted to run to her and spin her in his arms with the joy of seeing her again, he remained rooted to the spot.

The roaring rain almost claimed her words. "You're Prince Calle Everdon."

Her expression begged him to contradict her. He remained quiet, even when his pulse thundered in surprise. How did she find out? Why was she here? Did she come alone?

But when no one joined her in their cloud of rain, he relaxed.

"I think this is a conversation best held indoors, out of the rain." He reached out to touch her but thought better of it and retracted his hand. Instead, he tied Skaja's stone to his left wrist, gathered up his weapons, and guided her inside. She followed.

The smell of old wood and musty books greeted them, with a hint of sweet leaf tea lingering in the background. Rain pattered against the rooftop, leaking through the worn patchwork in several places. One of the buckets began to overflow, so he picked it up off the ground, opened the wooden shutters, and tossed the water out before replacing it beneath the leakage.

When he turned, he caught Skaja staring at him from where she stood in the doorway. A blush filled her cheeks, and she quickly glanced away.

A wave of excitement and satisfaction churned within him. Perhaps he was starting to look how he used to years ago instead of gaunt and underweight. He quickly tried to push the feeling back down.

He disappeared beneath the folding screen beside the bed and pulled on a dry shirt and trousers. He came back out with a blanket tucked beneath his arm, only to find Skaja glancing about warily.

"I'm alone, if that's what you're worried about," he said as he handed the blanket to her and watched as she wrapped it around her shivering shoulders. "Cian hasn't returned from Heulwen yet, and his last letter hasn't said anything about him returning soon."

When she still said nothing, his mouth worked its way into a frown. He crouched beside the hearth, wishing to start a fire with his magic. Instead, he settled for flint and steel. A fire quickly sparked to life. He moved to the stove next and poured a couple cups of tea. Still warm, though not as warm as he would have liked.

Skaja took the cup from him and stared into the hearth as the flames continued to rise. While she sat on the sofa, he perched cautiously on the arm.

"It's good to see you," he said finally, breaking the tense silence between them. "I wasn't sure if I would. How did you find me?"

She gave him a teasing half-grin. "I just located the stench of fae slave and followed."

He cracked a smile at her humor, grateful for the jest. "I don't stink. Anymore," he amended as he thought of how long he'd gone without a proper bath in the Pits. "How did you really find me?"

She nodded to her dagger he'd placed on the kitchen table. "My dagger has a pair. It located its other half. Why else do you think I gave it to you, other than to be able to find you and finish my original job?"

"You can't kill me," he chuckled. "I think you left it behind because you couldn't help the urge in your blood."

The air once again stiffened with tension. Dozens upon dozens of words swirled in his mind, but he couldn't grasp onto any long enough to form a proper sentence. How were they supposed to start this conversation? What did she want to know? What lines should he avoid stepping over?

"You never told me your name," she accused finally, giving him a characteristic glare.

He shrugged and took a long sip of his tea. Its naturally sweet flavor coated his tongue. "I didn't intentionally hide my identity from you. I honestly forgot. In the Pits, it's easy to lose yourself. You start answering to 'slave' or 'worthless cretin'. No one has called me by my name in a very long time."

"Calle. Everdon."

His body hummed pleasantly in response to the way his name fell from her lips. He liked hearing it. A lot.

Reaching across several feet to the hearth, Calle grabbed a fire poker and encouraged the flames to grow with a few prods. "I want to think you came to visit because you like my company…" He turned to grin at her. She did not appear amused. "Tell me the real reason why you're here."

She tucked herself further beneath the blanket as if to make herself smaller. "The valkyrie leader, Paula, confirmed your story. She stole me from my parents. To give me a life of freedom rather than servitude. And I'm…angry." Her jaw clenched and her eyes grew misty. "Angry at her. Angry at you. Angry at my parents. Angry at myself." She whispered, "I'm so confused."

Her head dropped into her hands, her wings drooping where she sat. Caution led his actions as he set his tea aside and slid onto the cushion next to her. He warily lifted his hand and placed it on her shoulder as she had once done for him. Instead of shifting away like he thought she might, she leaned into his touch. He dared to trail his fingers across her shoulders while trying his best to avoid touching her blanket-covered wings. When he had her firmly in his grasp, he slowly pulled her toward him until her head rested against his chest.

A different kind of tension filled the cottage. Heat crawled up his body and encouraged his heart to beat faster and faster until he was certain she might hear it where her ear rested against him.

He wasn't sure what surprised him more—his own reaction to her proximity, or the fact that she didn't move away.

"Will you tell me about them?" she whispered. "I want to learn about my parents."

He swallowed, his gaze far away as he tried to figure out where to start. "Avonia and Typheal had a special bond with my family. They were my parents' personal guards, though more like family than anything. They laughed with us, ate with us, played with us." A smile lifted his lips as he recalled the fond memories. "I remember playing with you too, as much as a six-year-old could play with a one-year-old."

She inhaled sharply, and her body stiffened, but she still didn't retreat.

Continuing, he said, "Our parents often joked that I would choose you as my bride when I turned twenty-one because of how often I sought you out. But then..." A storm of emotion clouded his memories, and the room grew colder despite the roaring fire in the hearth. "You were in the courtyard, but then suddenly...you were gone. Your parents were frantic. The entire palace searched for you for a long time. Months. Years. They left no kingdom untouched."

"I always thought..." She shivered against him, but he didn't dare pull her any closer in fear she would retract from him completely. "I always thought they abandoned me. Paula led me to believe it. I feel…cheated. Betrayed. So very confused."

The pain in her voice constricted his heart. "You certainly weren't abandoned. You were very loved." Another wave of heartache crashed into him as he recalled their despair. "They were never quite the same afterward. Never had another child. Withdrew from many activities with my family. At least until my parents were killed in a shipwreck when I was sixteen. They took it hard and often blamed themselves for not being there with them. The two of them became family after the incident, as if they were my own parents."

He shifted to hide his gathering emotions when she glanced up at him. He cleared his throat and continued. "I knew something awful was going to happen the day Nyana was killed. I told them to let Liam have his way with me. I knew it would put them in danger if they interfered. They fought by my side despite my plea."

"What happened to them?" she asked hoarsely.

His gaze darted to the plume of white feathers sticking out of the blanket. "Avonia was allowed to remain working at the palace. Typheal's wings were…taken, and Liam cast him out of the kingdom and branded him as a traitor."

Skaja's eyes widened in horror, and this time she pulled away from him and climbed to her feet as if to put distance between them. "They severed his wings?"

The alarm in her expression kept him from nodding, but she must have taken his silence as acknowledgement. All too suddenly, her shock turned to anger. A part of him expected her to slap him, but her hand remained within the confines of the blanket.

"Why didn't you release them from their blood oath?" Her voice hitched, on the verge of shouting.

Knowing her temperament, he forced his own voice to remain calm and steady. "To offer is considered an insult, Skaja. Harpies are...prideful...and they consider it an honor to serve. If your parents wanted to be released, they would have made a formal request in front of the council."

"Why would anyone want to serve the likes of you and Liam?" she shouted. "Paula was right to take me away. I could never serve a monster against my will."

Monster...

The likes of you and Liam...

No one had ever compared him to his brother in such a way. Pain slammed its fists against his heart as he stared back at Skaja in the stony silence of the cottage. When the fire crackled in the hearth, they both jumped.

The pain in his chest festered like a bleeding sun. But still he tried his best to remain calm. "Skaja, I know you're angry, though I'm not sure why your anger is directed at me. What have I done to warrant being a monster?"

"I didn't mean you." She twisted a ring on her finger, and he caught the faintest glimpse of gold. "But you could have helped them."

Now it was his turn to place his head in his hands. "You don't know Liam. He's worse than he sounds." He rubbed the sudden ache in his temples. "Harpies swear themselves to fealty to protect the royal family. What happens when two brothers are trying to kill each other? Whose side do they take? Who do they protect? Each harpy had to make a decision. I can't imagine it was easy." He lifted his head and met her eye. "What was I supposed to do, Skaja? They made their choice. But in the end, I couldn't help them. I couldn't even help myself."

"Because Liam sent you to the Pits."

He nodded. "My brother would never subject me to an easy fate like death. He wanted me to suffer."

"And perhaps he also believed you threatened his position on the throne." She stared down at her hand and twisted the ring on her finger again. This time he caught a glimpse of the sun star.

He gasped and jumped up to snatch her hand. He turned the ring, so the sun star faced him. "Where did you get this?"

When she tried to tug her hand away, he held on tighter just to make sure. Yes, this had come from Heulwen. Only those in the king's service were allowed to keep them.

"It's my trophy."

In other words, she'd killed the man who had previously worn the ring. But why?

As if hearing his unspoken question, she explained, "Heulwen soldiers keep attacking our home, and I wasn't sure why until now. I think your brother knows you're no longer in the Pits."

The blood drained from his face, and he finally dropped her hand. "He thinks the valkyries are keeping me prisoner?" They wouldn't have found his body in the Pits. The next guess was either he escaped, or the valkyries had taken him. But what was Liam's goal? To kill him and finish the job? Or to force him into a fate worse than the Pits? He couldn't possibly imagine a more dreadful suffering.

He felt as if he stood in the middle of a triangle, and no matter which way he turned, his enemies came at him in all directions. Liam likely didn't know where he was, and his best guess was with the valkyries.

"Are your valkyrie friends all right? Is anyone hurt?"

She raised an eyebrow high and loosened her grip on the blanket until her shoulders and the top of her wings peeked out the top. "You are worried about my friends? You do realize they would sooner kill you than allow you to live?"

"Yes, but..." His throat constricted when she allowed the blanket to drop entirely at her feet. Her beautiful wings extended halfway as if in an attempt to dry them by the fire's glow. His gaze lingered on her bare shoulders and the metal beadwork clasped around a delicate neck.

"But?" she urged, snapping him out of his stupor.

His gaze darted to her eyes, and he tried his best to keep it there as he stood. "Valkyries saved my life. *You* saved my life. I vowed to worship the very ground a valkyrie walked on and kiss the daylights out of them." He smirked when her gaze darted to his lips. "But I realized that would sooner earn me a blade to the gut."

"How very right you are." Despite her words, he didn't miss the flush that crawled up her neck.

"What I'm getting at is this—valkyries have my respect. I consider you my friend. I consider all of you my friends."

Skaja laughed out loud, holding her belly as if she'd never heard anything funnier in her life. "You can't be serious," she snorted. She slowly advanced on him until she backed him up against the wall, and although she pointed a finger at his throat, he felt as if it were a dagger. "You are delusional, fae prince, if you think you can ever be friends with a valkyrie."

"I stand by what I said." He held his ground and met her glower unflinchingly. "You. Are. My. Friend."

"I don't make friends with men."

"Then why are you still here?"

She slowly lowered her finger, and her glower transitioned into uncertainty. "I can't go back," she said miserably. "I can't face Paula right now."

"You can stay with me."

"Here?" Her damp wings snapped close to her body, spraying droplets of water across the wood floor. Her gaze traveled around the small cottage, likely built with one person in mind who never received visitors. Each room was conjoined into one large one, offering very little livable space.

Her hands rested on her hips as she spotted the bed. "I can't stay here with you. You are a man."

Despite her legitimate concern, his lips twitched in amusement. "And?" He sat on the edge of the kitchen table and crossed his ankles. "I've been accustomed to sleeping in a rocky cave with sharp pebbles digging into my back. I think I can manage sleeping on the sofa for a bit."

"But..." Rain pounded on the roof in their momentary silence, and she bit her lip as she turned in another full circle. "What if your friend returns?"

"What about it?"

"Where would I go then?"

Calle quirked his head to the side as he studied her. A jolt of surprise traveled through him when he realized she really didn't want to go back. She must have been more upset about her situation than she let on.

He pointed to the floor in front of him. "Here. You always have a place here."

Before she managed a reply, he crossed the room to the small desk tucked into the corner. Crisp edges and crumpled papers brushed his fingers as he searched, and the scent of ink followed his progress. Finally, his fingers closed around an opened envelope. He grimaced as he handed it to her.

"I admit I was far too eager to hear from your parents, even if it hadn't been meant for my eyes. Avonia—your mother," he amended in case she forgot her name, "sent this letter to me to give to you if I saw you again."

"Me?" she breathed as she traced the edges of the envelope with her fingertip. "How does she know already? I only found out the truth for certain yesterday."

The entire universe halted when she glanced at the envelope, and then at the fire. Was she...? She wouldn't, would she? He wasn't sure if he could quite recite the contents of the letter by heart if she destroyed it.

In the end, she crossed the room and gazed out at the rain pounding against the window and bathing the cottage in a clean start. Her eyes became glassy. Emotional. Uncertain.

"If you want...I could read it to you?"

Drip. Drip. Drip.

Raindrops broke through the anxious tension as they fell into the bowls throughout the room. Skaja's wings drooped as if in tune with her mood. Her finger traced each edge of the envelope. The somber expression on her face broke his heart in two.

"I'm not sure I can do this."

"That's fine." He gave her an encouraging smile. "Perhaps hold onto it for a while. Think about it."

He started toward the door, and the moment his hand touched it, she called after him. "Where are you going?"

Giddiness fluttered through his stomach, surprising him. He still couldn't believe Skaja had come back. This time, he hoped she wouldn't leave. "To get more firewood."

CHAPTER
14

The letter inside Skaja's pocket grew heavier with each passing minute. The rain refused to abate, which cooped her up inside far longer than she liked, with little to distract her other than the weight bearing down on her person.

She rifled through medicinal and other types of volumes on the shelves. Several books lay open on the kitchen table about the properties of magical brands. Was Calle trying to find a way to remove his brand? The only ways she knew how were for his slave master to willingly release him or to kill his slave master entirely.

She continued scouring every inch of the cottage until she knew the layout, the weaknesses, and the strengths. A floorboard beneath her foot creaked, and as she opened and closed the front door, she frowned when it made no sound. It opened far too easily for her comfort. If someone snuck inside, she likely wouldn't know until it was too late.

Bang! Bang! Bang!

She jumped at the sudden clamor. Calle must have climbed onto the roof. Judging by the slowing pace of one of the drips from the ceiling, he was fixing the shingles.

When she crossed the cottage, the floorboard creaked again. She knelt down, snapped open her dagger, and dug the tip of the weapon into the crack. With a couple heaves, the board came loose and revealed the valuables inside the empty space.

Sacks of coins. Stacks of letters. A golden ring with a strange symbol on it. A jeweled dagger.

"Too easy," she muttered as she rifled through the letters. Typheal's name on some of the letters shocked her. Her father. The reminder of her parents only burned her through her pocket.

"Who owns this cottage again?" Skaja shouted, and the banging above her ceased suddenly.

"Cian," he called back.

"Well, tell your friend, Cian, he should find a better hiding spot for his valuables. I found them in minutes."

She swore she heard him chuckle through both the layers of roof and the pounding rain.

She continued to shamelessly rifle through Cian's belongings. Something dark and glittery caught her attention in the furthest corner of the hiding space. Wings flattening as she dug deeper, her finger touched the corner of the object, and then another finger, until she managed to grab a hold of it. She pulled it out and inspected it.

A book.

Not just any book. It was heavy, and not in the normal sense. A great magic lay within its pages, some dark, some light, and some in between.

A plume of dust tickled her nose as she blew off the top layer of grime. The book had no title, but the author's name rested at the bottom of the cover in shimmering silver letters— *Killian Graves.* Beautiful gold, black, and green designs decorated the edges and spine. The dried ink sparkled when she tipped it every which way.

The book pulsed with life, with energy. It sang beautiful ballads in her mind. It beckoned her toward the unknown. Toward the peaceful. Toward the frightening. Darkness. Light. Mystery.

She opened it to the first page.

A gasp of wonder caught in her throat. Each margin was hand-painted to depict images of humans, fae, beasts, and more, with numerous symbols. Roses. Stars. Fangs. Moons. Apples. Strings of gold ribbon. Mountains of silver. One page was dedicated to Heulwen's sun star. Each of the twelve points symbolized something different, and the star as a whole symbolized strength.

She continued leafing through the pages and soon realized the book was divided into sections. Sun Fae. Forest Fae. Ocean Fae.

Her fingers traced over purple and silver lettering of the next section. Shadow Fae.

The magic lying between the pages of this section pulsed with darkness. With many horrible and dreadful things. With lies and death and secrets.

She slammed the book shut and dropped it to the floor. Her understanding of magic was minimal, but even she felt the raw, dark power within the pages.

Another shimmer in the darkness of the hiding place caught her eye, and although her heart still thrummed in her throat, she reached for it. Her fingers closed around a stack of metal sheets. They were silver, but the images on them flickered in different shades of gold.

Her heart constricted in surprise when the images moved as if they captured a single memory. The top sheet caught her attention. Two little boys laughed as they chased each other around a tree, though she couldn't hear the accompanying sound. They stopped suddenly, and the taller of the two wrapped his arm around the other. They couldn't have been more than five or six years old.

Without needing confirmation, she recognized the younger of the two as Calle. He had the same haircut as he did now, shoulder-length with two braids on either side of his face. But the boy next to him was unfamiliar. A friend, perhaps?

Though, she couldn't begin to guess which one. He apparently had innumerable friends.

"That's me and Liam, if you can believe it," a voice said over her shoulder.

Blindingly fast, Skaja reached for her lone dagger and snapped it open. The tip of the blade touched Calle's chest. His eyes widened, and he slowly held his hands up placatingly.

"Never sneak up on a valkyrie," she warned as she sheathed her weapon.

The door needed rusty hinges, she decided. She hadn't heard him enter the cottage.

She bit her lip when she realized she all too easily let her guard down around him. Something about him made her feel comfortable, which also created a pit of discomfort.

Like the first time she'd seen him upon their reunion, she couldn't help but stare. Wet, auburn hair slicked across his forehead. His damp clothes clung to defined muscles—muscles she was positive hadn't been there two months earlier. And his amber eyes suddenly became hot liquid, ensnaring her in its molten lava.

Her wings ruffled as a shiver ran through her, and only when she forced herself to break eye contact did her wits return to her. This feeling was...unfamiliar. Strange. Admittedly pleasant.

And wholly unwelcome.

She returned her attention to the metal memory. "But you two look so happy."

"We were." He settled down beside her, so close, but not touching. "I was five years old then. I came into my magic at age six. At first, Liam was excited, because he thought he too would come into his own magic. He didn't. Each year that passed, he became more and more bitter toward me."

"Magic put a wall between the two of you."

He nodded. "A very tall, sturdy wall."

She flipped to the next metal sheet to find a lovely young woman with long curls and big eyes. Her large smile literally caused flowers to open their petals as she bent to sniff their fragrance.

Beside her, Calle stiffened. "I'd rather not watch this one."

"Why not?" She turned to find him gazing at the wall with a troubled expression on his face. But when she returned her attention to the image, her question was quickly answered. A younger Calle snuck up behind the woman, his smile larger than the moon itself as he pressed a rose to her lips from behind. And just as quickly, he sauntered off as if he didn't want to get caught in the act. The young woman stared after him dreamily.

"Nyana..." she murmured, remembering the name of Calle's deceased sweetheart. "Whose memories are these?"

He flexed his fingers and then moved to play with an errant thread on his damp shirt. "They're mine—some of my more favorite memories. I captured them with my own magic, though in a slightly different perspective. I didn't realize someone had saved them from Liam."

Not wanting to intrude on his memory of Nyana any longer, Skaja set it down and watched the next one. Perhaps she should have left them alone, but her curiosity got the better of her. Besides, Calle wasn't trying to stop her.

In this moving image, younger Calle knelt on the ground with his arms and head resting against the arm of a chair. In the chair sat a winged woman with light hair. She couldn't tell what the color was when only different shades of gold twisted the image into movement. Young Calle smiled, and the image shifted slightly to show that the winged woman held a baby in her arms.

"What did you name her?" older Calle murmured beside her in sync with younger Calle's soundless lips. Then the woman spoke, and Calle recited, "Scarlett Ebony Svera."

A gasp escaped her. She pointed to the sheet. "This is me?" When he nodded, she peered closer for a better look at her mother's face, but the angle was wrong, and mostly rested on the sleeping child in Avonia's arms.

"If all of the sheets are there," he said, motioning to the rest of the stack, "then I believe there might be one or two more memories of you. Or at least, you would be in them. Of course, you're very young still."

She cursed her trembling fingers as she moved to the next in the stack. The last thing she wanted was to show weakness. But Calle didn't seem to care.

She breathed a sigh of relief when the next didn't depict her. Rather, it showed Calle at about age fifteen sitting in a tree with another boy. Golden streams of magic escaped the boy's flute and created detailed illusions of men battling sword against sword.

Young Calle bit through an apple as if he were a carefree child enjoying spending time with his friend.

"Joel," Calle said beside her, motioning to the other boy. A smile grew across his face and chased the shadows of the earlier memory away. "Growing up, we were inseparable."

"I think I can count on one, *maybe* two hands how many friends I have," she said, giving him a sideways glance. "How many do you have?"

He shrugged and gave her a charming half-smile. Her stomach reacted by tying itself in knots. "I might need a few more hands to help me count."

"A few dozen," she corrected, which earned her a laugh. She couldn't help but smile.

And then a thought struck her.

"If I want to be released from this blood oath, would I have to appear before a council?"

He shook his head, though the tilt of his head indicated his curiosity. "There is nothing formal about us. Our setting. Our friendship. Our history. If you want to be released, all you have to do is ask me."

Her mouth opened to ask, but the words halted on her tongue. This blood oath had brought them together in the first place. If she lost it now, how much more would she lose? What would happen to her future? "I'll keep that in mind," she said instead as she pulled out another silver sheet.

The next memory caused her heart to stick in her throat. Calle didn't explain it to her, and he didn't need to. Two harpies stood in the sunshine, both with smiles on their faces. The man held a little girl above his head and repeatedly tossed her into the air while she flapped her wings.

"My parents." She swallowed and ran a finger over each of their wings. "They're teaching me how to fly."

"Is that what they were doing?" he murmured before he pointed to the young boy perched in the tree above them, reaching out to touch her wings each time they flapped. "You never did fly. You were probably still too young."

"Probably..."

The letter in her pocket burned hotter and hotter as if in tune with her emotions. Her parents had cared about her. From what it looked like, they'd loved her. Very much. They hadn't abandoned her. Calle had told the truth.

Without a word, she gathered up the memories and sought refuge on the bed, where the smallest sliver of a dresser gave her some privacy. In the gathering darkness, she lit the lantern on the bed side table and slowly pulled the letter from her pocket. The envelope was addressed to C.E. which must have stood for Calle Everdon. But as she unfolded the letter, the words staring back on the page knocked the air out of her.

The opening of the letter had Scarlett crossed out and Skaja printed just above it. The paper rattled in her trembling fingers. Tears gathered in her eyes, and for a moment, she wondered if she had the strength to read it.

She swiped the moisture away and read.

My dearest Skaja,

I am at a loss for words. When I'd heard of C.E.'s survival, my knees buckled. When I learned you were still alive, and he knew where you were, I felt as if I drew my first breath since you were taken from us.

We searched for you for years. My heart shattered. It still hurts that I was not able to watch you grow up. Something absolutely precious was taken from me. From your father. Something we can never get back.

But this wonderful news brings me so much joy, and I hope more than anything C.E. will be able to deliver this letter to you.

We would like to meet you if you would allow it. Please consider writing back. It would make me the happiest person in the world.

Your loving mother,
Avonia

Skaja stared at the page for seconds, minutes, hours—she wasn't sure. When exhaustion finally bore its weight on her shoulders, she laid down on the bed and stared at the wall. Her parents wanted to meet her. But did she want to meet them? She feared they would be nothing but strangers when she longed for love and connection.

And her father...

She swallowed the lump in her throat. He was a man. How was she supposed to face him? The only man she felt comfortable around was Calle. The rest she preferred to meet an untimely end at the tip of her blade.

In the lantern light, the beautiful golden swirls of each memory on the silver sheets caught her eye. Her heart grew heavy as she watched her mother smile down at her as a baby, and then as both her parents taught her to fly.

Weight continued to pile on after she switched the silver sheet. A deep, aching, foreign desire entered her heart as she gazed at the scene of Calle and Nyana. The beauty of it. The love. It was wrong to wish it were her instead. So very wrong.

She twisted the golden band around her finger, the one that always reminded her of Calle. No matter what way she angled the silver sheet, she couldn't envision her own face in Nyana's place. She and Calle were very different people. She was a valkyrie in this life, and in another life, she would have been his servant.

She blew out the lantern and turned on her side in resignation as darkness bathed this part of the cottage. Flames still continued to flicker on the other side, popping and crackling and spreading the warm scent of hearth. Rain pattered against the roof, and she listened for small plops of rainwater hitting bowls but didn't find any.

When she started to turn over again, she paused. "I can feel you looking at me," she called toward the sofa. "What do you want?"

Calle's voice answered back. "I'm curious. How do you sleep without crushing your wings?"

"It's not hard, fae prince."

A pause. "What is it like to fly?"

She lifted her head, and an unexpected surge of warmth flooded her when she met his gaze. "Wouldn't you know? I flew you out of the Pits."

"I don't remember much of it."

Memories flashed across her mind's eye. Calle being whipped. His bloodied back. His pale, gaunt face. How little he'd weighed when she'd picked him up. The nightmares in his eyes.

"It's...freedom."

Their conversation ended there. The long flight from her valkyrie home crashed on her, and she started drifting off far too quickly. She cradled both her ring and her mother's letter to her heart. Very little made sense anymore. And for the first time in a while, she wasn't sure what to do next.

CHAPTER
15

Darkness shrouded him like a thick, wool blanket. Suffocating and heavy. Shadows bounced and curled and clawed as they stalked toward him. Calle tried to outrun them, but his body refused to move. Not even a flicker of light pierced the thick shadows. No matter which way he looked, unending black pulled him into its depths.

Dark.

Dark.

Dark.

And then he was falling.

He scrambled to find something to break his fall, but his fingers only raked across loose rocks and sand made of ebony nightmares. A scream escaped his mouth when suddenly, his throat opened up. He smashed hard into the ground.

Dizziness climbed up his body and shook his limbs as he managed to shakily climb to his hands and knees, even though every bone in his body felt broken and bruised.

"There you are," a deep, chilling voice said.

His heart leaped from his chest and wilted into dried petals as he turned his head, only to find the hard, unforgiving face of Arlo Stokes staring down at him.

Arlo snarled menacingly. "You can never run far. You belong to me."

The slave master raised his whip, and it cracked so fast through the air that he couldn't follow its movement. Another scream escaped him as it struck his back. His limbs collapsed beneath him, and before he attempted to crawl pathetically for refuge, a boot stepped on his neck and pinned him to the cold, sharp ground.

Air refused to enter his lungs no matter how hard he tried to draw breath. A heavy weight dragged him underneath frigid waters. Cold. Dark. Hopeless—

Calle gasped and shot up into a sitting position. He clawed at his throat to remove the boot, but instead of finding a rough leather boot, he touched soft, warm skin.

"Shh," Skaja soothed as she touched his hands, his face, his hair. "It was only a bad dream."

Her face finally came into focus in the darkness. Pinched, concerned brows. Pursed lips. Hair falling across her forehead.

He shook his head, suddenly aware of the perspiration that clung to his skin. His back ached where he'd been whipped. His throat still burned for air. The slave brand on his forearm rippled with heat. "N-n-no. It w-w-wasn't a d-d-dream."

"It was," she said in a soothing tone, and for the first time since they'd met, her eyes were kind and gentle. Her fingers stroked either side of his hair. She was touching him... And not just an uncertain, awkward touch. A compassionate caring lingered in her caress, and he couldn't help but lean into her hand.

She stilled.

"Please don't stop," he whispered.

A pause. But then her fingers continued their exploration. Her light touch skimmed his hair, his eyebrows, his nose, his cheekbones. They hesitantly touched his earlobe before she more daringly traced the shape of his long, pointed ear.

His heart slowed into something calmer. Something safer. The fear in his soul settled to the bottom of a clear, placid lake. The pain in his back and throat ebbed. The burn on his forearm died slowly like a waning fever.

He breathed in Skaja's scent of jasmine and cool midnight skies and breathed out a river of calm. She was right. It was only a dream.

Yet, it had felt so real.

A flash of darkness passed across his mind, and as if he once again found himself in the deep ravine of the Pits, his hands began trembling. Skaja's gentle touch trailed from his ear, to his shoulder, down his arm, before she clasped his hand. Her touch felt so good. Like a breath of sunlight after being caged in the darkness for so long.

"Do you want to talk about it?" she murmured, and the gentle tone of her voice further coaxed him into the waters of safety. "The Pits?"

He shook his head, even as darkness clouded his haunted expression.

"I can handle it," she insisted.

"I know you can. But I can't." He placed his other hand on top of hers, closed his eyes, and released a long breath. "I wish I could forget."

They sat in the darkness for a few minutes, the safety of silence between him. He hung his head as her presence chased his shadows away. Her thumb circled the back of his hand, and as if emboldened by the way he drank it in, she picked up his left hand and smoothed the anxiety out of it as well.

She flipped his hand over and stilled. He opened his eyes to find her staring at her stone tied around his wrist. "You still have it."

He nodded, silently hoping she wouldn't release him yet. He craved her touch. He wanted more. "I followed your counsel. I squeeze it in my hand throughout the day, for hours every day. It has helped strengthen my hand considerably."

"Let me see."

Like the first time, she threaded her fingers through his, but she didn't twist his wrist until pain misted his eyes with tears. Instead, she waited.

The inevitable pain didn't scare him quite as much because he found it more bearable. He squeezed her hand. Harder. Harder. Harder. Until agony rippled through his wrist. He hissed and allowed his muscles to go limp.

"Much better," she commented. "You may be able to improve its condition a little further."

When she still didn't release him, his heart leaped to the skies and burst to life in a shower of red and white fireworks. He didn't stop the heat of fondness from coursing through him. He didn't want to either. Instead, he breathed it in, the heat smoldering in his lungs.

Don't touch her, he warned himself, afraid she might scamper off like a frightened animal if he crossed any discomforting lines.

Though, he would never deny her if she crossed those lines first.

Like now.

Her finger trailed across the sun star tattoo on his wrist, visible in the approaching light of dawn.

"This is beautiful," she murmured. "What does it mean?"

He watched, transfixed as she touched him. It had been so long since he'd touched another, other than embracing Cian a couple of months ago, however fleeting. He craved the contact that made him feel alive again.

"It's tradition for Sun Fae to cover their scars with tattoos," he explained. "Only, we do not get to choose the tattoo, nor the accompanying color. Gold is the highest honor. Next is silver. Then bronze. All the way to black, which is disgraceful. This…" He traced a part of the star but made sure not to brush against her as he did it. "…is a word repeated over and over to form the star. It says 'sacrifice' in our tongue."

Her lips parted as if she wished to ask another question, but she quickly closed her mouth and retracted her hand. All too quickly, she stood and put distance between them. It was as if her loss of touch blew out the candle in his heart, allowing ice to climb through the cracked window.

"Your footwork is sloppy," she said as she crossed the room to gaze out the window. Rain no longer fell from the sky, but the gray clouds from yesterday still lingered. "Your weakness in your left hand clearly shows, as you do not do a good job at hiding it. It's obvious you have relied far too much on your magic. Your stance is more defensive than offensive, even when you are trying to attack an inanimate object. If you were faced with more than one opponent, you would surely lose."

He raised his eyebrows, surprised at the sudden conversation change. "Is there anything I'm decent at?"

"No." A wicked smile grew across her face. "But I will teach you."

CHAPTER
16

"Again."

Skaja watched as Calle's chest rose up and down with each labored breath. Perspiration dotted every inch of his skin and soaked his shirt. Strands of his damp hair clung to his face. His eyes blazed with determination as he jumped forward and struck his sword against her two daggers. Once. Twice. Three times. The power behind each attack took her by surprise, and she braced against it by planting her feet more firmly on the ground. He was certainly much stronger than he'd been in the Pits.

He'd been right.

Had he been at full strength in the Pits, combined with the element of surprise he'd possessed during their first fight, he would have won the battle.

She ducked his swing, rolled across the grass, and kicked him in the back of the knee. He stumbled in the opposite direction, and by the time he faced her again, she was already back on her feet.

"You are relying too much on strength," she said, both her daggers poised to attack. "Anticipate where I'll be before I get there. Move quicker when on the offensive and widen your stance when on the defensive."

"I don't want to hurt you."

She raised an eyebrow high. He was holding back? Exactly what would the enemy be dealing with if he had no reservations at all?

"You have no idea what I endured during training as a valkyrie. Fighting you is nothing in comparison."

Not giving him a chance to respond, she charged forward with both daggers. He managed to block her swing but moved too slowly and gave her the opportunity to stab him with her other dagger. The tip of the blade hovered above his belly button. He jumped backward and knocked it away with his weapon.

"Your left side was open again," she commented.

He ran a hand over his face and groaned. "I don't know how to cater to my weakness."

Several feet separated them as she met his eye, and then glanced toward the left side of his body. She tapped her lips with her fingers. "That's what shields are for. But I know for a fact you can't hold a shield. You'd be too busy dropping it all the time. Someone would kill you in your distraction."

He frowned, but otherwise said nothing.

"Hypothetically…" She met his gaze again, and a sliver of warmth snaked down her spine. The fae prince was handsome. Even more so since he'd first walked out of the barber shop in Oddwaran. "If you still had your magic, what could you do with it? Could you create a shield you could hold?"

Slowly, he nodded as if contemplating the feat. "It doesn't have to weigh much, but as long as my magic held, so would the shield."

"And you could summon it at will."

"Except I don't have my magic. And I'm not sure if I ever will." The feat to restore his magic seemed hopeless.

She attacked again. Right side, shoulder, throat.

Block. Block. Block.

Left side.

Stumble. Pause.

She tapped her lips again. "You would benefit from wearing armor on the left side of your body. But then again, you are already slow. The armor would only weigh you down."

His many weaknesses stared back at her like a bright, billowing torch fire.

This time, he surged forward and attacked her. She blocked with both daggers, but the strength of the blow caused her weapons to slip.

She cried out and dropped her daggers, clutching her arm as she crumpled to the ground.

Calle swore under his breath and dropped his sword. "Skaja, I am so sorry. Where—"

When he leaned down as if to help her, she hooked her legs around his and knocked him off balance. "Ha!" she shouted triumphantly before flipping him over in one fluid movement, taking him by surprise as he landed hard on his back. His expression turned from initial shock to wonder when the sunlight cast brilliant colors off her feathers. "Another weakness of yours—compassion."

"Compassion is not a weakness," he grunted. "It's a strength."

"Not in battle, it's not. I could have already killed you at least a dozen times today already. And I'm only one woman."

"A valkyrie."

"Imagine if there were two of me."

"If there were two of you, there would be twice the beauty to look at."

She stiffened. "What?"

"What?"

Heat spread across her face as she noticed their position. Her hands pinned him to the grass by his arms. She sat atop him, straddling him in a rather intimate manner. Their faces were too close. Only inches apart.

Panic clawed at her, and she reacted instinctively as she raised her hand and slapped him across the face. The sound echoed in the small clearing and off the stones of the cottage, almost louder than Calle's shock. Her eyes widened just as quickly. "Sorry."

She rolled off him and tucked her wings shyly against her person, only to find him climbing to his feet while cradling his hand to his red cheek. "Stop slapping me."

"Then stop..." She gestured to all of him, not knowing how, exactly, to express her thoughts or feelings.

He rubbed his cheek, and then his back as if it were also sore. "If you slap me for a simple compliment, I shudder to think what you'd do to me if I actually tried to kiss you."

Kiss...

The rhythm of her heart picked up speed as her gaze darted to his lips. Did he want to kiss her? Or was he simply teasing her?

She pushed her curiosity of what it might feel like to kiss him behind her shy wings.

He leaned his sword against the nearby tree and stalked away. "I'm exhausted and sweaty. I'm going to bathe."

She set her own weapons aside and followed in the direction he'd disappeared. A brief splash echoed over the cottage rooftop, and when she rounded the corner, she took in the sight of a murky, yet beautiful pond. Lily pads dotted the edges of the water while cattails stretched over the glassy surface. A copse of tall, leafy trees shaded the pond in a cloud of privacy and cast a shadow across Calle's surprised face.

The water appeared cool and refreshing, a waiting relief after a long morning of training. She reached behind her neck to unclasp the top part of her dress, and as she started to slip it off, Calle averted his gaze.

"What are you doing?"

"What does it look like?" she asked as she stripped to her undergarments and waded into the frigid pond until her feet almost couldn't reach the bottom. "We weren't done with our conversation, so I'm joining you." By the way he still maintained eye contact with the clouds, she felt like she'd done something wrong.

"No," he said finally in a raspy voice. "You should leave. Otherwise, you might slap me again. Times ten. Or a hundred." He splashed the cold water over his face.

Slowly, her attention drifted from his bare chest to her undergarments revealing plenty of her skin. "Oh…" A flush crept up her body until it flared hot in her cheeks. Her wings quickly curled around herself to hide from his view. "Valkyries bathe together. I'm getting the impression that men and women don't."

"Well, not usually." His wicked, roguish grin gave him away, though he still averted his gaze as he chuckled and released a long breath. "But you are certainly welcome to stay."

She rolled her eyes and splashed water at him, which earned her amused laughter. She refused to let him win, so she curled her wing further around herself to give her a bubble of privacy to wash.

Cold water rushed over her skin, refreshing her aching muscles after hours of fighting. She tipped her head back to immerse her hair completely in the water. "I've been thinking…" Splashing ceased momentarily as if he paused to listen. "You can't wear armor. You can't hold a shield. You can't hold two swords. What if you used a sword in your good hand, and in your other, you wielded a small dagger? One small enough to fit in your boot."

"Won't it cut me?"

She lowered her wing to peer over it. "Not if you…"

The words got lost on her tongue as her gaze raked over him. His back faced her, but until now, she hadn't noticed the beautiful golden tattoos across his back. The whipping scars from earlier were no longer visible beneath shimmering gold ink.

And when the sunlight broke through the clouds above, both his hair and the tattoos glimmered in a dazzling array of color.

"Not if you..." he urged, but when she didn't answer immediately, he glanced over his shoulder to catch her staring.

The tip of her wing snapped back up to hide the heat growing quickly across her face. Her focus dissolved immediately like a sugar cube immersed in hot water. Scalding hot water. The pond didn't cool her down in the slightest.

A curious, foreign desire fizzled up inside her. To look. To touch. To feel. She lowered her wing again, and as if hearing her do it, he glanced over his shoulder once more. This time, she didn't hide her curiosity.

"Those tattoos are new," she murmured, their previous conversation forgotten. Her heart skipped in surprise when she realized she'd taken several steps toward him. But it was as if a rope tethered them together, and it cinched tighter...tighter...tighter...

Until she stood only a heartbeat away.

The look he gave her scalded her from the inside out, intense and devouring.

"They might have been there before," he said through strained words.

"They weren't. Your shirt was practically ripped to shreds when we met."

Curiosity and unfamiliar desire led her actions as she slowly reached out. Her fingers hovered over a tattoo closest to his shoulder. "What does this mean?"

"Which one?"

He turned slightly to give her a better view. She trailed her fingers from his left shoulder to the lower right side of his back. His skin warmed her hand, her arm, her face, until fire smoldered in her belly. She had never touched a man like this.

"Endurance," he answered.

One by one, she drew a line across each tattoo with her finger, and he replied consecutively, "Honor. Courage. Bravery. Strength. Love."

Then she took his left hand and tugged until he rotated to face her. Her heart beat rapidly at his proximity, and his intense focus turned to her.

She traced the twelve-pointed star on his wrist. "And sacrifice," she finished for him. "Where are your black tattoos?"

"Excuse me?" His mouth twitched in amusement.

"You can't tell me you haven't done anything awful in your life. You couldn't have been all good."

A deep, musical laugh escaped him and sent a delightful shiver down her spine. "Black is reserved for the worst of the worst. I don't have any of those, but I do admit I have a couple of gray ones. I'm not proud of them, but it is what it is."

"Where are they?"

She glanced toward his legs, but she couldn't see through the murky water.

His previous amusement turned into a devilish smirk. "Do you want to find out?"

She blinked several times before his meaning finally clicked in her mind. She splashed water into his face and stalked away from him and toward the grassy shore, all while his laughter trailed after her. Her wings provided her modesty, blocking most of her body from his view. But the moment she stepped onto the grass his laughter stopped.

"What happened to your legs?" The amusement disappeared, replaced by a serious expression that could cut glass.

A frown formed on her face as her gaze traveled to her legs and to the ribbons of scars climbing her ankles and calves. "Training to be a valkyrie is…vigorous." She swished words in her mouth as she considered what to tell him and what to keep to herself. She was embarrassed to admit her shortcomings. "I'm an incredible flyer. But I'm a terrible jumper. You have your weaknesses, fae prince, and I have mine."

Without another word, she strode away and dressed behind the corner of the cottage, out of view. A splash followed as if Calle waded through the water after her. Moments later, she found him dripping wet and wearing only his trousers. Sure enough, a gray and white tattooed design of snowy mountains stood out on his ankle.

She found one. Where was the other?

He still stared at her bare legs with furrowed brows. There was a reason she wore long boots.

"What happened?"

Not wanting to be the object of his scrutiny, she pulled her boots on. "In the training arena, there are spinning blades that pop out of the ground. The object is to get from one side of the arena to the other without getting cut. I couldn't help but use my wings. Paula tied them down to prevent me from flying."

She paused, her gaze far away as she relived the horrible memories. Stinging pain. Ribbons of blood. Shrill threats. Tears of determination. "I failed over and over again."

"How awful…"

Jokingly, she said, "I should get them tattooed. I think a black design might look nice on my legs."

"Black?" He leaned away as if she'd struck him. "I can't imagine you ever receiving black ink."

"No?" She stood as tall as possible, but there was still quite a height gap between them. "Do you have any idea how many people I have killed? How much blood is on my hands? All the horrible things I've done?"

Horrible things she now wasn't sure were in the name of goodness. Her whole life was a lie. Were her motives a lie as well?

Her wings drooped. "I'm starting to think I deserve the blackest of black." She turned, and instead of allowing him to see her troubled expression, she spread her disconsolate wings. "I'll hunt for dinner tonight. I need time to think."

CHAPTER
17

Long hours turned into long days. Long days into long weeks. Calle was slowly losing his mind. But unlike his mind-numbing experience in the Pits, his insanity stemmed from so much waiting, so much training, and so much...Skaja.

He closed his eyes and took a deep breath when her sweet jasmine scent filled his nostrils and almost teased him into action. He longed to touch her. He longed for so much more than covert glances and close proximity. The wick of the candle inside his heart had been dried and wilted for so long, but Skaja set him ablaze.

"Get up," Skaja ordered as she pushed off from where she'd pinned him to the ground. "Do I even have to tell you that closing your eyes will get you killed?"

"There are other fun things two people can do with their eyes closed other than getting stabbed."

He knew he'd said the wrong thing the moment it escaped his mouth, because suddenly he was on his feet with his back to a tree, her strong, armored arm pressed against his throat.

"Holy embers," he gasped against the cold bracer on his skin. "You're fast."

Valkyries were terrifying, he decided as she snarled inches from his face. She looked as if she could cut his face to ribbons with a single bite of her teeth. Yet, she was alluring and far too beautiful for her own good.

"What are you doing?" she asked, confusion setting into her snarl.

Until then, he hadn't realized he'd placed his hands on her waist. Her tight-fitted clothing wasn't only good for flying fast and moving soundlessly, it seemed, because it showed off each of her lovely curves. Each of those curves which were pressed against him...

"You are killing me," he whispered, his voice either raspy with emotion or because he could hardly feel his throat anymore—he wasn't sure.

"I assure you, I'm not." Her grip on his throat loosened, and her hardened expression melted as she dropped her arm entirely. "I would kill you much quicker than strangling the air from you. Besides, I think at this point I wouldn't try to take your life, even without the blood oath in the way."

"That's almost romantic coming from you."

"Romantic?" Her eyebrows furrowed, and as he suspected she might, she lunged at him again. This time, he dodged beneath her arm, twisted her over his back, and pinned her on the ground like she'd done to him only a minute earlier.

Shock stared back at him in the endless brown pool of her eyes. Her chest rose up and down with each deep breath she took. Her golden-white wings fluttered beneath her as if half-heartedly fighting against his grip.

"You bested me," she said, and just the sound of her voice was too much. Not to mention the way her lips moved when she spoke.

Oh, holy saints above. He couldn't resist the temptation any longer. His hands slid along her arms, to her bare shoulders, grazing her neck, and then he dug his fingers into her hair.

And froze.

"What *is* this?" he gasped as he dug his fingers deeper into the pool of brown and gold. The strands wove around his skin as if he dipped his hands in warm, enticing water. It was so soft that he wasn't sure it was entirely there.

"Umm...my hair?"

"This isn't hair. This is liquid silk."

"I'm a harpy," she said as if it explained everything.

He scooped a handful of it and leaned forward to take the risk of kissing the daylights out of her when the beat of a drum in the distance startled them both. He climbed to his feet and glanced in the direction of the pounding rhythm. A line of thick trees blocked his view. Loud chatter and laughter followed the beat, quickly joined by other instruments. They'd been so secluded in their little cottage that he'd almost forgotten the rest of the village existed.

His eyebrows furrowed as he counted the days on his fingers. Could it possibly be...?

"It's the summer solstice," he chuckled, shaking his head in wonder. Dusk settled in the sky, splashing bold yellows, oranges, and pinks across the horizon. "It's an important day for the Sun Fae. You would think I would have remembered."

When he glanced over his shoulder, he found Skaja still lying on her back, staring up at the sky while breathing deeply. Her daggers lay several feet away, but she could move so fast that he doubted it would take less than a second to retrieve them if she tried.

"The summer solstice..." she murmured softly. "It's the day Liam chose his bride, and the day he sent you to the Pits."

"Yes." The scars on his back suddenly ached at the reminder, and his wrist began to throb. The pulsing pain climbed up his arm until the slave brand on his forearm burned. He clenched and unclenched his fingers, but the scorching heat remained. What did it mean? He wasn't even sure where to begin looking for answers.

"You would have chosen your own bride the year after."

This time, he nodded and turned his gaze toward the beautiful sky. He remembered that day in the Pits. The day when he'd felt so much despair and heartache for everything he'd lost.

"How does it work?" she asked, suddenly at his elbow. She stood close enough for her flowery scent to tantalize him once again. "Choosing a bride?"

He cast her a sideways glance filled with disbelief. But he reminded himself she had no experience in courting.

"The choosing usually happens long before the summer solstice with courting. But it's also said that magic helps it along. For example, my father planned to choose someone other than my mother. But when he laid eyes on her that very night, he thought of nothing else but her."

She wrapped her arms around her midsection, and if he wasn't mistaken, he noticed a somber look in her eyes. "I wonder what life would have been like if I had grown up in the palace."

Calle scratched his head and grimaced at the pang of guilt in his heart. If she had grown up in the palace, he reckoned choosing between her and Nyana would have been difficult. But then he reminded himself she would have been fifteen at the time. Probably too young to have caught his eye.

The guilt and confusion ate at him as he listened to the beat of the drum. Nyana had been perfect for the man he used to be. But Skaja? She encouraged him to be better, to do better, to become someone more, to do something more. She brought out his best self, and he liked to think that perhaps he possibly did the same for her too.

"Do you want to find out?" he asked as he offered his hand to her.

For a long moment, she stared suspiciously at his hand as if expecting a trick. "Find out what?"

"What life would have been like. I can't imagine the summer solstice celebrations in the village would be too different from what you would find at the palace."

Instead of taking his hand, she tucked her wings closer to her body, clearly uncomfortable with the idea. The rejection stung, and he slowly lowered his hand. Perhaps it wasn't a good idea to venture away from the cottage. The ward around the property protected and hid him from view. Even then, the wrong people might recognize him. But he needed to get away. He needed to sing, to dance, to live. And he found he couldn't resist the lure of the drum.

"Celebrations usually last until early morning," he said as he threw a cloak over himself and stuffed his hands in his pockets. "I suppose I will see you tomorrow then."

A part of him hoped she would race after him, but she didn't.

The unexpected pang in his chest took him by surprise. A lump of discomfort formed in his stomach. Allowing himself to feel anything warm for the valkyrie was a very bad idea. The future was so uncertain. He could lose her in an instant.

He wasn't sure he could survive the pain of loss a second time.

Yet, a part of him wanted to give in fully to the connection between them, even if he risked finding a blade between his ribs.

The drums beat louder as he wound through the thick trees until he found a well-worn path to the village. Chattering and laughter reached his ears. The delicious scents of honey cakes, sweet apple curd, and plum pudding beckoned him closer. When he broke through the trees, a large smile grew across his face when the entire village transformed before his eyes.

Tents dotted the space, some vendors selling sweets, some trinkets, and others fortunes. A long pole with ribbons fluttering from the top stood in the middle of the village, with a couple dozen people dancing along to the music.

Ribbons and flowers and skirts twirled about, transporting him to another time. A happier time. A time filled with less burden and heartache.

He allowed the magic of the night to sweep him up, to take his burdens and replace them with levity. All his anger and frustration and heartache melted like copper ore. Without another thought, he jumped into the throng of dancing, wrapped an arm around a young lady's waist, and twirled her in circles. His smile grew wider when she laughed in delight.

At least until her gaze landed on her face. Her smile immediately vanished. "Prince Calle," she breathed.

"Not tonight," he replied as he spun her again several times until her smile returned. He glanced about, hoping no one had heard her, but everyone else seemed too fully immersed in the festivities to recognize his face.

What he wouldn't give for a glamour to hide his identity. Where was Joel when he needed him to weave his magic of illusion?

He passed ladies around the dance floor, twirling and dipping and spinning. His feet remembered the movements. His ears recalled the music. As torches lit up the darkening skies, a new hand slipped into his.

He inhaled sharply as he thought he recognized the touch. He glanced down to find his beautiful harpy gazing up at him with determination despite the uncertain hunch of her wings. He tightened his grip on her hand as if she might slip away like water. But she didn't try to pull away. In fact, she moved closer to him.

"You have your weaknesses, and I have mine," she said, repeating her words from a couple weeks earlier. For a moment, he thought she referred to being near men, but he quickly realized the weakness she referred to was dancing.

A grin split across his face. "It's not too hard. I'll show you."

Slowly, he slipped his arm around her waist and continued to grip her hand. Heat flamed hotter in his blood as if he stood near a billowing torch. "I'll go slow. Just follow my lead."

When he stepped forward, he pushed against her gently to urge her backward. Her wings fluttered as she stared down at their feet. They moved at an unhurried pace, even as other dancers twirled past them, and the tempo of the song increased.

One step. Two steps. Twirl. One step. Two steps. Twirl.

And then her gaze fixed on him.

His mouth dried as he stared into her eyes. The light of flickering fires mingled with the golden specks in her irises, so dazzling as to pin him to the spot.

Though her hand remained touching his, she spread her fingers, so they rested lightly against his. Palm to palm. Finger to finger. Curiosity entered her expression as she stared at their hands. Along with something warm. Likely the same warmth that echoed back in his own heart.

"We stopped," she said, pulling him out of his daze.

Indeed, they stood directly beneath the pole of ribbons, no longer dancing, but standing much closer to each other than only minutes before.

Someone bumped into his shoulder, and he stumbled forward, barely managing to catch himself against Skaja. Perhaps the middle of a crowded dance floor wasn't the best place to create sparks with a harpy.

He held onto her hand as he led her toward the vendors. Although he didn't have much money, and what he did have wasn't entirely his, he wanted to give her an experience she'd never forget.

He didn't release her hand as he bought her honey cakes and a bottle of wine. The night passed in great conversation, laughing, dancing, eating, drinking, and merriment. For the first time in six long years. He was happy. Immensely happy.

And it was too late to prevent himself from falling for the beautiful harpy who brought the sunshine back into his life. He owed her everything. Absolutely everything.

CHAPTER
18

Skaja felt as if she floated on air, gliding into a warm, bright ball of sunlight. Her head felt light, her heart giddy as Calle pulled her along by the hand into the quiet embrace of the trees. An irrational, foolish desire took hold of her when she realized she would follow him anywhere.

What a foolish, very unvalkyrie-like notion.

Her wings flared on either side of her, giving away her attraction and interest in the fae prince. Although she was no expert in the goings on between a man and a woman, she would be blind to miss his lingering glances and constant touches.

Heat nestled into her cheeks when he guided her over slippery rocks, across a languid stream, and over a fallen log. For a moment, they faced each other, close enough to catch the faint trace of his earthy scent. All she wanted to do was make a bed in his scent and lie down in it.

"We're almost there," he said, breaking her out of her daze.

But she quickly reentered the foggy haze when he placed his hand on her lower back and guided her into a clearing filled with green, inky grass dotted with pearly white flowers. Moonlight rippled across alabaster petals, giving them a silvery glow.

The warmth from Calle's touch fled from her back the moment he retracted his hand and sat on a smooth, charcoal rock. Hesitant feet warred with the desire to move mountains for this man. He was giving her a choice—join him beneath the starry sky or return to the safety of the cottage.

A sense of longing struck flint against her heart. Perhaps this would only end in disaster, but it was a disaster worth experiencing.

In the end, she joined him on the rock, and he rewarded her with a warm but triumphant smile. He opened the bottle of wine, took a swig, and swished it in his mouth for a moment before swallowing.

"I think I was spoiled at the palace. This isn't quite as good as the golden goose wine at court."

He passed her the bottle, and she took a sip. The wine passed over her tongue, and she detected more sour than sweet, with a slightly bitter aftertaste. "Is everything in your kingdom gold and silver?"

"Well..." He grinned and shrugged as they each took another turn drinking from the bottle. "Mostly. Did you know certain types of magic have a color? Mine is—was—gold."

When their shoulders touched, her heart stilled in surprise before racing faster than a valkyrie's blade. This was...pleasant. Exciting. And a little bit nerve racking.

She took a long swig from the bottle and welcomed the flush of heat that followed. It made her feel warm, safe, and a little bit reckless. Perhaps a dangerous combination.

"Are you going to reply to your mother?" he asked suddenly. Sobriety fought against the liquor's influence, and so far, it was winning.

"I don't know." She stared at the blades of dark grass dancing in the gentle breeze. She wanted to leave it at that, but her desire to draw closer to Calle had other plans, and her heart spilled out instead. "All my life, I hated my parents. I now know it was under false assumptions, but the hurt is still there. I'm not sure how to come back from a lifetime of pain."

"Understandable." He rested his forearms on his knees, but the action only put more of her arm in contact with him. She didn't want to move away, but rather leaned into him. "I hope someday you might give them a chance."

Me too...

But she didn't say it out loud.

"You know... That golden goose wine is starting to grow on me. How much is left?"

When she reached for it, he held it out of reach. "You've had more than half the bottle already."

"I have not," she argued. "You are hoping to hoard a little more for yourself."

She reached again, her wings flapping slightly to give her more lift. She placed one hand on his shoulder and continued to reach, all while he chuckled at her vain efforts. How were his arms so long?

But when she turned her head to complain, the words died on her tongue when she found herself mere inches from him, nose to nose. His amber gaze softened, and she felt hers follow suit. She knew she should hop off the rock and put distance between them. She knew she shouldn't give into the urge to lean closer. But when he cradled her face in his hand, her good senses flew out the window.

"Skaja," he whispered moments before his lips brushed against hers.

A waterfall of emotion rippled through her. Surprise. Giddiness. Warmth. Need. Her hands felt along the contours of his muscles through his tunic. His hair grazed her fingers as she moved to his shoulders.

Clink.

The wine bottle touched the rock as if he set it down, and now both his hands tangled in her hair. His fingers left fiery trails of hot embers in their wake. His kiss scorched her lips and filled her with undying heat. The desire to explore, to touch, to kiss enveloped her, the need so great it shocked her into breaking the kiss.

Her breath felt heavy in her lungs as she stared back at him in the moonlight. She wasn't sure what to do, what to say, so when her hand lifted to slap him across the face, it did so on its own accord. But he caught her wrist mid-strike, much to her horror. She hadn't meant to do it.

"Ha ha!" he laughed. "I saw that coming from miles away." He grunted and jerked away suddenly. "Ow! Skaja, why?"

Her eyebrows furrowed in confusion. "It wasn't me." But then she spotted the fist-sized rock that had struck him lying at their feet.

Blindingly fast, she jumped to her feet, drew her daggers, and snapped them open just as several knives whizzed out from the cover of the trees. *Clink, clink, clink!* She batted them away as if they were stones while standing protectively in front of Calle.

Battle cries shook the gentle air, turning the clearing into a war zone rather than the romantic glade it had been moments earlier. A dozen men burst out of the trees, some with bows, others with knives and swords.

"Run!" She pushed Calle's shoulder and he stumbled forward. Together, they raced through the trees, leaped over rocks, and splashed through the frigid river. Icy water soaked her boots and dress. She never slowed her pace.

Her gaze darted to Calle's belt. Another wave of dread soaked into her to find it barren. "Where's your sword?"

"I don't have it," he wheezed, out of breath already.

"Calle!" she shrieked. "Always, *always* have a weapon!"

"I have the one in my boot."

"You think that measly thing is going to help?"

She scanned the way ahead while simultaneously glancing behind her shoulder. Her pursuers weren't very fast, but just quick enough that losing them wouldn't be easy. One of the men nocked an arrow and pulled back the string. She pushed Calle out of the way. The arrow soared right past him where his shoulder had been moments before.

"Hold your arms out," she instructed.

Her wings spread out on either side of her, lifting her into the air. She hooked her arms around him. When she attempted to pull him upward, her wings screamed at the effort. Twice more, she attempted the feat, only to gasp in a lungful of air. She dropped back to the ground.

"You've gained too much weight since the Pits. I can't carry you."

Their pursuers raced closer, now starting to catch up.

"Go!" he panted as he trudged through a thick layer of mud while she allowed her wings to help lift her over it. "I don't want you getting hurt."

She cast him a disbelieving stare as she hurtled over a smaller runoff stream. "If you think I'd abandon you, you are an idiot."

"Then let me be an idiot for once."

"Once? You've been an idiot more than that already."

His next sentence came out as a wheeze. "Just go! Those are Arlo Stokes' men."

Her eyebrows furrowed in determination as she moved closer to him rather than darted in the opposite direction. She would sooner die than allow him to return to the Pits. Although she wasn't sure if it was herself or the blood oath speaking, she knew she would fight for him to the death.

The trees broke ahead into what looked to be a clearing. If they could get past it, they might be able to lose the men behind them.

They raced out of the forest, only to be met by a steep cliff that dropped off into the sea. Violent water battered against sharp rocks below. The only way out was either down or to face the enemy.

Knowing she wasn't strong enough to carry Calle, she spun around with both daggers drawn. She stood protectively in front of him.

"Please." The devastation in his tone gave her pause enough to glance over her shoulder. The brand on his forearm glowed an angry red. "I can't lose you. I can't...do this again."

Like most times, she ignored him and widened her stance, ready for the oncoming bloody brawl. Arlo's men finding him wasn't a coincidence. But she didn't know how magic worked. She couldn't even begin to guess how they'd been discovered.

Her grip on her daggers tightened when the men rushed out of the trees. They slowed when they noticed they were trapped. More men followed. And more. And more. Until several dozen trapped them against the cliffside. Most of them wielded swords. A few carried spears. A couple handled bows, arrows nocked but pointed at the ground.

If she were alone, she would have already charged forward and taken out the archers, and then those closest to them. But she didn't dare leave Calle defenseless. Not with only a knife to protect himself from the enemy.

She eyed the swords in the enemies' hands. Calle wouldn't be defenseless for long.

A chilling voice cut through the thick tension and bloodlust, enough for the blood in her veins to curdle. "Did you really think you could escape?" Arlo Stokes laughed. He stepped out of the crowd, slow and unhurried as if he thought he'd already won the battle. "Do you even know what your slave brand does?"

Behind her, Calle glared. The tick in his jaw gave away his fear.

The slave master continued, "Locating you wasn't easy. Wherever you were hiding out, a magical ward protected you. But once you stepped out of the ward..." He clapped his hands together. The crashing sea almost drowned out the noise.

"What do you want?" Calle growled.

"I thought it was obvious." Arlo grinned wickedly like a cat playing with a half-dead mouse. "My slaves don't run away and get to live. Besides...the Sun King has paid me a handsome price to make sure you're dealt with. He's no longer interested in keeping you in the Pits."

Calle produced the knife from his shoe. Despite the brave action, a chorus of laughter rushed over them.

Skaja couldn't help but smirk at the audacity of these men. If they could only see her valkyrie tattoo in the dim light, none of them would think twice about laughing.

She only had seconds to act before chaos would ensue. She spread her wings blindingly fast. One of them hurtled into Calle and knocked him off balance. He stumbled over the edge of the cliff.

And landed on a safe ledge against the cliffside.

Arrows began firing in her direction. She leaped into the sky to avoid being hit, arced back down, and sliced one of the archers across the throat with her blade. She stabbed, sliced, kicked, and punched her way through the mass of men. Only after she'd killed six of them did they get over their initial surprise and fight back.

Metal met metal, creating a symphony of screeching weapons. Her daggers ripped across flesh. Blood spurted and spewed in all directions, speckling herself and the enemy. She jumped and ducked and wove in and out of her attackers.

Out of the corner of her eye, she noticed Calle climbing back over the edge of the cliff as a couple of men moved in his direction. She ducked beneath the arc of a spear. The moment her fingers curled around the handle of a sword lying on the ground, she tossed it toward Calle. He scooped it up and joined her in the fight.

The two of them fought side by side. Effortless. Predictable. They knew how the other fought, what the other would do next.

With a start, she realized there was no other person she would rather fight beside. If he died tonight, she would die with him.

Despair washed over Skaja when many more attackers arrived behind the ones they had defeated. They weren't going to make it out of this alive. Even she had her limits.

"Caw!"

A crow landed on Calle's shoulder, startling everyone into lowering their weapons for a few moments. The prince gasped and glanced behind him. She followed his gaze to find a swarm of black feathers headed in their direction.

"Caw!"
"Caw!"
"Caw!"

An angry chorus of cawing and flapping feathers created an ebony cacophony in the sky. The birds flew fast.

With the intent to attack.

She moved forward with the hope to break a line through Arlo's defenses and escape, but Calle's hand closed around her arm. "Do you trust me?"

After a pause, she nodded.

"Then keep fighting. The birds won't touch you."

Men screamed the moment the swarm descended upon them. The flash of silver weapons mingled with the flurry of black feathers. Through the thick cloud of crows, men carelessly swung their blades to fight the creatures, only to hurt one another in the process.

This time, Calle led the way and she followed. They met blade against blade within the screaming chaos. She hurried and scooped a fallen bow from the ground and strapped it as well as a quiver holding a single arrow around her shoulders.

However, the moment she straightened, a curtain of dread and panic closed over her eyes.

Calle was gone.

She sprinted over slick blood and crow carcasses. Only…her feet passed straight through the birds. They weren't real. They were illusions.

"Calle!" she shouted, but the chaotic din drowned her voice.

Her feet slipped. In an attempt to catch herself, she dropped one of her daggers. Two men rushed at her at the same time. She sliced one across the chest, her blade scraping against bone, and stabbed the other through his eye socket. By the time she turned, her dagger was gone.

A hulking mass of a man charged at her. She ducked beneath the swing of his mace and stabbed her dagger upward through his ribs.

It got stuck.

The man stumbled over the edge of the cliff, taking her dagger with him.

It was as if time moved slowly when the crow illusion broke enough for her to spot Calle locked in battle with two opponents. By the way he struggled to keep up with their blows, he was going to lose.

She turned and spotted Arlo watching the battle with amusement on his face. He was convinced he would win. And he would.

Unless...

Unless Calle got his magic back.

With trembling fingers, she pulled the bow off her shoulders, strung her only arrow, pulled back the string, and let it loose.

It whizzed through the air and struck Arlo in his grinning mouth. He fell backward at the same moment a sword entered her side. A wave of fiery pain gripped her. Her head spun, and the men and crows around her became a haze.

She fell...

Fell...

Fell...

Until the ground smacked into her back. Feet trampled her wings.

And the world became dark.

A surge of energy burst through Calle as if a dam broke. Strength returned to his body. Magic pulsed and pushed against every inch of his core until the heat burned him too much to keep it inside.

Golden magic exploded on all sides of him, burning everything it touched. The men around him screamed as they caught fire before falling over dead. Many more jumped over the edge of the cliff as if to douse the flames in the unforgiving sea below. With his magic returned to him, he threw aside his sword and instead fought with streams of golden magic.

He felt powerful. Unstoppable. Like a force of nature.

When his opponents began to flee toward the safety of the woods, he started to chase after them.

Only to realize the expectant flutter of wings didn't follow.

Panic effectively smothered his magic like a flame without oxygen as his gaze darted around the cliffside. Dozens of bodies lay on the ground. Blood soaked much of the once-green grass.

And then the flash of white punched the air out of his lungs. His entire body froze at the sight of Skaja unmoving on the ground.

He gasped in a ragged breath when it felt as if a knife slashed his heart open and let him bleed out. Tears stung his eyes. His feet broke through the ice of his shock as he stumbled toward her.

"Skaja!" he cried, shaking her shoulders.

Nothing.

Blood covered everything from her wings to her hair to her clothing. He almost didn't notice the thick red liquid escaping a wound in her abdomen.

He placed his fingers against her neck to feel a faint pulse. She was still alive.

His tears blinded him as he picked up her limp body in his arms. His wrist screamed in protest, but the pain was nothing compared to the festering ache in his heart.

"Calle!" a voice shouted, and he turned his head to find his childhood friend, Joel, racing over the fallen bodies toward him.

"Joel." His voice didn't work right. Everything hurt too much to speak correctly. "Help me carry her to Cian's cottage. I need to get her somewhere safe."

Together, they managed to carry her back to the cottage and laid her on the kitchen table. When Joel played his flute, orbs of golden light lit up the darkness to reveal the damage done to Skaja. It was worse than he'd originally thought. The wound still bled, but her wings...

They looked bent and broken beyond repair.

"Help me get her cleaned up," he ordered as he took charge and cut away the fabric of her dress nearest the wound. It had been so long since he'd used magic, but it greeted him like a long-lost friend, pleasant and eager to please.

He took a deep breath, closed his eyes, and placed his hand against the wound. His magic raced into her body, feeling, seeking, healing. He located the root of the damage and poured his magic into it.

"Don't die on me," he begged.

Perspiration dripped down his forehead and soaked his chest, both at the exertion of not using magic after so long and from fear of losing her.

Pulse.

Pulse.

Pulse.

Her heart beat far slower than it should. He could feel the very essence of her life slipping through his fingers.

He poured even more magic into her until miraculously, it caught hold. It seemed as if hours passed as he concentrated on healing the wound, and only when it healed enough to keep her alive did he stop and move to her wings.

Joel had cleaned the blood from her hair, body, and wings, which revealed no further wounds. For a moment, he spared a glance at his friend. He looked much older and muscular than the scrawny nineteen-year-old he used to be. His brown hair fell in waves over his ears. His bright green eyes reflected the gold from his magical orbs. His jaw was more angular, and he might even have grown a couple inches since that fateful day six years ago.

"Do you think you can save her wings?" Joel asked, bringing his attention back to the tragic damage.

"I don't know. I hardly know anything about harpies. Do you?"

"No."

Except over the past couple of weeks, Calle had watched how her wings moved in combat, how they stretched and glided through the air, how they bent and how they folded.

If he did nothing, she would surely never fly again.

Together, they stretched each wing and set the broken bones. While Joel held the wing in place, Calle reached out with his magic, healing just enough to mold the bones in place. When he could do nothing more, he poured his remaining magic into her.

"Hand me a knife," Calle said, gesturing to one on the counter. With the small weapon in his hand, his heart beat faster. A part of him grieved his next actions. If he followed through, he might lose her.

But if he didn't, he still might lose her.

He slashed the tip of the knife against her palm. Blood dripped over her fingers and joined the pool of blood on the floor. He lifted her hand to his lips and sucked the metallic liquid into his mouth before spitting it onto the ground.

"Scarlett Svera." His voice shook, along with his suddenly weary left hand. "I, Calle Everdon, release you from your blood oath." He caressed her pale and unconscious cheek with the back of his finger and whispered, "You are free."

"This is her," Joel murmured. "Typheal's daughter."

Calle nodded, not trusting his voice. Skaja looked so broken and battered, even in his oversized shirt Joel had changed her into. Her chest rose and fell with each breath, but still, she did not wake.

They gently moved her to the bed, careful not to jostle her wings. From there, he poured the rest of his magic into her until the well dried and flickered out for the night with nothing to fuel it.

"You saved our lives," Calle said when his heart calmed a fraction. He wrapped a scrap of white fabric around Skaja's hand to bind the small wound. "Thank you, Joel. Really."

His friend shrugged. "It wasn't me. I just provided the distraction. Scarlett lost her weapons in the brawl and used her only arrow to kill Arlo."

Emotion clogged his throat, and he blinked back the moisture in his eyes. Skaja had risked her life to set him free.

"She goes by Skaja now," he said, not able to tear his gaze away from her unconscious face. "How did you find us?"

"Typheal brought me back to Heulwen and sent me to you. When I didn't find you here at the cottage, I went out looking. I..." Joel cleared his throat and glanced away as a guilty grimace pulled on his features. "I found you. But you were a bit...busy, so I thought to come back later when I saw Arlo's men." Joel's green gaze met his own. "I apologize for hitting you with a rock. I wanted to warn you about the danger without giving away my position."

Calle rubbed his throbbing shoulder after the reminder of what he'd first assumed was Skaja hitting him. "You always had impeccable aim with slingshots."

"And you always were a showoff with your magic."

"Me? You were the one creating fancy illusions for the ladies at court."

The two of them laughed together, but Calle quickly sobered as he glanced toward Skaja once more. When she began shivering, he draped several blankets over her and held her hand for a long moment.

"I'm not sure I like the summer solstice," he said quietly as he brushed an errant strand of hair away from her face. "It felt like history was repeating itself."

Joel gestured to Skaja. "Because you fell in love again."

"No, that's not—"

But he stopped himself just as quickly when he realized Joel was right. When he fell in love, he fell fast and hard. He'd been trying to hold back his growing feelings, but somehow, they still managed to punch him in the chest. If he lost Skaja, he would be absolutely devastated.

Joel's hand on his shoulder startled him. "You look awful. Go get washed up and changed. I'll watch over her."

His gaze traveled down his bloodied clothes. Red flecks dotted his skin, dry and crusted. He tried not to think about whose blood it was, especially because some of it belonged to Skaja.

"Then you'd better watch from a distance. If she wakes and sees you, you're a dead man. Even if she's injured."

He looked down at her sleeping face for a moment, wishing for the sun to rise faster to give him the strength to help her again. If only he had been faster. If only he hadn't been so foolish as to leave the safety of the cottage. If only he knew more about Cian's medicinal herbs to better care for her.

He leaned down and placed a soft kiss on her forehead. But when tears pricked his eyes, he turned around quickly and exited the cottage.

Sweetness lingered in the air, but each breath he took tasted rancid. He shucked off his clothes and dipped himself into the frigid pond. With Joel no longer watching, a wave of emotions crashed into him. Despair. Guilt. Sadness. Love. They trailed down his face and dripped into the pool. He hadn't been so panicked and heartbroken in, well, six years.

Releasing Skaja from the blood oath had been the right decision. That way she wouldn't make any more foolish choices to keep him alive.

Blood crusted his left arm, and when he washed it off, his heart jumped in surprise when he noticed the slave brand had disappeared completely. He truly was free.

And it was all thanks to Skaja.

She had saved him from death multiple times. She had freed him from his slave bonds. He owed her everything.

CHAPTER
20

Skaja's body swayed as if she lay on a raft in the middle of the sea. The gentle rhythm of the waves pulled her further out into the water until sunshine rained on her face. She shifted to better feel the warmth, but all too suddenly, it transitioned into blazing fire. The raft burst into flames, scorching and searing and burning.

She gasped and bolted upright, only to cry out at the pain in her wings. The sudden scene change from ocean to cottage jarred her into momentary panic.

Calle's head shot up from where it rested on the edge of the bed beside her. His bleary eyes quickly found hers. "Skaja," he said in a raspy voice. "Thank the stars."

Her heart pounding, she glanced around to find herself back at the cottage rather than lying in a field of blood.

Daylight streamed in from the window, a stark contrast to the midnight skies she last remembered.

Confusion pulled on her features as she glanced down at herself, only to discover she wore someone else's clothing. It smelled distinctly of forest and sunshine. Calle's shirt...

When the pain in her wings became too great, she slumped back against the pillow as her gaze traveled to where hers and Calle's hands connected. She stared at the tendrils of golden light that swirled around each of their wrists.

Magic.

Calle had gotten his magic back.

Images of the fight flashed across her mind. Arlo's men trapping them against the cliffside. Fighting side by side. Shooting Arlo. And then the black void of darkness.

Her gaze once more met his. "I thought I was supposed to be dead."

The grip on her hand tightened as he shook his head. "You made a wise but foolish choice by killing Arlo. It released me from my slave bond and returned my magic. But you were badly injured. I can't..." A pause as he swallowed, and when he spoke again, the thick, watery tone disappeared in favor of an intimate rasp. "I couldn't allow you to do something like that again. I released you from your blood oath."

She blinked several times as she tried to comprehend his words. "What does that mean?" she asked quietly despite her heart pounding far too loudly. For the first time, she noticed something had shifted within her. She felt lighter. The intense desire to protect had vanished, but in its place remained a deep-rooted worry.

He confirmed her suspicions. "You are no longer bound to me. Not as a guard. Not as a protector. Nothing. You are free." A flicker of uncertainty passed across his eyes, and she wondered if he was worried she might try to kill him and succeed this time. Or…if he was worried she might leave.

To know he had released her without her permission created a deep ache within her. A surprisingly deep ache. They weren't bound anymore.

I like being bound to you, she admitted only to herself.

"You shouldn't have released me, Calle. How does that serve you at all? What do you gain from it?"

"I hope you are never forced to choose between my life and yours again. I also hope to gain your trust. And…" He swallowed again, shifting closer from where he sat in a chair beside the bed. The amber of his eyes enthralled her, melting her like wax in the hot summer sun. "I want to earn your affection without an oath in the way of our relationship."

Relationship…

Heat seared her face like a hot brand, and as hard as she tried to break eye contact, she found herself powerless against his captivating stare.

"Valkyries don't form relationships with men," she murmured finally.

"They also don't save their lives or escort them to safety." His mouth lifted in a devastating grin. "Or kiss them."

She scowled past her blush. "I will smack you."

"And you won't have anything holding you back either. Try to go easy on me."

Pushing aside the playful banter, she grimaced when her wings burned once more as she shifted. But a cooling relief battled against the pain. She glanced down at their hands, and more specifically, his magic touching her, threading through the very fibers of her spirit. A warmth. A gentle caress. "You're healing me."

He nodded. "I'm doing my best. It's been a while since I've used magic. I'm a bit rusty."

A grateful sigh escaped her as she leaned back into the pillows and closed her eyes while focusing on Calle's gentle touch. The magic that flowed through her had his distinct feel. Attentive. Gentle. Kind. Charming. Despite the silence between them, it felt as if their spirits intertwined and communicated in an intimate way.

Opening her eyes, her gaze passed across the shadows beneath his eyes. "How long have you been doing this?"

Giving her a shrug, he rubbed his eyes with his free hand. "Hours. But I'm afraid if I stop, your wings won't heal properly. I can't risk you never flying again. I'll happily give up a bit of sleep for you."

Emotion lodged in her throat. "But won't your magic run out?"

A bright smile spread across his face as he motioned to the sunlight streaming into the room from the open window. It bathed him in a brilliant light. "Not if I have a constant source of energy. However, come nightfall... My well of magic will dry up." A jolt shocked her heart when he leaned down and brushed a kiss against her hand before he rested his forehead against her arm. "Thank you for this gift."

She knew he meant restoring his magic, but she couldn't help but think many more layers weaved into his words.

After a few moments, he lifted his head and said, "So…how was it?"

"How was what?"

"Our kiss yesterday."

A shy smile lifted her lips as she stared at anything but his face. The bed sheet. Their connected hands. The freckle on his thumb. "I've never kissed a man before." She briefly glanced up at him before lowering her gaze. "I liked it. Very much."

She finally gained the courage to meet his eye, only to find his expression soft and filled with a fond warmth. He opened his mouth as if to say something when the door opened and hit the wall with a loud crash.

Calle jumped to his feet but continued to hold tight to her hand.

"Sorry," a man grimaced, one with similar ears to Calle's. "I expected the door to have a little more resistance." He quietly closed the door behind him.

"Bloody crows, Joel!" Calle shouted as he gestured to the sword leaning against the nearby wall. "I was ready to run you through. Can you not knock first?"

"Knock?" Joel grinned as he looked between the two of them. "Is there something going on here?"

Skaja looked questioningly at Calle. "Another friend of yours?" In another life, her first reaction would be to kill him. But the urge fled her completely.

"Yes."

Joel fingered a flute, his shoulder resting against the wall. He grinned. "I see how it is. I'll stay in the village tonight and you two can share the cottage."

"It's not like that!" she sputtered, her face blushing crimson.

When she glanced at Calle, she caught him nodding and mouthing *yes, it is*, but he quickly started to shake his head and mouth *no* when he noticed her attention on him. She scowled through her fluster.

"Hello, I'm Joel. I would shake your hand, but I was told in doing so, I would meet an untimely end."

She narrowed her eyes at him. "Who are you? Where did you come from? How did you find us? If you hurt Calle, I will kill you."

Joel's eyebrows lifted high into his wavy brown hair. "I thought you released her from the oath."

"I did," Calle said, though she didn't miss the twitch of amusement at the corner of his mouth. He gave her a reassuring look. "He's my good childhood friend. We can trust him. In fact, he came to escort us to Heulwen. When we're ready."

Which meant when *she* was ready. But she wasn't sure if she wanted to accompany him. Then again, she wasn't sure she wanted to leave him either.

Joel left the cottage, and a few moments later, a jaunty tune followed on his flute. The sound became increasingly quiet as if he traveled in the opposite direction.

Slowly, the sun sank below the distant mountains, and the sunshine in the window faded. The golden magic that connected their wrists like a binding unity rope flickered out and died, and at last, Calle's shoulders drooped with exhaustion. "May I lie down next to you?"

A couple weeks ago, she might have hesitated at his question. But she nodded all too quickly, desperate for his comfort.

The bed dipped as he climbed up and settled beside her. The slight jostle caused another wave of burning fire through her back.

"My wings really hurt," she whimpered. She tried to shift them, but they refused to move more than a couple inches. "Will I never fly again?"

He draped an arm around her waist and scooted closer, so they were nearly nose to nose. "I can't pretend I know all too much about how wings work. They were...very damaged. Joel and I set the bones and I've been healing them the best I can. I don't know, Skaja. But I'm trying so very hard to make sure that's not the case."

"Thank you."

She reached for him and mimicked the way he held her, with fingers lightly brushing against his back. Being near him like this...it wasn't uncomfortable or terrifying. Rather, she found it pleasant and easy. And for one vulnerable moment, she wasn't a tough valkyrie, but a woman who needed her friend. Or perhaps, more than a friend. She wasn't sure.

"You haven't tried to slap me yet," Calle chuckled.

"I don't have it in me. Otherwise, there would be plenty of slapping."

"Oh? And here I was starting to think you actually liked me."

When her whole body ached, she only managed a smile before she shifted enough to rest her head against his chest. His scent wrapped her in a comforting embrace, further securing her within his arms.

Violent images flashed across her mind, effectively killing her smile. Bodies vacant of life. Blood coating every inch of her daggers. The instinct to kill and protect.

"Do you think I'm a horrible person?" she mumbled miserably. The bridge of her nose puckered in pain. It had been a while since she'd felt so awful. Years, even. "Am I the blackest of black?"

"You're really worried about that?" he murmured against her hair.

She nodded. "I thought I was a good person. I don't know anymore."

His fingertips skimmed her shoulder. "If your intentions were good, then yes, you are a good person."

She nodded again, this time gratefully, and closed her eyes as a couple of tears leaked out. Exhaustion prevented her from wiping them away, but only moments later, warm, gentle fingers caught them on her cheeks.

"I don't feel so good."

The caress against her shoulder stopped, and he lifted his head. "Is it your wings?"

Yes, but… "In here." She placed her palm against her heart. "I don't quite feel like myself."

His hand moved to cover hers, providing her with a comforting warmth. "A lot of changes at once can do that. Maybe it all finally caught up."

A comfortable silence fell between them as she pondered his words. So much had changed in such a short time. She'd befriended a man. She'd learned of the lies in her past. She'd left the only home she'd ever known. She'd sacrificed herself for someone she cared about. She'd been released from a blood oath. And now she wasn't sure if she'd ever fly again.

It was too much to take in.

"Do I want to ask why I'm wearing your shirt?" She desperately needed the distraction of humor and was rewarded with Calle's dashing grin.

"Your outfit was bloody. I don't know how you make all your clothing work with your wings. We had to cut holes in the shirt to accommodate them."

"Most of my clothing is bare on my upper back. Makes it easier."

The pain in her wings and back was enough to bring a valkyrie to tears. Her weak hands clutched Calle's shirt, and he responded by moving even closer, so not a single inch remained between them. His arms tightened around her, slowly shifting her until her head rested on his shoulder.

She breathed in slowly, and when she let it out, exhaustion pulled her deeper into its waters.

"Just wait until morning when the sun rises," he said, his voice cutting through the fog of sleep. "You'll feel a bit better. I promise."

She already felt a bit better now in his arms, but before she managed to tell him, her exhaustion won out and she was powerless against sleep's influence.

CHAPTER
21

Calle woke to the feeling of energy both entering him and leaving him. He found himself nicely snuggled against Skaja, his hand resting on the wound on her stomach. Sunlight streamed in from the window and caressed his face. Golden magic exited his fingers and threaded through her, and to his relief, her expression looked much more relaxed than it had the night before.

As he watched her sleeping face, he could deny it no longer. He really was in love with her. The emotion frightened him. Love had the power to hurt. Fiercely.

And with the future so uncertain...

She shifted slightly and murmured, "Calle."

"I love when you call me that," he whispered, as she had usually only called him fae slave or fae prince up to this point.

He nuzzled his nose against hers, earning him a flicker of a smile, but otherwise she remained asleep.

His lips curved into a soft smile. He wanted to wake up like this every morning. Beside Skaja. Smiles and sunlight and happiness. Minus her injuries, of course.

Noticing her still-fragile wings, new fears swirled like dense black fog in his head. The fear of losing her. The fear of never reaching his end goal. The fear of never gaining her affection.

His gaze darted to her dagger harness that lay on the table. Her daggers hadn't been in there when he'd carried her back to the cottage. That must mean...

The last place he wanted to venture was to the cliffs where she must have lost them. But he knew how much she loved her weapons. It was worth the risk just to witness her smile when she woke up.

"I'll be right back," he whispered. Her eyebrows crinkled when he stopped the flow of healing magic, but she continued to breathe deeply in sleep.

He padded across the wooden floor of the cottage, pulled on his boots and cloak, but then he hesitated at the door. Uncertainty pulled his mouth downward as he glanced at his sword leaning against the wall. Did he need it anymore when he had his magic?

Skaja's voice echoed in his memories. *Always,* always *have a weapon.*

At the moment, he had his magic. She had nothing.

Not wanting to leave her without a means of protecting herself, he leaned the sword against the side of the bed and quietly slipped out the door.

The early morning sunshine greeted him like a friend he hadn't seen in years. His skin absorbed its power like a man desperate for a drink of water. It fueled his magic, flowing through every vein and every pore. Nothing blocked it anymore. He was blessedly free.

He lifted his face toward the rising sun and breathed in the fresh, woodsy air. Birdsong twittered in the boughs. Dewdrops glistened on fat green leaves. Small, woodland creatures scampered across his path. Despite the horror from a couple of nights ago, a few moments of peace reigned in the heavens.

At least until the overpowering stench of death and decay smashed into him.

Calle lifted his cloak to his nose in an attempt to block out the foul odor. His eyes watered and his stomach heaved. Streaks of blood littered the forest floor. A trail of bloodied weapons followed. And then bodies.

In the night, the bodies had been large lumps in the darkness. But in the daylight, they were bloodied people with reeking flesh.

A wave of nausea gripped his stomach as he scanned the damage from the night before. Dozens of bodies littered the cliffside, eyes staring vacantly in their twisted positions as flies feasted on their remains. He knew for a fact he'd only killed a few men.

The rest must have been Skaja.

His eyes widened at what a valkyrie was capable of. And with only two daggers. Not to mention she'd protected him at the same time. If he hadn't been with her, how many more people would she have killed? How much more blood would be on her hands?

Am I the blackest of black? she'd asked the night before.

Now he understood why the topic concerned her.

He wasn't entirely sure what to think, only that they'd been cornered by the enemy. Neither of them had had much choice but to fight.

A low growl sounded on his left, and he spun around with a start, only to find a pack of wolves scavenging for a meal. He backed away slowly. The wolf lowered its head, but it kept its eyes on him.

Wary of the wolves, he gingerly stepped across the mounds of bodies, searching for a pair of familiar daggers. He kicked a couple knives out of his way. He sifted through a pile of swords and spears.

But then the glint of familiar metal caught his eye.

Skaja's dagger lay beneath a man, nearly every inch of the weapon coated in blood. The sticky substance stuck to the handle, and as he stooped to pick it up, he wondered how many lives had been taken by the blade.

A faint power pulsed through the dagger. Reaching. Calling. Summoning. A desperate need to reunite with its other pair.

He allowed the power to guide him. But he stopped short at the edge of the cliff. Waves crashed below him, tearing and clawing at the sharp rocks below. More bodies remained stuck between the unforgiving depths of the ocean and the jutting rocks. Dark red slicked the very bottom.

His stomach heaved again.

Wherever the dagger lay, it was likely long gone by now. Skaja would be disappointed.

However, the magic inside the dagger continued to call out. He hesitantly pulled on the tiny thread. Without warning, the second dagger shot out of the depths below, hurtling his way, and he barely managed to duck in time to avoid the slicing blade.

The tip of the dagger embedded itself in a nearby tree with a *thunk.*

"All this time and I didn't even know," he chuckled to himself as he braced his foot against the tree and yanked the dagger out. "Where did you get this, I wonder?"

When one of the wolves growled again, he turned around and left the cliffside at as quick of a pace as he dared. The creatures didn't follow. The further he traveled, the fresher the air. His stomach settled into a calm relief.

A burbling stream caught his attention as he stepped within earshot. Soft forest foliage carpeted each of his footfalls. Birds continued to sing in the boughs above him. Sunshine broke through the trees overhead in lovely spurts. The promise of a new, happy day smiled down from the skies.

And his mind filled entirely of Skaja.

Her laugh. Her smile. Her dedication. Even her occasional awkwardness. He loved it all.

He crouched beside the small river and dipped the daggers into the water to clean them. Tendrils of red billowed off the blades, disappearing with each dunk and each splash. Giddiness rose within his chest as a blanket of warmth when Skaja's possible reaction entered his mind. She would be happy to see these. He knew it.

A small, reflective circle shone on the tree in front of him, and his eyebrows furrowed in confusion. It reminded him of his younger years when he and Joel had used knives to reflect light into the faces of nobles during a feast.

The back of his neck prickled with awareness, and with a start, he realized someone stood behind him.

His magic reacted on instinct, forming a long, sturdy rod between his fingers. He spun around just fast enough to block the stabbing movement of a dagger aimed for his back.

The blood in his body turned to ice. Cold, despairing fear crawled into his trembling fingertips. Dark brown eyes, almost black, stared back at him. In the darkness of the Pits, she had been weaponless and far less terrifying. But seeing her now in her fierce valkyrie leathers right after witnessing what *Skaja* was capable of...

Inari's eyes widened in recognition the moment her gaze landed on his hair. "You!" she gasped. Slowly, a grin spread across her face. Evil. Excited. Triumphant. *"You."*

"Bloody daggers," he groaned moments before she delivered a lightning fast, expert kick to his stomach. He stumbled backward and barely managed to catch himself against a tree before she attacked again.

She swiped her dagger at his neck, and he dodged out of the way only for the tree to receive the slice.

In his awkward, unprepared stumbling, he struggled to recall the things Skaja had taught him. *Anticipate where I'll be before I get there. Move quicker when on the offensive and widen your stance when on the defensive.*

He ducked beneath her next attack before squaring his shoulders and planting his feet. Inari moved wildly in a dance of silver and feathers. He blocked one attack. Then the next. And when she spun, the feathers in her hair fluttering from the movement, he sidestepped with fancy footwork he'd learned from Skaja and struck Inari in the side.

She gasped and stumbled several feet before spinning back around with one hand clutched to her side. "I know that move. What have you done with Skaja?"

Before he answered, a feral screech escaped her mouth as she produced the staff strapped to her back, swung it with impossible speed, and smashed it against the side of his skull.

Dizziness spun with the shadows in his head, but he didn't dare give into its tempting pull. He caught himself on the ground and rolled out of the way of her staff as the wood scattered the dirt where his face had been moments before.

He scrambled to his feet and allowed his magic to flow through his fingertips. The transparent golden rod in his hand elongated and sharpened into something deadly. If he didn't kill Inari first, his hair would hang from her staff like the dozens of others swaying with each of her swings.

Fear pulsed in his veins as he desperately tried to keep himself alive. He'd seen what Skaja was capable of. If Inari wanted to finish him quickly, she would have done it already.

They met each other blow for blow, his golden sword against her dagger. Pain hissed through his arm when he left himself open on his left side. Warmth trickled down his skin. He didn't dare take his eyes off Inari to look.

Calle ducked behind a tree to put an object between them. But it was as if she moved through the shadows because one moment, she ran toward him, and the next, she trapped him against the trunk.

Swipe. Swipe. Swipe.

One swing he managed to block. Another hacked the tip of his hair. And the next sliced his cheek.

Stinging pain briefly clouded his mind. One moment his back dug into the rough bark of the tree, and the next, he found himself on the ground with Inari poised with her dagger above him.

His magic rushed to protect him, and instead of holding a sword, he carried a golden shield. Her image shimmered like a mirage as she stabbed downward. The shield held.

She stabbed again. The shield cracked.

After one more stab, the magical shield shattered like fragile glass. His heart thundered in his chest as he willed his magic to pool to his fingers, but it wasn't rushing to him fast enough. He'd already used too much.

Inari lifted her hands and was about to stab downward when a blade pressed against her throat. The valkyrie froze.

"Kill him, and consider our friendship over," Skaja said in a deadly calm manner, but the dark intensity in her eyes betrayed her fury.

And her fear.

He scrambled for the knife in his boot and pointed it at Inari's stomach. Even then, he felt far too defenseless, as he doubted even a simple knife could stop her.

"Skaja?" Inari gasped as she slowly climbed to her feet. "You've been gone for *weeks*! Paula sent me to find you. I thought...I thought this man might have hurt you. He had your daggers."

Skaja never lowered her weapon, though she stepped between them as if to act as a protective barrier. Her wings drooped considerably. Dirt coated the tips of her feathers from dragging on the ground. Although she wore one of her own outfits, she wore no shoes, which revealed the ribbons of scars on her legs.

Her knees trembled, whether from weakness, fear, or something else, he didn't know.

His own hands shook with the realization that he'd almost died. So quickly, a radiant morning had turned to bloodshed.

He swiped at his cheek, only for a smear of blood to come back on his hand.

"Why are you protecting him?" Inari asked, peering over her shoulder where Calle attempted to pick himself off the ground. He found it difficult between all the cuts he sustained, his spinning head, and ringing ears. "He's a man. The very one I have been looking for. You already know that."

"I don't care."

Inari's eyes widened. "What have you done, Skaja? Did you...? You rescued him from the Pits! And you lied to me about it. You said you never saw him."

"Yes, I lied. But so did Paula." Skaja glanced over her shoulder at him. Fear still remained in the depths of her eyes. "By valkyrie code, I lay claim to this man. You cannot harm him unless you want to face me in a duel to the death."

Claim...

A duel to the death...

Heat scorched his neck at the lengths Skaja was willing to go to protect him. He knew for certain he had released her from her blood oath. Something other than duty spurred her actions.

"I claimed him first!" Inari argued. "In the Pits."

"No, you didn't. Not officially."

They argued further. Skaja kept her sword raised.

In all his life, he had never been fought over by two women, and definitely not by two valkyrie women with one intent on taking his life and the other intent on protecting him. Although he had no desire to harm Skaja's friend, he would if it meant keeping his locks of hair off her staff. He'd come too far to end up a valkyrie trophy.

"So...what?" Inari finally said when she threw up her hands in resignation. "You've been hiding out here? With him? Is he your lover?"

Skaja's ears turned red. "No. He's my...friend."

"*Friend?*" The other valkyrie's expression twisted into shock and appall. "You're willing to die for him and kill me for him. He's not just your friend."

Her ears turned a brighter shade of red, and for one moment, hope slithered past his trembling fear. Perhaps she returned his affection more than he realized.

Sticky blood trickled down the side of his face, blinding him in one eye. He wiped it away, only to realize his head stung and ached. Inari had given him a good beating. Exhaustion weighed down on his shoulders. Exhaustion and dizziness. She'd clubbed his head hard.

"Put your weapon away," Skaja ordered. "Go back to your home."

"It's your home too. You're coming with me."

"No, it's not. Not…anymore."

Thankfully, Inari tucked away her dagger, and Skaja lowered the blade. He took several staggering steps toward the river where he'd left the weapons. A ray of sunlight broke through the trees above, and he latched onto it, breathing it into himself until it smoldered in his core like fire. Magic healed him enough to walk straight.

But what he wouldn't give for somewhere to sit. Or lie down.

He glanced over his shoulder to find Skaja watching him with worry in her eyes, but she remained standing between him and the other valkyrie.

"Then I'm not leaving here without you," Inari continued, arms crossed. "And I promise I won't harm a hair on your beau's head." She muttered under her breath as she stared at his hair. "No matter how much I want to."

Through the haze of red still dripping in his eye, he pointed one of Skaja's daggers at her. "Don't think I won't be ready for you next time. And why would you try to kill me if you think I harmed your friend? Wouldn't you try to get information first?"

Inari grinned. "Kill first. Ask questions later." But then her smile fell. "Skaja, what happened to your wings?"

"It's a long story," she sighed.

But even so, she gave a quick summary on their way back to the cottage. Calle followed behind the two valkyries, not daring to turn his back on Inari for a single second. His dizzy mind still spun. His body ached. More than one cut leaked trails of blood. Although Skaja kept glancing at him worriedly, she did nothing to help. Almost as if she were afraid to show any amount of concern in front of her friend.

When they finally reached the cottage, he slumped onto one of the few logs surrounding a dormant fire pit. A fierce ache pounded in his temples, and his caution of Inari flew out the window as he lowered his head into his hands.

How many times had Skaja saved his life now? He was useless without her. His fighting skills were average, and somehow, he ran into danger at every turn. On his own, he couldn't imagine himself surviving a single fortnight.

"Here," Skaja murmured as she sat beside him and pressed a cold cloth to his head.

He winced at the pain, but kept his eyes closed to hide the way the sting summoned tears to his eyes. She dabbed at the wound before moving to the one on his cheek.

"A shallow cut," she commented. "Might not leave a scar on your pretty face."

"Huh?"

He opened his eyes to find her blushing from head to toe. A grin twitched at his mouth.

"I didn't mean to say that out loud." Her gentle hands continued to dab at the cuts, but her gaze evaded his. As if to change the subject, she said, "Inari went off to find the griffin she left behind. She promised not to kill anyone while here, especially not you or Joel."

"I'm glad to hear it. Also, I think you are beautiful."

The red in her cheeks darkened. Once again, she tried to change the subject. "I was right. You would never make it on your own. I've had to save your sorry arse too many times now."

True and true.

"I will have you know…I fought against three chupacabras and lived. You were definitely wrong."

When her gaze darted to him in her initial surprise, his entire being melted. He desperately wanted to close every last inch between them. He caressed her jaw with the non-bloody parts of his fingers, holding her face captive between his hands. Wide, brown eyes stared back at him, but rather than a frigid storm glaring back, warmth burned hot and bright. Her lips parted, and even in her injured state, her wings moved slightly in response to his touch.

His words escaped as a husky whisper. "May I kiss you again?"

"Calle…" A sweet vulnerability claimed her expression, and her hand covered one of his. "You are covered in blood. Perhaps you should worry about healing your injuries first."

"I can't. I'm saving my magic for you."

"You shouldn't."

He opened his mouth to say he loved her but shut it just as quickly. Too soon.

Much too soon.

Instead, he jested, "I rescued your dagger from the sea, and a pack of wolves stared at me as I did it. Not to mention facing the wrath of a valkyrie. A kiss on the cheek then? Hand maybe?"

Her eyes closed and her chin trembled, inciting a frown rather than a smile. "I was so scared," she whispered. "Inari is my friend but being on the other end of her blade is a dangerous place to find yourself."

"How did you find me?"

A shrug lifted her shoulders, but then she placed her free hand over her heart. "I felt it in here. My heart was calm, and then suddenly it wasn't. As if I was feeling your fear."

Gingerly, he removed her hand from her chest and replaced it with his own. His other hand rested on his chest. Surprise jolted his heart, and in turn, hers skipped to the same beat.

"Synchronized heartbeats." His smile grew wide, and despite how the action pained his face, it remained steady. "My healing magic is flowing through you, still attaching you to me. It's only temporary. But we can make it permanent."

The coy innuendo hugged the space between them.

"What do you mean...permanent?"

"By binding two souls with a blood exchange."

For several long moments, she stared back at him as if trying to understand it in her mind. "It's magic?"

"Perhaps a magic of the universe, but not my magic."

"Have you...done this with anyone else before?"

Her voice betrayed her hesitancy and wariness, and he knew she thought of a certain young woman with blonde hair and blue eyes. "If you mean Nyana, no. I haven't done it with anyone. But I'm willing to do it with you."

"Why?"

Their hearts beat quickly as one as he lifted his hand to hers. Finger to finger. Palm to palm. "I thought I already made that plenty obvious."

Someone a little way behind them coughed gently, and then hacked before they jumped apart.

Joel.

That bastard.

"Oh! I didn't see you there," he wheezed, coughing once more into his fist. He stood at the edge of the clearing, dressed in a green tunic with brown pants, boots, and a matching forest green cloak over his shoulders. A packed bag was slung over his arm.

Joel's eyes widened when he glanced at Calle. "What in the hell happened to you?"

Inari chose that moment to walk into view with one hand carrying her staff of hair and the other leading a griffin by leather reins. She grinned from ear to ear the moment her gaze landed on Joel's hair. "Well, hello there."

Skaja pulled Calle to his feet and led him away from the other two. He glanced over his shoulder, his heart racing with concern.

"We shouldn't leave them alone."

"Inari promised to play nice," she reassured, finally pulling him around the corner of the cottage and out of view. "I wanted to give you something before I can't anymore."

His eyebrows furrowed quizzically before he inhaled sharply as she wrapped her arm around his neck and pulled him down for a kiss. Sparks of heat burst to life where their lips touched.

Despite her bold advance, her hands hovered with uncertainty. He grabbed them and placed them on his shoulders. His fingertips skimmed her back, her sides, and then he pulled her closer to him by the waist.

Every ache, every fear, every uncertainty fled his mind as he wrapped his arms tighter around her, never wanting to let her go. He dug his fingers through her silky hair and pulled gently to tip her head at an angle to give him better access. His tongue skimmed the seam between her lips, requesting permission.

Her body froze against him, once again uncertain.

But the moment her lips parted for him, he explored slowly. Carefully. The faintest whimper sounded in the back of her throat. The heat of desire smoldered in his core as he tasted her scent of jasmine and midnight skies.

The quick taste wasn't enough. He wanted more. Much more.

However, he needed to take this slow with her. Agonizingly slow. No matter how fast she slipped into his heart.

He kissed her tenderly a couple more times, and on the last sweet kiss, she held it for a few long moments before she broke it and hurried away without looking back.

A soft smile tugged on his lips as he touched his mouth and watched her beautiful golden-white wings disappear around the corner of the cottage. His heart thrummed quickly, and he knew his wasn't the only one dancing to a wild beat.

And she hadn't even slapped him.

CHAPTER
22

The black thorns of trepidation dug into Skaja's side with each footstep. It ached and festered in the wound in her abdomen. It cut and clawed and cramped. Her wings fared worse. Every inch of them burned. Lifting them to prevent the tips from trailing on the ground proved to be a difficult feat. A part of her suspected only Calle's constant magic flowing through her made it possible.

The four of them had been traveling for a couple of days already.

"I'm nervous," she murmured, out of earshot of the other two who walked further behind them. Lush, forest floor slowly transitioned into rocky stone. Peeking out of the trees every now and again was a magnificent view of Heulwen in the distance. Bright. Golden. Nestled on top of glistening falls, with clouds that sparkled like rainbow dewdrops.

She'd seen fewer things more beautiful in her life.

And this was her home. Her true home. She wanted it back.

"You shouldn't be." Calle gave her a flirtatious grin as he gripped her hand tighter. The moment a ray of sunlight hit him his healing magic grew momentarily stronger. "I'm not *that* scary."

"I'm not talking about you." With a scowl on her face, she smacked him in the ribs. He winced. "I'm talking about my parents. What am I supposed to do? What am I supposed to say? What will they think of me? What if they're disappointed? What if I am?"

Joel's slow, calming melody on his flute bounced right off her, unable to take the edge off her anxiety. His music hid the four of them and Inari's griffin from view in both sound and body, he'd explained.

Whatever that meant. She still kept her eyes and ears alert for any sign of danger, ready to draw her daggers in a moment's notice.

"I can't see any reason for their disappointment." Calle gave her hand a gentle squeeze, followed by a reassuring smile. The cut on his face had already healed a great deal with his magic, as if his body couldn't help but take some for himself as he gave it to her. "You are beautiful and fearsome. Your *harpy* parents will appreciate how well you wield your daggers. But more than that, they will be ecstatic to meet you. Their hearts have been broken for a long time with your absence."

She'd heard harpies in the Sun Kingdom were great warriors. She worried she might not live up to her parents' expectations, even as a valkyrie.

She bit her lip and gazed out at Heulwen again through a break in the trees. "What should I do? Hug them? Shake their hands? Do nothing? What do they expect me to do?"

"Whatever feels natural. Don't do what you think they expect. But what makes you most comfortable. I know they'll understand."

Shaking her head, she squeezed her eyes shut momentarily and pinched the bridge of her nose. "It's more likely I'll do something embarrassing around my father. I'm bad with men."

"Not all men." He flashed her a devastating grin, his expression full of teasing and mirth.

Before she managed a snarky reply, someone cut across her.

"Friends don't hold hands either!" Inari shouted with an irksome, gleaming smirk, dangerous, dark undertones in her feral gaze. Joel's note stuttered as he snorted, but he quickly resumed the song.

Skaja glared momentarily before shifting her gaze to their clasped hands. Golden tendrils of magic snaked up her arm and pressed cooling relief to her shoulder blades. If she released his hand, she feared the accompanying pain, and the awful reminder that she may never fly again.

The thought alone crushed her spirit. She greatly valued her freedom. Without it...the burden would be a painful one to bear.

A glint of gold from the corner of her eye broke her out of her foreboding thoughts. She inhaled sharply when Calle presented her with a shimmering, golden rose. She gingerly took it from him, surprised to find it solid with the energy of his magic surging through it. The smooth, glassy stem warmed her fingers, and each petal danced in a shimmer of gold when she tipped it one way, and then the other. Bringing it to her nose, she breathed in Calle's familiar, earthy scent.

"This is pretty," she murmured. "How long can it stay in this shape?"

Something shifted in his eyes. The amber color swirled with happiness and a sliver of hope. "Forever if I will it. A rose signifies someone's intention to court another person."

Skaja's heart beat fast as the predator of alarm chased her. Her hand reacted by itself as she threw the rose to the ground, and it shattered into golden dust at her feet.

Shocked silence. From both of them.

"Oh," he said finally as they started forward again. "All right."

"I'm so sorry. I panicked." She lifted her head to stare wide-eyed at him, but instead of finding anger on his face, amusement lifted the corners of his mouth and crinkled the skin around his eyes.

"At least you didn't slap me."

Her thoughts drifted to the silver sheets back at the cottage containing Calle's memories. The one with Nyana, in particular. The first time she laid eyes on the memory, she'd wanted it for herself. Badly. She still did. With Calle. If she agreed, she knew a part of her valkyrie self would crumble.

When so much of her identity would wither with it, and with nothing else keeping her grounded, would anything remain?

After a long stretch of silence other than the crunching of shoes against rocks, she said, "Valkyries are like the female Praying Mantis. They have a little fun before killing their mates."

He grimaced and rubbed his neck with his free hand. "I'd like to keep my head. Thank you."

"What I'm saying is this—courting is not something we do. I don't know the first thing about it. I'm a valkyrie, Calle. Not a lady. Not a princess. A valkyrie."

She released his hand, and the pain from her wings crashed down on her like violent waterfalls. Her body threatened to droop, but she forced herself to remain upright to prove her point.

Despite directing her message at him, she withered beneath her own words. She'd grown up as a valkyrie. She would forever be a valkyrie. She knew little else. A relationship between them would never work.

Right?

The slow, languid beat of her heart hurt nearly as much as her wings. But it wasn't her heartbeat she felt. It was Calle's. Despite his warm smile, his chest ached.

And it was her fault.

He replied with a change of subject. "Just wait until you see the falls up close one day. When you stand at the top, you feel as if you are standing on the very top of the world."

Inari came up behind them and slung an arm around Calle's shoulders. He stiffened at her touch.

Her obsessive gaze landed on his hair moments before she ran her fingers through his auburn locks. She gave him a look between a smirk and flirtation. "I've been with several men," she said as she stroked one of the strands of hair, and then another. "Such fun times."

His mouth lifted in disgust. "You stay away from me."

A surprising prick of jealousy goaded Skaja into stomping toward them. She grabbed her friend's arm and threw it off him. "Leave him alone, Inari."

"Why?" Inari cackled and held up her staff of hair. "He would complete my collection. I think I would be satisfied for a few years after his lock of hair joined the others."

"Go home," she snarled, pointing in the direction of the valkyrie islands.

"No. Not without you. I promise I won't kill anyone. Or tell Paula what you've been up to. But if you ever change your mind about this one..." Inari licked her bottom lip hungrily as her gaze raked down Calle.

"Never."

"Quiet," he hissed suddenly as he grabbed her by the waist and pulled her to the side of the road beneath the shadows of a nearby tree.

In all her arguing, she hadn't noticed the *crunch* of boots on rocks or the *clink* of weapons against armor. Joel still played his flute, but now his eyebrows furrowed with concern and a trace of fear. The tempo never stopped. The melody remained the same.

A half dozen soldiers appeared around the bend dressed in red and gold armor. All wore swords on their belts. A few carried painted shields to match their uniforms. She noted four of the soldiers were male, and two were female. She refused to allow a single drop of female blood to stain her hands. But the men were another story.

Slowly, she reached for the daggers at her shoulders. Although she didn't dare draw them and risk creating noise, she still held on tight to each handle. Watching. Waiting.

The six soldiers approached. Her heart beat fast like the flapping wings of a bird. Or perhaps it was Calle's heart. She wasn't sure.

As the soldiers passed their group, none glanced their way, nor did they notice the way Inari's griffin looked as if it wanted to snatch one of the men by the neck and eat it. Knowing Inari, it probably would if she willed it to.

After they disappeared, their group released a collective sigh. She and Inari likely would have been able to erase the threat. But the noise from fighting would have given them away and put Calle in danger.

"Come on," Skaja said, her heart still beating hard. "Let's get going before we run into anyone else."

"Wait." Calle stopped her with a hand to her shoulder. "Now...where we're going, there will be men. Good men." He gazed earnestly into her eyes. "Probably a lot of them."

"I won't kill anyone. Neither will Inari."

He nodded as if satisfied with her answer.

They continued forward at a faster pace, and all the while, Joel didn't miss a single beat on his flute. He eventually led them off the path and deeper into the woods. But all too suddenly, they stopped.

She glanced around in confusion. Large trees stretched across the space in front of them. Dirt and leaves littered the forest floor. A rabbit scampered into a green and red bush.

Joel's music ceased at the same time Inari cackled. "Oh, there is something here," Inari said, her mouth spreading into a wide grin. "Something big. I can feel it."

Skaja's fae friend's connection to the forest always astounded her.

Joel moved forward and pulled out a knife. He cut his finger, and as a drop of blood trickled down his palm, he placed his hand against a tree. In the blink of an eye, a couple trees turned into a large stone arch. One by one, they passed through the arch, and a large set of stone steps led downward. A man and a woman stood guard in front of two large, rounded doors, spears in their hands. Their long, pointed ears revealed they were Sun Fae.

The moment their gazes locked on Calle, their eyes widened, and they dropped to their knees, heads bowed.

"Your Highness," the woman murmured. Tears flowed down her cheeks, relief shimmering in the trail they left on her skin.

The man backed toward the door, still bowing. "I will tell everyone the true king of Heulwen has arrived."

After he disappeared, the woman pulled open the doors for them and ushered them through. They entered a dim corridor and descended a wide staircase, large enough to accommodate the griffin.

Her pulse spiked when Calle leaned close enough for his breath to caress her ear as he whispered, "King Calle has quite an awkward ring to it. Don't you think?"

Despite her trepidation growing with each step into the unknown, she grinned. "Prince Calle does sound much better. It's a good thing you haven't taken the throne yet." Her smile fell. "Do I look all right? Should I have worn something fancier? Am I showing too much skin?"

"You are perfect." Her face grew warm when he placed a kiss on her cheek. The space between them became far too cold when he moved away.

Torches flickered to life as they came across another stone hallway, followed by a second flight of shorter stairs. Where was everyone? She'd almost expected to be met by hundreds of rebels with a ridiculous amount of fanfare.

Unless they were being led into a trap.

She stepped closer to Calle, ready to snap open her daggers at the first sign of trouble.

Two more people bowed at the next arched door as they opened it to let them through. The small hallway opened into a gigantic cavern filled with beautiful light, almost as if the structure was far above ground rather than below. The ceilings stretched high in a series of arches, the mysterious windows letting in light.

A wide, red carpet led up several stone steps and into another room. But her heart stopped completely when she noticed the hundreds upon hundreds of people crammed in the room with them. Each person exclaimed with excitement, followed by a deep rumble as each of them fell to their knees in subservience.

Calle parted from their group of four, and instead of following him like she wanted to in case of an attack, fear held her back. Two of these very many people were her parents.

And she was scared.

She slipped further behind the griffin to give herself a safe place to partially conceal herself from so many eyes.

"Thank you for your warm welcome," Calle said, his voice echoing off the stone walls, thick with emotion. "I am finally here. And I am ready to lead."

Hundreds of voices burst to life all at once, some greeting Calle, others welcoming him back home. He took in their appreciation modestly and with an immense amount of kindness. This man...he'd been born a leader. A leader with a kind heart.

Watching him interact with others endeared him to her even more, but it didn't erase her anxiety of what was sure to come.

"Calle, my sweet boy," a woman said, pulling him into a crushing embrace and kissing every inch of his cheeks and forehead like a mother might do for a son they hadn't seen in a very long time.

Breathing became difficult. Swallowing impossible. Her gaze raked across the familiar but unfamiliar woman. Dark blonde hair threaded with silver. Brown eyes. Golden-white wings.

A blanket of cold anxiety draped over her. This was her mother.

Chapter
23

Avonia pinched Calle's cheek, then his side as tears of happiness swam in her eyes. "You are too skinny. You need to get some meat on you."

"I'm working on it," he chuckled as he pushed her hand away. "You should have seen me a couple months ago if you think this is bad."

Her expression filled with the heartache of loss, and she wrapped him in another fierce mama bear hug. And then she stilled and released him slowly, her eyes wide as she stared at the stone arch doorway they had entered through. Calle followed her gaze to find Skaja in a defensive stance, a wary expression on her face as she half hid behind the griffin.

"Avonia, may I introduce you to—"

"My Scarlett," she breathed. She pushed him aside and approached all too quickly to Skaja's obvious discomfort.

"Scarlett. Skaja." And then Avonia pulled Skaja into a fierce hug, her shoulders shaking with sobs. The tension in Skaja's body lessened, but she didn't return the embrace.

When Avonia pulled away, tears continued to trail down her cheeks. Happy tears. Tears of relief. But her happiness melted into concern. "My darling, your wings."

Skaja flinched away when Avonia reached for her, but Avonia was persistent and tried again. Calle might have laughed at the way Skaja leaned precariously away from her if it wasn't for her immense look of discomfort. Though, she seemed to relax, if only slightly, when Avonia gently spread her wings and felt along the bone structure.

"My, my," she murmured as she traced the top of both wings with her fingers. "Six breaks along here and one bad break in the right scapula. You must be in so much pain."

His heart leaped to the skies when Skaja finally spoke.

"It wasn't easy getting the fae prince here," she replied in a joking manner, clearly avoiding mentioning her pain. "He's more trouble than he's worth."

He grimaced and explained, "My slaver showed up with his men. Your daughter is a fierce warrior. You would be proud."

Avonia's eyes began tearing up. "I am."

Skaja glanced away, something unreadable in her expression. But the way his heart ached in sync with hers gave away how much seeing and speaking to her mother hurt.

As if oblivious to Skaja's discomfort or willfully ignoring it, Avonia said, "You must see Cian. He can likely heal all this damage. Otherwise, I fear your right wing will never function the same again. You will fly lopsidedly or not at all."

"Where is Cian?" Calle asked, trying to help take some of the pressure off Skaja's shoulders and putting it on his own. "He never returned to the cottage."

"In the healer's quarters. There is much to do here."

Fast-paced footsteps echoed down the corridor and filled the room with still-curious people remaining. Typheal skidded around the corner, breath ragged, his gaze jumping wildly around the room until it fell on Skaja.

Calle's eyes widened, and he shook his head in warning while repeatedly dragging a hand across his throat. *No! Stop!*

Typheal ignored his warnings. He rushed toward Skaja as if to embrace her, but at the same moment, her eyes hardened, and she snapped her daggers open in a blindingly fast movement. Typheal deflected her blow at the last second.

Clang!

Surprise lighted the man's expression before his eyebrows furrowed in determination. A glint of exhilaration marked her own face. While her initial reaction may have been instinctual, she actually seemed eager to fight him.

Skaja struck again and again. He blocked each attack before he started to fight back.

Calle's distress melted as he watched, mesmerized at the way Skaja moved. Earlier, she had sparred with him, and he had watched her daggers. But now he watched *her*. She moved fluidly around Typheal like water around a sturdy but menacing rock. She bent and dipped and fought with admirable grace.

237

"She's not going to kill him, right?" Avonia asked worriedly beside him.

"Nah." But then his mouth contorted into uncertainty. Skaja was often unpredictable. "Of course not."

"I'm not sure what to do. Should we try to stop her?"

He grinned and casually draped an arm around Avonia's shoulders. "Skaja is incredibly awkward when she interacts with men. Let her fight. It's her way of saying hello."

His attention slipped to Typheal and the black tattoos dripping down his face like tears. *Traitor. Disgrace. Worthless.* His stomach twisted when he noticed the man's shirt. No wings stretched out proudly from his body. He'd really lost them.

Skaja managed to kick Typheal in the stomach, and he stumbled backward. She threw one dagger over his shoulder while attacking with the other. The first dagger arced in the air and curved like a boomerang as it spun and twisted back toward them. Typheal ducked the incoming blade, and Skaja caught it in her free hand.

The attack took Typheal off guard enough for Skaja to roll across the ground, kick the back of his knee, and the moment he stumbled, she placed one dagger against his throat, the other against the back of his neck.

Calle held his breath, and Avonia clutched his arm with a death grip.

"Do you yield?" she asked, hardly out of breath.

Typheal dropped his sword and held up both his hands in surrender, which caused a murmur of excitement to rumble through the crowd. "I yield."

She sheathed both her daggers. Instead of expressing shame or anger from losing, immense pride shone in Typheal's eyes. Pride for his daughter.

"That could have gone worse," Calle said quietly to Avonia. "A lot worse."

"Then let's be glad it didn't."

He kissed Avonia on the cheek in farewell and joined Skaja where she began to walk away from her father. He steered her in another direction where Avonia had pointed him, and a woman soon led them toward the healing quarters.

"He's a lot better than you," Skaja commented.

He rolled his eyes and playfully pushed her shoulder. "He's a harpy. One of the best guards and fighters in Heulwen."

She sighed into her hand. "I can't believe I attacked him. I knew I'd do something stupid."

"But you feel better, no?"

The slightest shift of amusement on her mouth answered his question.

"Why..." Her expression sobered. "What are those tattoos on his face?"

"They are meant to shame him in public." He frowned. "The tattoos brand him as a traitor to the crown. But to me, he is the bravest man I have ever met."

Although Skaja said nothing more, her expression revealed her sorrow and contemplation. He knew better than to interrupt. She needed to work this out on her own, and if she needed help, he would remain by her side whenever she needed him.

He loved her. And the more he got to know her, the more he knew his feelings would never change.

When they rounded a corner, Skaja's wings drooped, and pain rippled across her expression. He took her hand, and she let him. Although he knew his magic refused to heal the damage in her shoulder blade for some unknown reason, he was glad that when his golden energy entered her body, the pain on her face lessened.

It wasn't much, but it was the only thing he could do.

****

Remaining strong proved too difficult of a feat for Skaja. Her pride, her anxiety, her trepidation had kept her grounded until this moment. But now she wanted to collapse and sob into her hands from the weight of her pain and overwhelming surroundings. Or into Calle's shoulder. Both were safe places to break down.

Only his healing magic kept her on her feet.

The underground hideout stretched for what seemed like miles. Her feet dragged. Her wings drooped. And when she stumbled, Calle caught her by the waist and didn't let go.

He scooped her into his arms until her feet dangled several feet from the ground and her feathers ceased collecting dirt from the floor.

"Put me down," she mumbled half-heartedly into his shoulder, but even as the protest left her lips, she closed her eyes. In Calle's arms she felt warm, safe, and relieved.

"Not a chance," he murmured into her hair. "Though, I might consider it in exchange for another kiss."

She responded with a grunt.

Worry leaked into his voice. "You must be feeling awful. No slap? No threatening me at dagger point?" No answer. His grip tightened on her. "The fight with your father must have taken everything out of you."

The lull of the safety he offered might have dragged her down into sleep, but the fire clawing at her back like a caged animal prevented the temporary relief.

The air pressure changed as if they stepped into another room. Incense wafted past her nose with its sweet, citrus-like fragrance. She opened her eyes to find herself in a large, dark room filled with candles and several occupied cots. Bloodied bandages covered an unconscious man. Bruises dotted a woman's face and body, a haunted look in her eyes as they passed by. A child lay curled on another cot, so small in comparison to many others.

An older man hunched over a patient, but the moment he noticed them, he quickly dipped into a bow. "Your Highness. I heard you made it home." The man's gaze darted to Skaja's wings, and if any energy remained, she might have squirmed under his scrutiny. "And Skaja. I'm pleased to make your acquaintance."

"Cian," Calle murmured, his voice as soft as candlelight. "I've done what I can. I don't know what else to do."

After a lingering glance to Calle's unbranded forearm, the man nodded and gestured for them to follow. He led them into an unoccupied room. A dim lantern lit a table full of strange metal contraptions, a rickety cot, and a large cabinet.

"Have a seat, Skaja."

241

Calle set her down on the cot, but when Cian reached for her wings, she smacked his hand away and glared. "I don't want you to touch me. Give me a woman healer."

The two men exchanged concerned glances before the old man spoke. "There are none. It's why I have not returned to my cottage. I am needed here."

Her glare remained. "You will not touch me."

"Then you will not fly."

She hesitated at his blunt comment. The idea of being touched by a strange man made her immensely uncomfortable. But was it a worthy trade to be able to fly again?

"Find me a woman."

"Skaja," Calle murmured soothingly, and just the sound of his voice eased her nerves. "Would you allow me to touch you? Cian can direct my hands."

Again, she paused as she gazed back at the earnestness and kindness in his eyes. He had proved himself trustworthy. He had healed so much of her body already. There was no one she trusted more.

Finally, she nodded. "Only you."

The warmth from his hands settled on her shoulders as he silently directed her to lay on her stomach, her wings furled out on either side of her. Her left wing felt heavy and tired, but her right wing hung uselessly off the cot. Pain crackled through it like lightning. Simply moving her body coaxed tears from her eyes. She closed them to hide her agony from the other two. But by the way Calle's thumb caressed her cheek, he likely felt the way her heart stuttered in pain through their temporary soul bond.

"I believe I was able to heal the stab wound in her abdomen," Calle began. "Her upper wings accept my healing magic just fine, but it avoids this area." His finger lightly skimmed below her shoulder blade. "I've tried to heal it, but it's not working."

Cian grunted far too close to her for comfort as if inspecting it himself, but true to his word, he didn't touch her. "Likely because the bone is not set. It's a harder one to do. Less noticeable and from the looks of it, it's very inflamed. As for the other bones, you did a good job. I have something to speed up the recovery process."

"And her right wing?"

"You will have to set the bone and heal it enough to keep it in place. I will be able to speed the recovery on that too if you do it correctly."

Calle released a long, anxious breath. "I'm not confident. Skaja, are you sure you want me doing this?"

"Only you," she reiterated. If there were no female healers, then she would take the next best thing.

He swallowed audibly. "Cian, tell me what to do."

"First…" the old man said, and she opened her eyes to find him rifling through the cabinet until he pulled out a small glass vial filled with purple liquid. "This will be immensely agonizing, Skaja. I recommend consuming this for the pain. It only takes a couple of minutes to take effect. But it will also put you to sleep."

"So you can break your promise and touch me in my unconscious state? I'm not swallowing whatever it is. I will sooner cut off your hand."

He and Calle exchanged another look. The old man raised his eyebrow as if they conversed silently.

Finally, Calle crouched down to her level. The kindness in his eyes remained, along with anxious fear. "I don't think my heart can handle this job if you are screaming. Take it for my sake. And I swear I will not let anyone touch you except me. Not Cian. Not Avonia. Not Inari. No one."

"You promise?"

"I promise. And when you wake up, you will be much closer to flying again than ever before."

Hesitancy gave her pause. She wanted to fly again. She feared her injury made it impossible. But being healed by men went against her valkyrie ways.

Then again, so did her entire association with Calle.

At last, she nodded, took the vial, and downed its contents in one swallow. In only a few moments, a heaviness pressed on her head, a fog of dizziness clouding her eyes. Panic fumbled around in her mind at losing control of herself, of her body, her mind, her consciousness.

She stumbled to her feet, but only managed to knock over several unfamiliar instruments on the table.

The old man reached for her. She snapped open her daggers instinctively and took a swipe. She missed. Or at least she thought as much. Her world swayed, so she couldn't tell. Her movements were sluggish as if she moved through water. Her throat constricted and the air in her lungs felt heavy.

First her arms drooped, and then her knees collapsed. A pair of hands caught her.

And then darkness.

****

"What's wrong with her?" a voice cried behind Calle, and he spun to find both Avonia and Typheal in the doorway—almost as if they couldn't stay away from their daughter for more than a few minutes.

"She's receiving medical treatment," Cian reassured as he pulled out a white handkerchief. The tip of his nose dripped blood from the scratch Skaja had delivered with her blade. He was lucky to be alive. The moment he pressed the handkerchief to his face, he turned on Calle. "How are you still alive? She tried to kill me within five minutes of meeting me."

"Me too." He chuckled, now laying her down carefully on the cot. Avonia rushed forward as if to help, but he held up a quick hand to stop her. "I promised I wouldn't let anyone touch her. I intend to keep my promise."

"There must be something I can do."

"Perhaps you can assist Cian. But you mustn't touch her."

Cian nodded while he still held his bleeding nose. "We must hurry. The elixir won't last long."

Calle rolled up his sleeves and placed his hands on her bare back just below her right wing. "Tell me what to do."

CHAPTER
24

When Skaja woke, everything hurt...less. The arch of her wings pulsed lightly with pain, but not much. Her shoulder blade obeyed her when she tried to move it, and her wing no longer hung at a precarious angle.

She bolted upright and found herself in a dark room, lying on a bed with soft sheets. Her hand instinctively reached for the other side of the bed, expecting to touch a sleeping Calle's shoulder. Only...he wasn't there.

She nearly laughed at herself, but she didn't refrain from rolling her eyes. How was it possible a valkyrie like herself had come to depend on his constant, comforting presence?

Slowly, she edged off the bed and lifted her wings. They obeyed her. The muscles in her back pulled in protest when she spread them on either side of her. She flapped them once, twice, before pulling them back to her body.

Tears of gratitude pricked her eyes. Calle had done this for her. She was indebted to him.

The last place she remembered was the healing quarters. If Calle had kept his promise, he must have carried her back to this room himself.

Noticing her dagger harness on the bedside table, she picked it up, along with both daggers, and slipped out the door wearing only her dress and bare feet. A part of her wished to find herself wearing Calle's clothes again.

Darkness slithered on all sides of her like crawling shadows. They followed her as she crept through the hallways, blindingly trailing the faint tether that connected hers and Calle's heartbeats.

She frowned as she crept down one hallway, and then another, her feet silent against the cold stone floor. Wherever Calle was, it was far from her room. Not being near enough to protect him concerned her.

The light from two torches flickered on the wall further down the corridor, moving closer and closer.

By instinct, she ducked behind the corner and tucked herself as close to the wall as possible. She held her breath as two guards passed by with swords *clinking* against metal armor. Only when the light disappeared around the bend did she roll her eyes.

"What am I doing?" she whispered into the darkness. "I'm allowed to be here."

Still, she continued forward silently and avoided notice until she stood in front of a plain wooden door. The golden handle appeared to be rusted, even in the pitch-black corridor. She grasped the handle...

And paused.

Shaking her head, she murmured again, "What am I doing?"

Her gratitude could wait until morning rather than her waking Calle up just to say thank you.

She slid against the wall until she sat on the ground. Her feathers ruffled around her, getting comfortable to pass a night's sleep in the hallway when the door opened suddenly, and Calle's head poked out.

"Why are you in the hallway?" Even in the darkness, his eyes twinkled with amusement.

With a shrug, she played off her confusing attachment to the fae prince. "Didn't want Inari to make good on her threats. Your hair looks better on your head."

"I agree." He paused. "You know, the stone looks awfully cold. It's warmer in my bed."

"Is that an observation or an invitation?"

He grinned, his white teeth gleaming in the darkness. "Obviously, an invitation. I would have stayed with you in your room, but people were watching. Your father put your room *way* on the other side of the fortress. I don't quite appreciate it."

Laughter escaped her, but she quickly clamped a hand over her mouth and glanced back and forth down each end of the hallway. Silence.

Flickering torchlight steadily moved back in her direction like the first time. Before the guards could catch her outside the prince's room, she slipped inside, and he softly closed the door behind her.

"It better be warm," she said as she climbed onto the bed and snuggled beneath the covers, "because my feet are cold."

"Where are your shoes?"

"I'm not sure. My room was dark."

His smile gleamed again as he joined her beneath the covers. "Always, *always* have a weapon on you, you said. I thought the same rule applied to having shoes in case you need to run or something."

"I can fly. I don't need shoes."

Her heart tumbled in her chest as he moved closer to her, his arm draped around her waist and his warm feet covering her cold ones. His warmth seeped into her. Beckoning. Inviting. She felt safe and comfortable in his arms, but something else lay beneath the surface of her skin. Searing heat. A desire for more snuggles and laughter and kisses.

"I can feel your heart," he murmured as he gently trailed a finger across her eyebrow, down her cheek, and caressed her jaw. "I think you might actually like me."

"That's your own heart you're feeling." Though the way her pulse pounded in her ears betrayed her.

"Most definitely a bit of both." His mouth quirked with disappointment. "The soul bond is already starting to fade between us. I rather enjoy this connection with you."

"Why?" she dared to whisper.

SYDNEY WINWARD

He didn't answer. Instead, he gazed into her eyes as he trailed his fingers through her hair, over her shoulder, and caressed the tips of her wings. The intimate touch of her feathers spurred a fast-paced, irregular rhythm in her chest. She tipped her face up to level it with his. An invitation.

One he didn't hesitate at.

He kissed her lips softly as if they were two rose petals brushing together in a gentle breeze. Although she wasn't very good at this, she tried to mimic what he'd done. Her hand trailed up his back and her fingers tangled in his hair.

He released a groan against her mouth and deepened the kiss. Her insides quaked in response to his touch. To his kiss. A foreign desire erupted within her. To touch him everywhere. To be touched everywhere.

Her hands slipped under his shirt, feeling his toned muscles and chest hair beneath her fingers. His skin burned with a desire to match her own, their hearts beating in sync. Their tongues danced in a passionate frenzy. Their bodies fit together like midnight skies and starlight. He stroked her wings and her hair, and when he grabbed her arse, she inhaled sharply in surprise and broke the kiss, stopping them from going any further.

"Sorry, too much?" he whispered beneath her. His dark amber eyes pooled with desire, and she felt as if a single wrong word from her would snuff the light all too easily.

"No." She bit her lip, but a smile broke through anyway as she tucked a strand of hair behind her ear. "I am simply not accustomed to being touched by a man."

He raised an eyebrow. "By women?"

"No," she laughed, falling onto her elbow, her head resting against her hand as she gazed down at him. "Not by women either. Though Inari..."

"You don't need to tell me about her romantic pursuits," he chuckled, and she closed her eyes and sighed when his fingers brushed her cheek. His voice turned into a raspy whisper. "You are so beautiful, Skaja."

She flicked him in the shoulder. "You most definitely are a cat if you can see me in the dark." As she placed her hand over his heart, she sobered. "Thank you for healing me. My wings hardly hurt anymore. You...aren't like any man I've been led to believe was evil. You are good and kind. And...I'm sorry for trying to kill you in the Pits." A surprising sadness washed over her, and her chin trembled when she thought of a life without Calle in it. Why did it hurt so much? "It would have been a horrible mistake."

Taking a few moments to reply, Calle reached for the covers pooled at their ankles, and she spotted the gray and white tattoo of a snowy mountain range before he tucked her in beside him and held her close to his body.

He kissed her forehead, her nose, and lightly kissed her lips. "I can't be too upset when you rescued me and are with me now like this. I'm happy. I haven't been this happy in a very long time."

"Me neither." Comfort and joy charged the following silence in the room. Calle's body heat enveloped her, lulling her into relaxation. She thought he might have fallen asleep when his breathing deepened, but she ventured to ask, "I saw the tattoo on your ankle. What does it mean? And where are the other bad boy tattoos?"

"Bad boy?" he laughed. Seconds later, a magical golden orb floated in the air with a gesture of his hand, casting a yellow light over his face. He sighed. "I'm not proud of them, but no one is perfect. They are reminders of my past and how I can do better in my future." He gestured to the foot of the bed. "I left my friend stranded in the mountains to save myself. It was a selfish thing to do. When I got back to the castle, they sent out a search party. My friend lived. For a few years, at least. And then he got killed by a valkyrie."

She grimaced. "I hope more than anything it wasn't me."

With a shake of his head, he replied, "It wasn't. She had lighter skin. I only wish I had done something to stop it." He sighed, but then pulled his waistband down a few inches to reveal the tattoo below his left hip bone—a gray rose with drops of red on the petals. "Confessing to an elder who is also your tattoo artist is like confessing to a priest. My friends dared me to try to seduce the daughter of a visiting foreigner. Things went poorly when I took her to the falls. She...fell in and the falls swept her over the cliff. She was gravely injured, but she survived. Our visitors left quickly after that. I am ashamed of myself to this day."

"How old were you?" she murmured, tracing the buttons of his shirt.

"Fifteen."

"Fifteen..." Flashes of red streaked across her vision as memories assaulted her mind. "When I was fifteen, I killed my first man. It was awful. He'd been a lone traveler. Hadn't done anything wrong, necessarily. He was just in the wrong place at the wrong time." She swallowed while trying to push the horrid images from her mind. "I like to think I'd have been a better person if Paula had never taken me. Perhaps we would have grown up as friends. Perhaps I would have protected instead of killed."

"There is still time to change." He stroked his fingers up and down her spine. "The past is not there to haunt us, but to help us. To learn from it. To become better."

She lifted her head to look at him. "Do you truly believe that?"

His throat bobbed up and down as he swallowed. "I try my best to. It's not always easy."

Those words ran through her mind as she lay her head on his shoulder. "Then I will try as well. To move forward. To become better."

He kissed her head. "It's all we can do."

CHAPTER
25

"Get up! You have a lot to do today," a woman said in a sing-song voice moments before a bright light blinded Skaja. Her eyes flew open right as Calle groaned and turned away.

Light entered the room from what looked to be windows, likely an illusion in the underground fortress. Her mother, Avonia, turned but then froze. "Oh!" Her eyes widened in shock as she looked from her, to Calle, and back to her where they cuddled on the bed.

"Five more minutes," Calle groaned again. He reached for Skaja's wing and spread it so her feathers bathed his face in shadow to block out the bright intrusion.

Avonia's mouth moved, but no sound escaped. Although Skaja's daggers lay on the bed side table only a foot away, she knew her mother was no threat. So instead, she rested her head back on the pillow beside Calle while watching her mother warily. Embarrassment heated her cheeks, though she felt like she had done nothing wrong.

"What...?" her mother finally breathed. "What are you two doing? Together? In here?"

He yawned, exposing all his teeth to her. "Obviously, she was scared of the dark. Came in here to bother me. Didn't get much sleep because she snores."

Skaja laughed and kicked him in the foot. "I do not. You slept like a valkyrie after midnight watch. Why are you so tired?"

He yawned again. "Other than you chatting my ear off all night? I'm making up for six years' worth of bad sleep." He started drifting off, but she kicked him in the shin. "Ow!"

"Fall asleep again and it will be my knee to your groin."

He opened his eyes to glare at her. "Coming from you, I know you're serious."

At last, he shifted in the bed until he sat up and his bare feet smacked the floor. His clothes were rumpled from sleeping in them all night, similar to hers. "Brr! This place is cold. Brings back some rather unpleasant memories." His hair stuck out in all directions, his eyelids halfway closed.

Avonia cleared her throat. "Prince Calle, you're needed in the council room. I'll just..." She blinked a couple times in confusion as if she didn't know what to do. "I'll step outside for a minute."

The moment the door closed behind her, Calle said, "Your poor mother. Can't chastise a prince for sleeping in the same bed with her daughter. Can't chastise her daughter because there is no motherly relationship there."

Guilt swam like piranhas through her blood. Though, it wasn't her fault they had no relationship. It was Paula's fault. She didn't know how to fix it. She didn't know if she wanted to.

"I'm glad it wasn't your father," he continued as he rifled through his drawers. "Or another male servant."

"I already promised I wouldn't harm anyone while I'm here."

He raised an eyebrow at her, his eyes still squinting through the haze of bright light. It seemed even after a few months of being above ground, he wasn't quite used to it. "I know you will intentionally keep that promise. But what about unintentionally? Your first instinct is to protect yourself by killing."

She frowned because he was right. "It will take some time, Calle."

"I know." Despite his squinting eyes, his expression softened. "I never thought any of this would be easy. But I'm glad you are here."

"Me too." Nervous? Yes. Uncertain? Yes. Uncomfortable? Also, yes. But still glad. And she was grateful to him for making this transition easier. "Where do I fit in here?" she asked as she slid off the bed and stretched her wings. A smirk grew across her mouth when she caught him watching with wide, mystified eyes.

After several blinks, he said, "I don't know how to answer that for you. In another life, you would have been a personal guard to the royal family. But we're in this life instead. I don't want you as my guard."

Her wings ruffled as she took his comment as an insult. "Why? You don't think I can protect you?"

He chuckled and leaned one shoulder against the wardrobe as he gazed across the room at her. "I warned you about the blood oath. Harpies are prideful when it comes to their duties. A harpy must ask to be released from a blood oath because it is an insult to suggest otherwise. I should have given you a choice when I released you from the oath."

"Yes, you should have. A choice would have been nice."

With a sigh, he shook his head and gave her a look sad enough to twist her gut. "You tried to give your life to save mine. I absolutely will not let it happen again."

"I would have done it even without the oath."

Shocked silence.

But it was true. Just the thought of him coming to any harm created an ache inside her heart.

With a start, she realized it was her own heart she felt, and not Calle's. She couldn't feel his heart at all. The temporary soul bond had vanished.

The knife twisted further in her gut at the loss of connection. No blood oath. No soul bond.

"I wish I could do the same for you," he replied finally. "I would definitely try, but we both know I'm a lousy fighter."

"Yes, you are," she laughed, playfully shoving his shoulder. "You stand a chance against another lousy fighter, but not against a valkyrie."

He grimaced and shuddered. "I know. You are terrifying. Inari is terrifying. I almost lost my head twice. And like I said before, I like it much better on my shoulders." He paused. "And...for what it's worth...there's no one I trust more with my life than you."

Emotion clogged her throat. Tears swam in her eyes. Never in her life had she imagined a man saying those words to her. It was almost as if she held his magical glass flower in her hands again, and this time, she cradled it close to her heart. The object was far too fragile to risk breaking.

"Now get out of here," he said with a devilish grin, waving his folded clothes in the air. "Don't watch me get dressed." He mouthed, *Or do.*

She rolled her eyes. "I've already seen you naked."

"Half naked," he corrected. "You couldn't see the other half in the water."

"How was I supposed to know men and women don't bathe together?"

"Well, now you do."

He waggled his eyebrows and mouthed, *Join me anytime you want.*

She smacked his arm with her closed dagger and left the room in a huff, even as his laughter trailed after her. She jumped when she found her mother leaning against the wall, far too close to the door for comfort. Had she been there the entire time? What had she heard?

Her playful mood died instantly, replaced by wariness in her mother's presence.

Still unsure whether she was friend or foe, she sized her up with one sweep of her gaze. Her golden-white wings matched her own exactly as if she faced a mirror. Her hair and eyes she'd inherited from her father, but she recognized herself in the shape of her mother's face.

They stood facing each other awkwardly, neither knowing what to say.

"Are you hungry?" her mother finally asked with a nervous smile. "I'll take you to the banquet hall. The food isn't too fancy. Feeding hundreds of people is difficult, but we make it work."

With a nod, Skaja followed her down the hallway, trusting Calle would find his own way.

She gave her mother a sideways glance. Her shoulders slumped with fatigue. Dark circles rested behind her eyes. "You haven't slept," she commented.

Avonia shook her head sadly. "I still work at the palace, and I just returned from my shift. I have to keep this place a secret. And my relationship with Typheal too."

Her wings ruffled in surprise. "Why?"

A sad smile. "If the wrong people find out I've been meeting him, I will be branded a traitor as well."

"You've been meeting him in secret for six years?"

"I have. He's my husband. Well, he was, but the king broke our marriage after the incident with Calle." Her expression turned wistful. "I'm looking forward to the day I can remarry him."

"Why not remarry him somewhere else?"

"It's not so easy as that. No priest in any kingdom would marry us when he has those tattoos. It would be putting a target on their own heads."

They passed people in the hallway. Many were men, and the discomfort of it caused her to walk closer to the wall with one dagger in her hand, ready to be snapped open. Many of them stared at her as if curious.

Without tearing her gaze away from potential threats, she asked the one question burning in her mind, "Why didn't you have another child?"

Avonia's eyes watered and her chin trembled. They stopped for a moment when she reached out to the wall as if strength fled from her, and she only just barely managed to keep herself in one piece. "Because you were our miracle baby. W-w-we—" She took a deep breath and cleared her throat. "We struggled for years to have a child. Succeeding a second time was not possible."

Uncomfortable with the sudden display of emotion, Skaja ducked into her room to retrieve her shoes, and when she reemerged, Avonia stood waiting. They continued to the banquet hall.

Several long tables stretched across the room, many of them occupied. Like the antechamber, large windows let in light from the high-vaulted ceilings. The low hum of conversation filled the room, and even as she piled a plate with bread, cheese, and dried meat, she never turned her back to anyone. She ended up standing rather than sitting at any of the tables. Avonia joined her.

Her heart skittered with anxious energy, and her wings stiffened the moment her father stepped through the doors. His gaze found them, but he didn't approach. He smiled. She didn't return the favor.

Perhaps someday she would find herself comfortable in his presence. That day wasn't today.

"What is this place?" she asked. Although her stomach rolled with discomfort, she tried her best to eat.

"An underground fortress. The portal's location can change at the caster's will. King Liam knows about the fortress. He knows our people are here. But he doesn't know where it is or how to find it. The people here are both loyal to Prince Calle and those who need refuge from Liam's cruelty."

"Where are your soldiers? I don't know how many men King Liam has, but I doubt what I've seen is enough to take the city."

"No, it's not." Her eyebrows furrowed. "There are more people loyal to Calle in Heulwen, but few will rise up if they think there is no chance we can succeed. Over the years, we have thwarted Liam's efforts. Raided caravans. Made threats. Stole food and money. Rescued people from the scaffold. It was all we could do until now. Before we knew Calle still lived. Now we can do so much more."

She picked at her food. "What will Calle do? Kill his brother? I'm not sure he has it in him. He's too...kind-hearted."

"Yes," she laughed. "He has always been that way. So very unlike his brother." Then she sobered. "But I've seen him try before. He had more at stake then. And he lost it all. Under similar circumstances, I'm sure he'd find the right motivation to do what's necessary for the sake of his people."

"Nyana?" The name on her tongue caused several needles of jealousy to prick her feathers. "Unless you know someone who deals in necromancy, I don't think it's a viable option."

Her mother shook her head and leveled her with a stare, tipping her head curiously. "Calle will do anything for someone he loves. Under any other circumstance, he is soft, and I fear he is too soft to overthrow Liam."

A spark of anger lit the kindling in her heart. "You would use him as your pawn?"

"No." Avonia looked upset at the suggestion, and Skaja remembered Calle mentioning they had a mother-son-like relationship. "But we need him to step up. We have no one else."

The silver sheets of Calle's memories came to mind. His smile. His laughter. His carefree demeanor. "I assure you he is much changed since the Pits. But I agree he is very soft. He'll do what it takes to save others and to save himself, but he lacks initiative."

The feathers in her wings ruffled in surprise when she realized she was having an easy, comfortable conversation with her mother. She excelled in battle tactics—a trait she now realized had come from the person who had birthed her.

"Calle released you from the oath?" Avonia asked suddenly.

Skaja frowned. So, she *had* been listening to their conversation. "It was after I was gravely injured. I was unconscious."

"Your wings look much better. How do they feel?"

Her eyes narrowed at her mother. The sudden topic change was strange. She also felt overwhelmed by the lack of knowledge on how to communicate with her own mother. "They ache a bit. But nothing compared to yesterday. Calle did a great job."

Her mother's mouth twitched. "I heard you threatened to cut off Cian's hand if he touched you."

"He's a man," she replied matter-of-factly.

"Calle is a man too."

"Yes, but he's…Calle."

A long pause gave her a chance to look over the banquet hall. More people entered. Voices competed over other voices in a louder hum than before. She knew who she searched for before she found him. Calle smiled at her from across the room where he conversed with Typheal. Warmth bubbled in her heart, and she returned the smile with one of her own.

"I don't mean to pry," her mother said slowly, "but what is your relationship with the prince? I'm not sure I can figure it out."

She closed off immediately, not wanting to talk to a near stranger about something so personal. She wasn't sure she entirely understood it herself.

Avonia frowned. "We searched for you. For years."

"I know. Calle told me everything. You don't need to explain."

"But I do. I am so happy you have been found." She placed her hand on Skaja's shoulder and squeezed gently. "I want to have a relationship with you. I want to be your mother."

Skaja shrugged off her hand. "All my life, I was told my parents had abandoned me. I know now it's not true. But it still feels true. You can't erase that."

"No...but perhaps we can try to move forward."

Thankfully, Calle approached and cut their conversation short. A smile grew wide across his face as he slung an arm around Skaja's shoulders. An immediate blanket of comfort wrapped around her at his touch. He was the only familiar thing in this sea of foreign chaos.

"We're needed in the council chamber. Immediately, it seems." He chuckled and led her out the door and down the hallway. She glanced over her shoulder to find Avonia, Typheal, and several others following them like guards might escort their charge.

"We? Don't you mean *you*?"

"I want you there, if you are willing."

"Why?" She cast him a suspicious glance. "Are you chaperoning me because you don't trust me not to hurt anyone?"

"No." His smile melted into a more serious expression. His fingers ever so lightly stroked the base of her wings in an intimate way, and a pleasant shiver worked its way down her spine. But his touch disappeared just as quickly. He leaned closer and murmured in her ear. "You are the single most important person in my life. I want you there, as well as your council."

Heat flared in her cheeks, and not knowing how to reply, she tried to jab him in the ribs with her elbow.

Of course, he side-stepped her attempt, chuckled, and slipped into a nearby room. With a huff, she followed.

A large, rectangular table sat in the middle of the room, chairs on all sides, and a half-dozen people sat in those chairs. They stood abruptly at Calle's presence and bowed.

"Your Highness," one of them murmured as he straightened. His long, lavish red robe spoke of wealth and position. His long brown hair tumbled down his back. A tattoo shaped like a diamond sat on his forehead.

A curious glance around the table revealed three of the six men wore the same tattoo. And she noticed they were all men. When Calle eventually took the throne, she would ensure at least half his council contained female members.

The thought inspired a frown. She still didn't know where she fit into Calle's world. So, she joined her mother near the now-closed door, acting as a guard while Calle approached the other six at the table. His gaze followed her path, and he wore his own frown. Had he expected her to sit beside him?

Other than her parents, two guards stood at the door on the opposite side of the room, and Joel and Cian sat in chairs beneath a window. Where had Inari gone? Hopefully not getting herself into trouble.

The red-robed figure, who introduced himself as Harold, began the meeting by presenting the last six years' worth of events. He skimmed over Liam's wife and two daughters as if they weren't an important enough topic to discuss before moving onto their efforts to thwart the king.

From how it sounded…

They were expecting this to last many more years before finally wresting the kingdom away from King Liam. She crossed her arms and ruffled her feathers in aggravation.

"Do you have something to say, Skaja?" Calle asked, and she jumped at the sound of her name. All eyes turned toward her, and suddenly the room became too quiet. Too still.

"I am allowed to speak?"

"Always."

She started to take a step forward but thought better of it when she realized all the other men would be too close for comfort. "Fine... What I see is a council sitting on their arses, spending hours debating whether they should drink water or wine. Do you know how long it took for us valkyries to plan out the attack on the Pits? A week. You've had six years, and from the looks of it, you're no closer to your original goal than you were from the beginning. I think you are too afraid to do what is necessary because you are deciding what will result in the best outcome. But there is no outcome at all without action."

"And how do you propose we take the city?" Harold asked, lifting his chin as if to say he was more important than her. What arrogance! Valkyries were all equals, and if Calle wouldn't be sorely disappointed in her, she might have been tempted to cut up the man's face a bit. "We lack a large army. Those we have recruited aren't all trained soldiers. Our prince is still recovering from the effects of slavery. Need I go on?"

"No." Her upper lip lifted in the faintest scowl. "You have made it quite clear you are willing to wait until Liam dies of old age or has an heir."

"Yet, you are making no counter proposals yourself."

"Give me the rest of the day to count stock and heads, and I'll give you one on the morrow."

Harold lifted a goblet of water to his lips and eyed her. "I'll hold you to it."

As if to diffuse the tension in the room, another council member rose from his chair and held out his arms in a show of peace. "Your Highness, we all spoke at length about your return, and we have come to a unanimous decision. We think it's best you take a wife before we make a move on the kingdom."

Calle choked on his water, and as if involuntary, his gaze darted in her direction. Their eyes locked, and her heart tripped over itself in both worry and fear. He couldn't get married. He wasn't…wasn't ready!

"Excuse me?" he finally gasped. "When was this decided?"

"A couple months ago. You are five years past the day you should have chosen a bride. But don't you worry, Your Highness. We have gathered all the eligible maidens willing to support you at your side."

As the man spread his arms again, the doors on the opposite side of the room opened, and nearly two dozen women entered wearing fancy dresses and crowns of flowers in their hair. They whispered excitedly amongst themselves, but as Skaja watched them, dread grew like an infectious disease in her stomach. They were all beautiful and elegant and poised. Their skin was unblemished, without tattoos or scars that she could see. And their faces radiated goodness and warmth.

Skaja self-consciously tucked her wings closer to her body and hid her hands beneath her feathers. Although no visible blood marred her skin, her hands had taken more lives than she could count. They were dirty and scarred and lacking light and goodness.

"He is to marry?" she finally managed to whisper to her mother, who eyed her curiously. More specifically, she eyed the way Skaja's wings spoke without her uttering a word.

Avonia nodded and replied quietly, "It was an idea proposed in the council a couple months ago after we found out he still lived. Knowing his romantic temperament, we thought it would give him more of a reason to fight. He mustn't know our reasoning behind it."

"But...won't marriage distract him from the bigger picture?"

"We think it might focus him more. Does that sound so outrageous?" Yet, her mother said it without looking her in the eye as if she had something to hide. More reason must exist for it than that.

"No. It...makes sense." *Unfortunately.* Her wings drooped in their misery. "However, it's a bad time, no? Why not wait? There is not a large selection of women here."

"It may not be a large selection, especially for a prince, but it is a good selection."

Skaja's stomach rolled again, fearing Calle would give into the pressure of the court and choose one of the twittering ladies. But then she turned her gaze warily to her mother. "What other secrets are you hiding from him?"

Avonia's jaw clenched, and she looked away. "Nothing."

She peered at her mother suspiciously. There was something she was keeping from the prince. But what?

Calle clapped his hands suddenly and the room quieted. He gave an apologetic smile and gestured to the line of suitors. "You are all very lovely young women." And then he turned back to the council member. "But there is someone else I'd rather marry." Skaja's feathers ruffled with envy, not unlike the envious whispers and groans escaping the suitors. But then he grinned and glanced her way. "Unfortunately, she told me she would sooner rip my head off like a Praying Mantis does to her mate."

A rumble of surprise and laughter shook the room, but Skaja only managed a blank stare as a current of shock rippled through her body. She stared at him, eyes wide. Her wings hunched to give away her vulnerability.

Me? You would choose me over all these better candidates?

But...but...but...

Heat climbed her body from her toes, up her legs, her torso, her neck, but before it settled in her cheeks, she threw the door open and slipped into the hallway.

Too fast.

Everything moved too fast. Rescuing a man from death. Finding out her whole life was a lie. Kissing a man. Sleeping in the same bed as a man. Meeting her parents. A man wanting to marry her.

The air suffocated her lungs. They grew heavy as if turning to brick. Drawing each breath became difficult. Black drapes fluttered at the edges of her vision.

Her feet led her blindly forward, and she barely spared a glance for anyone, not even the men she passed in the hallways. When she stumbled across a secluded bench tucked in a corner, she slumped onto it, her mind spinning. The faux windows cast a glow on her wings, catching the light just right so a shimmer reflected on the wall. The luster contradicted the swirling gray confusion overwhelming her soul.

Only a few minutes later, Calle turned the corner. He stopped when he noticed her on the bench, and his worried expression melted into relief. He approached and sat beside her. She didn't stop him.

"Sorry," he murmured, giving her a guilty grimace. "It was supposed to be a joke. Unfortunately, I have a higher opinion of my wit than you do."

"Saying you wanted to marry me was a joke?"

"No, that's very real."

She recalled the golden rose she'd unintentionally smashed to the ground. "I thought you only wanted to court me."

"True, I do want to do that too. But I want more with you." He reached out to touch her but hesitated as if giving her the opportunity to pull away. She didn't. His hand cradled her face, and she couldn't help but lean into the warmth his palm offered. His amber eyes gazed at her with kindness and admiration. "I love you, Skaja."

Her heart rolled in a pile of emotions ranging from excitement to nervousness to uncertainty. "Even if I threatened to rip your head off?" she joked, though her cracking voice betrayed the tears rising to the surface.

"Even then." He kissed her cheek. Heat climbed into her face, but perhaps it had never left. He kissed the corner of her mouth. A sigh of contentment escaped. And then his lips claimed hers. Gentle. Sweet. When he pulled away, he left her breathless and longing for more.

Her voice trembled. "Am I supposed to say it back?"

"Only if you feel it."

"I don't know what I feel."

"That's fine." The back of his fingers trailed across her cheek, then her jaw as his gaze flitted over her face. "I wanted you to know I would never marry any of those women. It's a tradition for those in Heulwen to choose their own brides, and the council gave me such an opportunity, but even I can recognize when something feels unnatural and forced."

Avonia's words rushed to her mind. *He mustn't know our reasoning behind it.* Betraying Calle's trust was much worse than betraying her mother's.

"There's something you should know." She captured his hand to force his gaze on her. "My mother doesn't want you to be aware of why they want you to marry. They think it would center your focus to battle your brother if you had something you needed to protect. While her words might be true, I can't help but feel like she's hiding something else." She squeezed his fingers. "She may be my mother but...be careful, Calle."

He frowned. It certainly didn't suit him. "I have reason enough to fight. I already said I would lead."

"Then lead." She gripped his arms and gazed earnestly into his eyes. "Don't wait for them to tell you what to do. Don't be a puppet who bows to their whims. You are a *prince*! And someday, you will be a king. A good king. I cannot help but notice you doubt yourself. Don't. March in there. Command the room. Make plans. Execute the plans."

"But..." He bit his lip. "I don't know enough about the situation."

"Then learn. We'll spend today interviewing people, counting stock and heads, and I will learn the layout of the castle. We can do this, Calle. *You* can do this."

"I'm not sure I can. Everyone expects me to...kill my brother. When the time comes, what if I can't?"

Softly, she pointed her finger to his chest, right over his heart. "You do what is best for you and your kingdom. Don't let anyone else tell you what that is. This recent meeting is a prime example of their flowery words and secrets and control. They think they control you. Show them they don't." She absently stroked his chest and lowered her voice. "Take initiative. Make plans. Execute the plans. Things don't happen when people sit around arguing."

His fingers grazed her hips. "You are very good at this. A natural leader. You have a lot of talents." The melancholy in his voice betrayed him. He must think he possessed no talents at all.

She tipped his chin up so they once again maintained eye contact. "You may not be the best with the sword or with leadership, but you are charismatic. People are drawn to you. You can charm an entire room with a few words."

He smiled and trapped her hand in both of his. "Then let's try to put one of my only talents to good use, and then hope I can learn the rest."

A laugh escaped her, and she couldn't help but pinch his side teasingly, which earned her an even larger smile from him. "You will. Starting now."

CHAPTER
26

Exhaustion hung over Calle's head by the end of the day as he headed back to his chambers. He'd talked to many people and counted supplies, weapons, and food. They had a shortage of everything, especially soldiers. A concentrated, small-scale attack would work best on the outside, and if they managed to get Avonia and Typheal on the inside, they might be able to pull this off without fighting Heulwen soldiers.

He jumped when someone brushed his hand, and he glanced down to find himself holding a piece of paper between his fingers. When his gaze darted up again, the hallway was empty. Most people had gone to sleep by now.

His heart pounded a fearful rhythm against his ribcage as he spun in a circle and glanced up at the ceiling in case a dark-skinned valkyrie waited to jump on him and cut the hair from his head.

Inari was nowhere to be seen.

Inviting Skaja into the fortress was one thing. But having Inari wandering about made his skin crawl with discomfort. So far, no one had been killed. Inari had pulled a few pranks but mostly kept to herself and groomed her griffin.

His eyebrows furrowed as he returned his attention to his hands and smoothed the crumpled paper.

Meet me in my room.

The rhythm of his heart transitioned from fearful to excited. He'd never seen Skaja's handwriting, but who else could it be?

He hastened back down the hallway and to the other end of the fortress. The hairs on the back of his neck stood up, but when he glanced over his shoulder, no one followed. With wary steps, he continued forward until he stood in front of Skaja's door. It opened suddenly, and two hands grabbed his shirt, pulled him inside, and slammed him against the wall just as the door closed behind him.

"Are you asking to be followed?" Skaja snarled only inches from his face. "Keep to the shadows. Be aware of your surroundings. Listen to both your surroundings and your gut. Be cautious."

"I had no idea you were following me. I didn't even see you. Was this…a test?" He shrugged sheepishly. "I suppose I failed, eager as I was."

"No." She smoothed his shirt with the brush of her hands while her lips twitched with amusement. "We got caught in your room last time. We're less likely to be caught in mine."

"To be fair, I forgot to bolt the door. Not a mistake I'll repeat again." He slid the bolt into place and gave the door a firm tug. It held steady.

"I don't know any man brave enough to lock themselves in a room with a valkyrie."

"Probably just pure stupidity," he joked as he slipped off his shoes. "I'm not sure how much bravery plays a part."

When he glanced up, he froze, and his heart stuttered. Skaja stood only feet away with one of her daggers open, her expression unreadable in the flickering candlelight. She stood still for a long few moments, simply gazing back at him. But then her expression softened when she lifted her dagger.

Bells of warning pealed in his mind, telling him to move, to defend himself. But he remained rooted to the spot. He trusted Skaja. She would not harm him.

A new bell of alarm banged loudly against his skull when she lifted her dagger to her own hand. His eyes widened, and he jumped forward to try to stop her, but she moved too fast. The blade sliced her palm. Red rivulets of blood streamed from the wound and coated her hand and fingers.

"Will you bind your soul to mine?" she asked quietly, almost reverently. "Not temporary this time. But permanently."

He swallowed as he watched a couple drops of blood hit the stone floor, but then his gaze moved to her face. Earnestness sparkled in her eyes. And immense warmth.

"Why?" his voice escaped as a hoarse whisper.

Her wings folded closer to her body as if vulnerability caused her discomfort. "Because when I think about losing you, it hurts. Because I look forward to seeing you every day. Because I would do absolutely anything to keep you safe. Because I need to be closer to you."

She loves me, he realized with a start. *She just doesn't know how to say it.*

He took a step closer. And then another. "You might hate it—being so connected to me."

"I liked it a little too much when the bond was temporary."

Shadows flickered across her hopeful face as he stopped beside her, gazing into her eyes. Silently, he took the dagger from her and inhaled sharply as he sliced his palm opposite her. Pain pulsed through his hand like an eager, living thing.

After setting the dagger aside, he threaded his fingers with hers, palms pressed together and blood mingling. "This is different from a blood oath," he said, maintaining eye contact. "In a blood oath, one person consumes the other's blood. However, a blood exchange is required for bonding two souls. It's like..." He swallowed, a flicker of fear passing over him like silent shadows as he placed his whole self on the line. "It's like the marriage of two souls, not in law or body, but in spirit. Do you still want to do this?"

Her feathers ruffled in nervousness or excitement, he wasn't sure. "The real question is, do *you*? There are many better candidates over me."

"No, there are not. And yes, I certainly want this. I'd have all of you, in law and body as well if you would have me."

277

She bit her lip, though she didn't outright refuse him like he expected. "I make a better valkyrie than I would a queen."

"You haven't had a chance to try."

More uncertainty, and he realized he pushed too much on her at once. It didn't matter what he wanted. He found it more important to move at her pace.

He squeezed her fingers. "I'll ask nothing more from you than the soul bond."

Finally, her shoulders relaxed, as did the tension in her wings. "How do we do this?"

Golden light flickered between their palms as his magic reached out to her. The magic snaked around their wrists like a unity rope. The shimmering light moved fluidly through their merged blood and gently caressed the essence of her spirit. Asking. Waiting.

"I can feel it," she whispered. Warm light reflected off her face and filled her eyes as she gazed back at him.

Swallowing the emotion in his throat, he nodded. "Magic isn't necessary to bind souls. But I want it to bind ours. I admit I don't know what the result will be, but I'm looking forward to finding out." The worst his magic could do in this state was heal her, but he hoped it would help create a stronger bond. A unique one.

"Me too," she breathed.

He took a deep, fortifying breath before speaking words in the Heulwen language, the same language printed on his wrist and back. The words rumbled deep in his chest like a trembling mountain before a rockslide. His very soul shook, quivering with anticipation.

He then prompted her to speak the same words.

The moment she uttered the last syllable, their souls stretched toward each other like two boulders rolling down from opposite hills and crashing into each other at the bottom. He gasped. His knees buckled at the same time hers did, and he barely managed to catch himself against the bedpost with an arm around her waist.

Heat coiled in his blood, burning hotter and hotter as his soul fused with Skaja's. He felt her everywhere—in their syncing heartbeats, in their rolling emotions, in their spiritual connection.

The fever of passion inflamed within him. One moment, he held her hand, and the next, his fingers tangled in her hair and his lips claimed hers in a searing kiss. Their hearts beat wildly. Their blood boiled hotter.

He gasped when Skaja's hands wandered beneath his shirt. Her touch left a trail of lava in their wake, and when her fingers skimmed the waistline of his pants, he groaned against her mouth.

All too suddenly, her mouth left his, leaving him famished and wanting for more. She pulled his shirt over his head, shucked it to the side, and unclasped the neck piece of her outfit. Her dress dropped to the floor. The sight of her in her undergarments spurred his heart into a frenzied rhythm.

He reached out with the intention to pull her against him and feel her soft body against his, but she gave his shoulders a good shove, and he stumbled backward onto the bed. She quickly jumped onto him, straddled him, and leaned down so her hair brushed his face.

A shiver of desire crawled through him, demanding more.

A shuddering breath escaped him when she kissed his ear, his neck, his shoulder. His hands traveled up the length of her thighs, but they started to tremble when he forced himself to think clearly for a moment.

Skaja had never kissed anyone before him. That could only mean she had never done anything more either.

"Perhaps we should wait until after the bond cools down," he rasped.

"No," she growled as she fisted his hair and pulled him into another kiss.

He lost himself completely in her touch, in her kiss, in the feel of her warm skin on his. Mindful of her wings, he flipped her over and now straddled her. He breathed heavily as he gazed down at her in the flickering candlelight. "You won't slap me? Stab me? Rip my head off?"

The corners of her mouth twitched in amusement. "Not unless you ask."

Not able to resist the pull of her for long, he kissed her again and dissolved into her fiery passion. He loved Skaja, and he planned to make her his queen if it was the last thing he ever did.

CHAPTER
27

C *alle.*

At the sound of his name, his eyes flew open, and he bolted upright. His eyebrows furrowed, and he rubbed his bleary eyes to glance around. Darkness filled the room, dawn likely still hours away.

He blinked back confusion when he turned his head to find Skaja sleeping soundly beside him, her wings stretched out on either side of her where she lay on her stomach. Her bare back peeked out from beneath the sheets. He wanted to kiss her smooth skin again. He wanted to run his hands over her soft feathers.

Slowly, he grazed his fingers over her lower back. He smiled softly as he recalled their passionate night together and the promise of more to come. The tips of his fingers trailed across the arch of her wing. She didn't stir.

Calle, the voice said again, causing him to jump.

His gaze darted about, but he soon realized the voice echoed in his mind, and not inside the room.

Who's there? he answered back with caution.

No reply.

Had he imagined the voice?

Just as he settled back onto the bed, the voice penetrated his mind, louder this time. A child's voice. He bolted upright.

Uncle Calle. I know you are out there somewhere. Mama needs help.

His eyes widened. Uncle Calle... Mama...

You are my niece? How are you speaking to me?

Through the strange mind-link, her teeth chattered as if in fear. *Magic. Don't tell Papa. He doesn't know.*

I won't. Are you frightened? What happened?

I heard Papa say he will kill Mama if you don't show yourself by tomorrow.

The blood drained from his face.

When? How? He mentally did the math. If this was his older niece, she was less than six years old. She sounded far too grown up for her age, and the reason why caused anger to clench in his fists. *I have heard nothing of this ultimatum.*

A sniff. His heart ached at her tears. *Papa threatens the rebels once a week. When you don't show your face, he kills someone. This time it will be Mama.* Another sniff. *Please, I don't want to lose my mama.*

Shock and anger drove him to his feet. In the heat of his fury, his feet felt warm on the cold floor. Skaja had been right. Avonia...Typheal...the council...they were hiding information from him. People were *dying* because he hadn't taken action against his brother.

Well, no more.

He refused to lose his sister-in-law because he was waiting around on others to make the decisions, to make the first move. This was his move.

He swallowed as he glanced toward Skaja's restful, sleeping form. He felt her heartbeat, slow and peaceful, reminding him how precious she was to him. He wanted to do this alone. No one else had to die because of him. He refused to put his dear Skaja in harm's way again. He could not bear the thought of losing her.

Slowly and quietly, he dressed, pulled on his shoes, grabbed his weapons, and slipped out the door. Only then did he dare speak through the magical bond in his mind as if Skaja might hear his thoughts and wake. Or even detect the tension in his heartbeat.

Where are you?

In the castle, the girl replied. *In Mama's room.*

Mama's room... His mind raced as he tried to make sense of her words and recall where she indicated. Were she and Liam sleeping apart?

The queen's chambers? he asked, dodging quickly around a corner and keeping to the shadows just as Skaja had chastised him to do only hours earlier.

Yes. Mama is in pain.

He clenched and unclenched his fists as he attempted to calm his anger and maintain a cool head. *Is she awake?*

A pause. Then, *Yes.*

Tell her I'm coming. Tonight.

Another pause, and only when Calle reached the entrance of the fortress did the girl answer. *Mama says don't come. But she's scared. I want you to come. I'm afraid of Papa.*

I will come. I promise. I don't care what your mama says. Tell her to be ready in an hour.

Could this be a trap? Absolutely. But the fear in his niece's voice punched a hole in his gut. He couldn't allow Liam to kill his wife nor hurt his children. What a sick, evil bastard. But his brother had killed Nyana and doomed him to a life of slavery. He had no doubts about him being capable of such a horrendous act.

The pause this time stretched far longer than the others. He walked slowly through the corridor beyond the entrance to prevent his footsteps from making any sound. His heart pounded against his ribs. Any moment, someone might turn the corner and stop him. He refused to be stopped.

Mama says whatever happens to please protect her babies. But I'm not a baby anymore.

No? Then you must be big and strong. Look after your mama until I get there. Also, what is your name?

Maisy.

Calle stopped as if a root of surprise shot out from the floor and wrapped around his ankle. That's what he'd wanted to name his child if he'd had a girl. Had Liam known? He'd never told anyone but Nyana. Then again, he now knew Liam had likely sent spies to follow them.

His heart pounded as he pulled one of the large, rounded doors to the exit open. In the darkness, two guards drew their swords, the metal singing on the way out of their scabbards.

He feigned a sheepish expression as he glanced between the two of them—the same two guards as when he'd first arrived.

"Prince Calle," the woman said, blinking in surprise moments before she dropped to her knee alongside her companion.

Guilt crept across him like midnight shadows as he now feigned embarrassment. "I didn't realize anyone would be out here. You see, I wanted to meet someone."

The other man spoke this time. "With all due respect, Your Highness, the woods are not safe. Perhaps if I retrieved Joel to hide you…"

"Absolutely not." He bit his lip. "Skaja already came out here. I don't want her to think I never tried to meet her."

"We didn't see the harpy."

"Probably because she's fast." Calle tried not to tap his foot impatiently. Every moment they wasted was another moment dawn crept closer. Little time remained. "I am not asking for your permission. I'll be back soon."

The two guards gawked at him as he disappeared into the forest. Once out of view, he turned fast on his heel to the left and headed in the direction of the castle. A wave of magic rippled over him as he crossed the invisible barrier that hid the fortress from outsiders.

A shiver ran down his spine as he traversed the forest floor with only a sliver of moonlight to guide his way. He didn't dare use magic to light the path, afraid someone might spot him.

He pulled the hood of his cloak over his head and climbed down the rocky ravine beneath the bridge leading into Heulwen. Torches flickered above him, and he held his breath, praying his feet wouldn't slip. A patch of dark green moss cushioned his footfalls. The fresh scent of stream water promised escape in the distance. And when he reached a horizontal grate in the rock face, only then did he release his breath.

He eased one of the thick metal bars loose and silently set it aside on the soft moss. As kids, he and Joel had discovered this passageway that led straight to the castle. Although he wasn't sure if Liam knew about it, he slipped through the opening and proceeded forward carefully.

Keep to the shadows. Be aware of your surroundings. Listen to both your surroundings and your gut. Be cautious.

Skaja's words echoed in his mind as a constant, comforting reminder.

A chill swept through the pitch-black corridor made of stone and moss. The dank smell of mildew and decay teased his nostrils. He lifted his cloak to cover half his face, partially protecting himself from the rancid smell.

He crept along the shadows, moving only as fast as he dared. One hand still held the cloak to his face while his other hand felt along the damp stone. Drips of water echoed in the distance, and wind howled down another tunnel. The darkness swallowed him whole as if he walked straight into the belly of a beast.

Not knowing how the mental link between himself and his niece worked, he cast a net into the black pit of the ocean.

Maisy?

No answer.

What felt like an entire mile passed as he weaved through tunnel after tunnel. His fingers brushed against an empty sconce, affirming he now traveled directly beneath the castle. So far, none of Liam's men showed themselves. But his hand lay in wait to grab the hilt of his sword at the faintest sign of trouble.

Maisy, he tried again. *Can you hear me?*

I can hear you.

Does your father know I'm coming?

A tearful reply followed. *I don't know. I grabbed my sister from the nursery and brought her into Mama's room. I don't know if anyone saw me.*

His foot hit a stone stair, and cautiously, he began to climb. Darkness still blinded his way. *Is the door locked?*

Papa took the lock off.

Calle's stomach churned with disgust at the meaning. Liam's wife couldn't seek refuge from his ill intentions. With each footstep up the long, narrow staircase, anger burned in his blood. How could his brother have turned into such a vile creature?

At the top of the staircase lay a closed door. He felt along the wooden structure until he found the handle and turned.

He winced as the door creaked open. He paused. Silence greeted his ears.

He took a deep, steadying breath before he pushed aside a long, red tapestry and stepped into the solar.

Darkness coated the empty room like dust. A sliver of moonlight entered through a gap in the thick, velvet curtains. The unlit hearth was clean, as if the room hadn't been used in some time.

A portrait hanging over the mantle caught his eye, and as he approached slowly, his heart suddenly trudged through mud. He and Liam stood with their parents, each face smiling. They were happy back then. If only things hadn't changed in the years since.

Crash!

Calle jumped out of his skin at the sound of shattering glass. He drew his sword and pointed it toward the door. No one entered.

Someone shouted in the hallway, and he slowly edged toward the door. The shouting grew louder.

"You good for nothing servant!" Liam roared, followed by more shattering glass. "How hard is it to find a few hundred people?"

"Th-th-they're using magic to shield themselves," someone stuttered. "Our disenchanters can't even find them."

"Why? Isn't that your job? To break illusions?"

The servant began stuttering again. "Y-y-yes but we no longer believe the magic is an illusion. They must be hiding in a pocket in another realm."

"Then find them!"

"Your Majesty," someone said, a female voice this time. "Why don't you get some sleep? The hour is still early."

"I will get some sleep when those damn rebels are found! Are the gallows ready?"

Gallows...

The pit in his stomach grew larger at the mention. He didn't dare breathe, afraid even the tiniest sound would alert them to his presence behind the door.

"Surely you don't mean to hang your own wife."

Bang! Shatter!

Liam snarled. "Either it will be my wife or my bastard of a brother. Send out another search party. Calle will come. I have no doubt. Always the perfect and noble one. He'll come."

Glass crunched against boots before the footsteps echoed in the opposite direction. The glass then scraped against stone as if someone began to clean up Liam's mess. During a particularly loud scrape, Calle opened the door quickly and shut it behind him, finding himself in a dim hallway. Torchlight flickered around the corner near the source of the commotion.

He ducked into the shadows and crept along the hallway in the direction of the queen's chambers. Every footfall mimicked each thud of his heart. He kept his senses alert, listening for the first sign of danger. It was strange to walk these halls again. He remembered every room, every corner, every turn. It was home.

Yet, it wasn't at the same time.

A rat scampered down the hallway, followed by the growl of a cat. But otherwise, the castle lay still in the early morning darkness.

Firelight flickered from beneath the door leading to the queen's chambers. Could he exit the castle as smoothly as he had entered? With three people to protect?

I'm here, he said in his mind, hoping Maisy heard his words. *Don't be frightened. I'm walking through the door.*

With one hand on the pommel of his sword and the other on the door handle, he opened the door, slipped inside, and closed it quietly.

A gasp.

Calle spun around, his gaze darting about the room. Two small girls shared a large armchair beside the fire, both looking haggard and tired and scared. And the source of the gasp...

He squinted against the firelight to find a figure huddled beneath a blanket, lying on a cot. A purple bruise lay on her cheek, her neck and swollen eyes faring just as badly.

It was as if someone punched him in the gut, and he suddenly couldn't draw a single breath in his shock. Blonde hair. Blue eyes. Small face. Tiny frame.

"Nyana," he choked.

CHAPTER
28

Skaja bolted upright when Calle's shock rippled through the bond, as if she plunged into an icy river in the dead of winter.

She knew in her gut something was wrong the moment she found her bed empty.

In less than a minute, she dressed, strapped on her weapons, and darted out of her room. Calle's emotions surged through her. Shock. Anger. Sadness. No, not sadness. Devastation. Where was he? With Avonia? Typheal? Certainly not Inari, otherwise she would feel his fear.

He should have taken one of her daggers so she would know where to find him.

Despair. More anger. Disgust.

Her gut churned with unease as she raced through the empty hallways of the fortress. Surely, no one could feel so many emotions in the span of minutes.

Despite exerting herself by running, her heart wasn't attuned to her own body. It was attuned to his and it beat much more slowly than it should.

When running proved to be much too slow, she spread her wings on either side of her. They still ached from both healing and disuse, but they obeyed her when she flapped them. Her feet left the ground only moments later, and she soared quickly through the halls.

Disgust. Tenderness. Unease.

Fear.

She flew faster when the outpouring of emotion nearly collapsed her wings and threatened to curl her into a ball.

As if sensing her panic, Inari ran out into the hallway right as she passed over her. Quickly, she landed and faced her friend. "Do you know where Calle is?"

Inari smirked. "Wouldn't you? You can't deny he's your lover now."

"I'm serious!"

Worry. Distress. Defiance.

"Who's there?" a voice growled moments before someone turned the corner. Typheal emerged with a torch in his hand, the black tattoos standing out against the shadows flickering across his face. He froze when he spotted the two of them. His eyes widened, and a flicker of hesitation crawled across his features. He looked as if he contemplated whether to draw a sword or run for the hills.

Uncertainty and distrust set aside, Skaja approached him in her desperation. "Calle is gone. I think something has—*is*—happening to him."

"How do you know?"

Swallowing, she held out her hand to reveal the shallow cut on her palm. "We are connected."

Inari howled with laughter while Typheal's brows pinched into a deeper furrow. "Tell me what you feel."

She recounted the way her heart beat and all the emotions Calle had felt in the last several minutes. When she finished, Typheal swore under his breath and motioned for her to follow him. They traversed a couple hallways before exiting the fortress altogether. Two guards scrambled to attention at the sight of her father.

"Prince Calle came out here." Typheal's comment wasn't a question, but rather demanded an answer.

The guards glanced from Skaja to Typheal with fear in their expressions. The man pointed to her. "His Highness said he planned to meet Skaja in a private place. He's been gone for an hour. Maybe more. He hasn't returned."

"Obviously, he wasn't going to meet me!" she growled as she raked her fingers through her hair but paused when she found her father doing it to his own. It seemed they shared the nervous habit. "Where is he?"

Even in the darkness, barely visible beneath the light of the moon, her father's face paled. "He went to the castle," he murmured, eyes wide. "No! He cannot find out like this. We must stop him. He'll get himself killed."

"Find out what?"

"We kept it from him for a *reason*. We knew he'd do something rash and stupid. He thinks, or perhaps thought, Nyana was dead. She's not. She's married to his brother. She's the queen."

All the blood rushed from her face, and she stumbled backward at the news. She caught herself against a pillar, and then combed through each of the emotions again. Calle's shock had been powerful enough to stir her from her slumber. He'd only just found out Nyana still lived. He was most certainly at the palace. But then what had driven him there in the first place?

Suddenly, the insistence for Calle to marry made sense. Before he found out Nyana was alive. He would be less likely to do something rash and stupid. Like now. Entering the palace without someone to protect him was both rash and incredibly stupid.

A small, insecure part of her flickered to life as her gaze lingered in the direction of the castle. What did this mean for her? Was she going to lose Calle? To his former flame?

She seethed. "I'm going to rescue his sorry arse just to kill his sorry arse."

Typheal reached out as if to touch her but retracted his hand. "You can't go by yourself."

"No, I can't." She marched back into the fortress, Typheal at her heels. Inari's bright eyes danced with enjoyment as she watched the drama unfold. "We need to act *now*. Wake the spellcaster who hides the fortress. Rouse your soldiers. We no longer have time to wait. Your prince's life is at stake."

Only minutes later, soldiers dressed in armor and weapons stood in the room with her. They shifted from one foot to the other as anxious energy pulsed across the walls. Some faces appeared excited, others frightened and pale. There weren't as many people as she would have liked, but it was enough.

She nearly expected either one of her parents to step forward to lead, but they didn't. All eyes fixed on her.

She slammed her hands flat on a table, and the entire room fell into a hush. "Your prince has made the first move to take a stand against the king," she said, her voice echoing for all to hear. Although, she skipped the part where she had no idea *what* he was doing or *why*. They needed to feel confident in their future ruler and not balk at his stupidity. "We may not have many soldiers, but we have enough to take the northern wall."

"And then what?" someone called out.

"We hold it. It's time to take back what is rightfully ours."

A cheer filled the room. She was surprised to find she meant it. *Ours...* This was her home too.

And she would make sure they succeeded.

"You didn't know," Nyana whispered, her eyes widening slightly in their swollen state.

He shook his head when words failed him. Tears blinded him and ran down his cheeks. "I had no idea you were alive. No idea you were married to Liam. I thought...I thought you were dead."

"And I thought you were dead until only a few weeks ago."

"Not dead. Just enslaved, starved, and tortured."

"Oh, Calle." Tears slipped down her own cheeks, and when she reached for his hand, he grasped on tight. Her grip was weak, her body frail. "My heart breaks for what you have endured."

He swallowed, his gaze passing over her face. "You have endured far worse."

She shook her head and winced as if the action pained her. "Not always. Only when he is angry."

However, the fear in her eyes told another story altogether. No one should fear their husband. "I'll get you and your daughters to safety. Can you walk?"

Another wince, and with the shake of her head, she said, "Liam broke my leg so I couldn't run." Sweat slicked her forehead, and pain rippled across her bruised face. But she remained stoic, either for her girls or because she was used to enduring such pain, he wasn't sure.

His jaw clenched as anger fueled him. His heart thrummed fast, pulsing white, hot fury through his blood. He squeezed her hand, intent on seeking her permission. "Will you allow me to take you and your children away from here?"

He glanced at the two girls. Maisy appeared to be five years old, her hair auburn and her eyes blue. The younger girl, perhaps age three, looked far more like Liam with her green eyes, though her blonde hair came from Nyana.

She swallowed and nodded as if in too much pain to speak. He stooped down and carefully scooped her into his arms while instructing the girls to hold onto him and not let go.

The door slammed. Calle spun around, his heart beating wildly when he found Liam casually leaning against the frame. Half his face twisted into a triumphant leer. Burn scars stretched across the other half of his face, still red and angry as if burned only yesterday.

"Well, well, well," Liam said slowly like a cat teasing its prey. "Look who managed to escape the Pits. I've heard they're inescapable. How did you do it?"

"A valkyrie saved me."

Nyana and the children clung tighter to him, their fear transparent on their faces.

"*Saved* you?" Liam's scarred face twisted into a snarl. "I thought they captured you."

He shrugged, and despite himself and the situation, he grinned. "I suppose I'm *that* personable."

Anger twisted his brother's features even more, but he didn't move forward. Instead, he eyed Calle's hands and winced as if remembering the day he'd burned his face. "Where is the valkyrie now?"

Calle's jaw clenched, and he spat at Liam's feet. "As if I'd tell you, you bastard."

"Always so much disrespect for your older brother." He smirked, though his eyes filled with contempt and hatred brighter than the sun. "How did you enjoy the Pits, Calle?"

Against his will, his breath became ragged. His body trembled. Horrible memories flashed across his mind. Darkness. Pain. Hunger. Cold. Misery. He snapped out of the horror only when Liam took a step forward.

"Stay back," he warned, moving slowly to put a table between them and their tormenter. "I will give you this offer only once. Step down from your throne, or I will make you do it."

Liam barked an ugly laugh. "You will *make* me do it? I may not know where the rebels are hiding, but I have a good estimate of how many there are. You cannot do what you threaten. Now, give Nyana back to me."

His grip tightened on his sister-in-law. "I won't allow you to hurt her."

"You will take her instead? She's my property. You have no right."

"She's no one's property. Especially not yours."

"She's my *wife*," he enunciated the word, slowly and clearly, with a grin pulling his lips into a lopsided smirk. "Those are my *children*."

The day he saw Nyana murdered by his brother's hand flashed back to his mind. He now knew it must have been an illusion to make Calle suffer mentally and emotionally while his body suffered physically in the Pits. Nyana had been meant to become his own wife at the time. His heart ached at the thought of Liam beating and mistreating her. She deserved far better.

"Why?" he rasped. It was as if a fierce, unyielding wind battered his heart. For what Nyana had endured. For her children who must have suffered so much already. "You had everything. You were the king. People flocked to you. You could have chosen anyone—"

Liam snarled and smashed his fist against the wall. The nearby painting rattled at the impact. "People flocked to *you*. Everyone loved *you*. Even the woman I wanted. Tell him, my love. The night you met him. Tell him about us."

Tears trailed from Nyana's bruised eyes, and she turned her face into his shoulder. She shook her head.

"Tell him!" Liam shouted, his anger flaring so suddenly that spittle flew from his mouth.

She began trembling in his arms, whether from a sudden chill, fear, or something else, he didn't know. "Liam and I spent a little time together. We shared a kiss. But then I met you and you were the only one in my thoughts. I didn't want you to know. I was afraid you would reject me."

A pit formed in his stomach, uncomfortable and nauseating. He'd had no idea. And now he felt like a fool. But still, he held her tighter against him. "It doesn't matter. I'm getting you out of here. You and my nieces."

The two little girls clung to his legs. Fear emanated from them as they stared wide-eyed at their father. Liam's fists curled and uncurled in sync with his snarling lips.

"You have been a pain in my life ever since we were kids," Liam said. Metal sang an eerie tune as he drew his sword from its scabbard. "I can either do this with Nyana in the way...or not. Your choice."

Disgust rippled through him as he stared back at his brother. "You would kill your own wife? Truly?"

"She can't produce me an heir. I have no further use for her. And when she's gone, it would be far too easy to blame her death on you—the rebel prince who broke into the castle to assassinate the royal family. The people won't love you so much then."

He backed away slowly, closer to the window. Two stories lay between the window and the ground, a dangerous feat for an escape. But enough magic swirling within his core remained to accomplish at least one more daring feat.

"Calle," Nyana murmured against him. "Leave me. Protect my girls."

"Never. I won't let you die a second time."

As if outraged by the sight of him holding his wife, Liam released a war cry and charged forward with his sword poised over his head. Calle's heart leaped to his throat, knowing he would never reach his sword in time when three people latched onto him. Burning hot magic boiled in his blood, and he managed to free one hand just enough to give the magic a channel for release.

Orange flames spurted from his fingers and caught fire to the rug in Liam's path. His brother leaped backward, which gave him enough time to break the nearby glass windows with a burst of golden flames.

The glass shattered at his feet, and without hesitation, he carried Nyana and after coaxing the clinging children from his legs, he guided them through.

A stairway made of gold magic and the blush pink of dawn greeted their feet. He urged it to crumble behind him as they ran down the length of the stairs and onto the grass of the courtyard.

The clamor of steel on steel caused his heart to jump out of his skin. Soldiers surrounded the northern tower, attacking each other in a sea of metal and chaos. Thick, billowing flames reached toward the skies from the eastern part of the castle.

The rebels...

When had they decided to attack? In his absence?

Two Heulwen soldiers broke away from the others and charged in their direction, blades raised. Panic lodged in his throat when he realized very little magic remained without sunlight to refuel it. But before he managed to lift a hand to fight back, a golden-white shimmer of wings swooped down from the sky. Calle turned the children's heads away before Skaja butchered the soldiers with her daggers.

"I'm going to kill your sorry arse for your stupidity, fae prince," Skaja growled as she provided a path forward.

He flashed her a charming grin. "Love you too." He motioned to the two children with a jut of his chin, both clinging to his clothing. "Can you carry them? And I'll take her." Nyana's head rolled against his shoulder, as if too weak to hold it up when covered in so much bruising. Worry gnawed at him, but he refused to give it a voice.

She nodded. Uncertainty, and perhaps envy, flashed across her eyes, but it disappeared quickly before she carefully picked a child up in each arm. "Together, they're still heavier than you were when I found you in the Pits."

"I've put on a little weight," he protested.

"According to my mother, you are still *too skinny*." A crash behind them. They continued their flight forward.

"You don't seem to think so."

No response, but he didn't miss the way her gaze raked over his body, followed by a faint blush in her cheeks.

"Keep moving, Calle, toward the gates. The caster moved the entrance of the fortress there. And I can't imagine your brother is happy you stole his wife."

His eyebrows furrowed and his lips pinched together. "You knew?"

They jumped over a pile of rubble. "I have known for less time than you, apparently. Your shock woke me up. Scared me senseless with your barrage of emotions. My father told me where he thought you might have gone, and I organized the attack."

The air rippled as they entered through the invisible barrier leading to the fortress. The guards ushered them inside. He noticed the insecure hunch of Skaja's wings, and only after they deposited Nyana and her children in the infirmary did he pull her aside while Cian rushed to the queen's aid. He cradled Skaja's face in his hands and gave her a tender kiss. Nyana may have been close enough to see them, but he didn't care.

He felt both discomforted and relieved that he didn't care. For years, he had mourned Nyana, wishing things had turned out differently. But he realized a life with her wasn't what he wanted anymore. Skaja brought out the best in him like no one ever had. She encouraged him to be better, work harder, do more. She held every inch of his heart.

"My niece called to me in my sleep," Calle explained at Skaja's accusing stare. "Said her mama was going to be killed if I didn't show my face. I sought to rescue them. I thought I could slip in and out because I know the palace so well. Liam was waiting for me. I didn't want you to get hurt, Skaja. I can't bear the thought."

Fear and anger rippled across her features as she gestured with both hands to his chest. "So, you disappeared without a trace? No word? No note? I didn't know where you were. Only that you were in trouble."

He sighed and caressed her jaw with his thumbs. "I admit I left hastily. I never meant to worry you. I'm sorry."

Her chin wobbled, but she still glared as if trying to hold onto her anger. "Are you going to go back to her?" She now gestured to where Cian treated Nyana's broken leg. Both his nieces held onto each other, tears trailing down their cheeks. "Now that you know she's alive? I know how you felt about her. Perhaps how you still feel about her."

He pulled her deeper into the shadows and lowered his voice. "I loved Nyana. But she's different. And I'm different. I don't feel the same way anymore. I love *you*, Skaja. If we manage to dethrone Liam, I still want you as my queen. And if we don't manage it, I want you as my wife regardless."

"It's too soon," she said in a wavering tone. Nyana's presence clearly affected her.

"I know." He kissed her forehead, her nose, and then her lips. "I only need you to know exactly where I stand with you. I won't push you into anything."

"But if I don't choose now, you will choose Nyana." A sheen gazed back at him in her beautiful brown eyes, and her heart echoed a range of emotions back to him. Longing. Fear. Desperation. Love. Sadness.

He realized she felt pressured to make a quick decision...

Gently, he placed his hands on her shoulders and gazed into her eyes. "Listen to our soul bond, and know I speak the truth. I have never bound my soul to another before. I have never been connected to another person like this. I have never felt this way about someone else. I will wait for you, Skaja, however long it takes."

"You say that now...but what happens if or when Liam dies?"

"Nothing will change." Again, he kissed her lips to finalize his words. "Now, I don't know about you, but I have a northern tower to take."

Her smile returned and her wings ruffled with excitement. She reached for the daggers at her shoulders and snapped them open. "You may need a guard at your back."

"Not a guard—an equal."

The expression in her eyes softened, and although she said nothing, he felt the stir of gratitude and happiness in her heart, linked with his.

They rushed back the way they'd come, confident Nyana and the children would be safe within the fortress.

Outside, sword fought against sword. Smoke curled into the dawn skies from where blazes caught fire. He and Skaja fought side by side until they realized gaining the tower looked more futile than possible.

A nearby granary caught his eye, and without a second thought, he ran toward it and started climbing. Several men tried to kill him on the way up, but Skaja quickly dispatched them with her daggers.

Using the last reserves of his magic, he created a golden, shimmering shield. He banged his sword against it as loudly as possible, and dozens of the "enemy" glanced his way. Some people stopped fighting altogether, their eyes wide as they stared up at him. The clamor reduced to cinders in comparison. Before it started up again, he called out to his people.

"I see some of you recognize me," he shouted to make himself heard. "Yes, I am Prince Calle. My brother, the king, sold me into slavery and lied to each of you about it, instead telling of my death. I am grieved by what has happened in Heulwen in my absence. High taxes. Unjust punishments. Fear day in and day out. I don't know about you, but that doesn't sound like a happy life."

People shuffled their feet, now uncertain. The fighting ceased altogether, and he now had a captive audience. He continued. "Shift your loyalty to me instead. When I am King, life will be happier. More just. Without fear. You can raise your families in a safe place. Fight for me instead."

A murmur moved through the crowd like waves of the ocean. Heulwen soldiers cast uncertain and wary looks at each other, as if no longer knowing the difference between ally and enemy.

"Kill them!" Liam shrieked near the castle, flanked by a couple harpy guards and several other regular guards. He pointed straight at Calle. "He's lying. He tried to assassinate my family. He's now holding them hostage."

Another murmur rumbled through the crowd. He felt their anger rolling off them like heat escaping a stove.

"My sister-in-law and nieces are under my *protection*," he corrected quickly. "The queen is currently being treated for injuries delivered by her husband."

The anger grew hotter, this time directed toward his brother.

"Death!" Liam growled, his glare made more menacing with a couple hundred soldiers between them. "Death will be the punishment for any who defy me."

Fear and uncertainty rumbled through the crowd like crawling thunder. It stretched endlessly across the sky, moving from one horizon to the other. The sunlight behind the mountains stained the sky gold. Just a little higher, and the sunlight could rejuvenate his magic.

Calle banged on his shield once again. "All who join me will be granted amnesty. You don't have to serve a monster like Liam."

Slowly, soldiers began to turn their backs on Liam. His heart surged with hope at the addition of more brave men and women to his small army.

He faced off against his furious brother in a deadly stare sharp enough to cut daggers.

Perhaps less than a fourth of the soldiers joined Calle's side. It would have to be enough.

Without warning, Liam gave a signal with his hand and his army charged forward in a deafening crash. Metal clashed against metal, and Calle once again found himself in the throng of danger. Both Skaja and Typheal fought at his side. And once the sun peeked over the mountains and caressed his face, he breathed in the light through his nostrils and felt the magic churning alive within his core.

His soldiers managed to get through the northern tower, kicking and fighting their way in. Metal clashed against metal. Weapons met blood and bone. Several bodies flew from the top of the tower and hit the ground with a sickening *crunch*.

Cheers lifted into the skies, and hope surged through Calle as he rushed toward the tower. But before he managed to reach it, Avonia grabbed his arm, pushed him hard, and he suddenly found himself sprawled on velvet carpet instead of rough cobblestone.

He was back at the underground fortress instead of the Heulwen castle. The invisible entrance swallowed him whole and spit him back out. Despite the eerie quiet, the crashing metal still echoed in his ears.

"What are you doing?" he growled, annoyed at being taken out of the fight when they'd found success and irritated at Avonia's secrets and lies.

"Hurry," she said, ushering him forward. "Our forces have found victory, but now we need your aid elsewhere."

He glanced behind him, and to his relief, he found Skaja following him with both daggers drawn. Wariness sat on her hunched shoulders, irritation in her brow to match his own. She was a fighter and being pulled early clearly irked her.

But still, he followed.

Avonia led him to the council chambers, but they stopped just outside the doors, her hand on his arm. "The council is holding an emergency meeting. We need the queen's input, but no one can convince her to attend."

In other words, she wanted him to do the convincing.

Anger coursed through him as he yanked his arm out of her grip. His expression wavered between a glare and devastation. Tears leaked from his eyes as he recalled Nyana's bruised and broken body, and the fear in her children's eyes. Yet, he stood tall and unbending.

"Is she the reason you and the council insisted so heavily that I marry? Tell me why."

The harpy's voice shook as she answered. "We didn't tell you she still lived because we feared you would do something rash and ruin everything we have worked for all these years. And if you were married, we thought finding out the truth would hurt less."

Skaja squeezed his hand comfortingly as more tears trailed down his face. He knew there was truth to Avonia's words, but he felt like her pawn. The council had used him and tricked him and once again, he felt like a fool.

"You have absolutely no idea the horrors I endured in the Pits. But one of the worst was hearing an alarming tale of my brother beating his wife so hard that she lost her child. I am disgusted and angry, and I feel betrayed. By the people who were supposed to be my support. My family. I haven't trusted anyone for six years. Not until I met Skaja. Quite frankly, I trust Inari more than I trust you. At least she's honest in her desire to take my life. You on the other hand…"

"Forgive me, Your Highness," she murmured with a bowed head.

"I am not your pawn. You don't get to decide what to tell me and what to hide." He turned to Skaja and held out a shaky hand. "Will you please come with me? I'm not sure I have the strength to face this alone."

Skaja's eyes widened, and he felt her heart beat with trepidation. "But…but don't you want to be alone with her?"

"It's been six years, Skaja. I meant everything I said to you yesterday. Today."

"Are you sure?" Her voice quivered.

"I've never been more certain in my life."

Finally, she nodded and slipped her hand into his. Together, they made their way to the infirmary where Cian and a couple other women rushed to and fro, one carrying bandages, another an elixir and healing herbs.

Calle found Nyana lying on a cot in another room, staring at the wall while her girls lay on another cot sleeping. She glanced up when they entered, but quickly returned to staring at the wall. The bruises appeared lighter as if in the process of healing, and her face no longer contorted with pain.

"Please leave," Nyana rasped as if she'd recently been crying. "I cannot bear for you to see me like this."

Ignoring her request, he pulled up two chairs beside the bed, and he and Skaja took a seat. "Like what?"

She swiped at her eyes. "Dirty. Broken. Defiled. Shamed."

He swallowed as his gaze passed over her. As if feeling his scrutiny, she pulled the sheets higher over herself. "I felt the same way, Nyana. Just in different ways. My imprisonment ended a few months ago. I've had that much longer to heal. Yours ends now. You'll recover. I promise." He reached for her hand and gave it a gentle squeeze.

Finally, she turned enough to face them, and her gaze flitted from him to Skaja. And then to their intertwined hands. He swallowed as he waited for her reaction. But instead of crying or shouting, she smiled.

"Will you not introduce me to your sweetheart?"

Relief washed over him. "Nyana, this is Skaja. She saved me from the Pits."

"It's good to meet you. Though, why do you appear angry with me?"

Only then did he notice the glare in Skaja's eyes and the way her nostrils flared. She gestured to the whole of Nyana. "This is what I fight against. This is why I kill men. To liberate women."

A startle flashed across Nyana's features before she glanced at the tattoo on Skaja's shoulder. "You are a valkyrie. The one Calle told me about."

"Yes. I want to butcher Liam for what he has done to you."

"You aren't the only one," she sighed tiredly. "I managed to shield my children from the worst of it."

Skaja seemed to all-too-easily understand the meaning. "By making yourself the target when his anger was directed at them," she murmured.

More tears leaked from Nyana's eyes, and for a moment, he wondered if she thought of the supposed child she had lost in her womb.

Calle squeezed her hand harder, his ache beating in sync with his soul-mate's. "Forgive me, Nyana. I failed you."

"No, you didn't." She glanced toward her sleeping daughters with a soft expression on her face. "I got my two wonderful girls out of this marriage. I will never regret that. I would not give them up for the world, not even to redo that horrid day."

What more could he say? He wasn't sure how to make this right, other than to protect her from Liam in the future. He couldn't take her back as his sweetheart—he didn't feel the same way as his younger self did, and she likely had moved on as well. He certainly didn't want to appear callous to her feelings and situation, but the longer he waited, the more people who could die.

"We need your help," he murmured. "I know you're tired. I know you want me to go away. But if there is anything you could offer to win this battle—information, tips, anything really—we would be in your debt."

Slowly, she started to rise into a sitting position, and Skaja quickly leaped up to help her. "I will give you anything you want, as long as my children are safe." She blinked rapidly as if to ward off tears. "And as long as you promise me you will make it so Liam can never touch me or my babies again."

"You want me to kill him?" The very idea created a discomforting pit in his stomach.

"I don't care what you do. Just free us from him."

Calle swallowed, thinking of all the people Liam had hurt or killed, and the many more who would face death if Calle failed. He would not allow Nyana to hurt any longer. "I promise I will try."

CHAPTER
30

The council room hushed when they entered. Nyana used a walking stick with Calle supporting one side of her and Skaja the other. All eyes followed them as they helped the queen into a comfortable chair.

When Skaja tried to move off to the side, Calle caught her hand and instead brought her to the table in the middle of the room.

As his sweetheart.

As his equal.

As his queen.

Heat claimed her face, distracting her from the fact that men occupied the table. Calle didn't sit, and neither did she. Her heart stuttered, and she blushed even more furiously as her gaze traveled up his long legs, slender waist, broad shoulders, and smooth skin of his neck. She had never been intimate with a man before. It was as if her wings had caught fire, but instead of burning, she'd ascended from ashes like a phoenix.

The council member named Harold began, "Your Highness, our soldiers have taken the northern tower, but they cannot hold it for long. What do you propose?"

Calle glanced at Skaja from the corner of his eye, but she subtly shook her head. He was the prince. This was his call.

"Do we know how many more men we have?" he asked.

"Ten times more, but it's still nothing compared to how many Liam has. They are controlled by fear. This is how the heartless bastard flourishes." Harold winced as he glanced toward Nyana. But her expression remained stoic, and she gave no indication the comment bothered her.

"Nyana," Calle said, and Skaja couldn't help but notice how he addressed her familiarly. He couldn't seem to help himself, especially when they used to be sweethearts. "What do you know about my brother? Does he have weaknesses? Holes in his defenses?"

When her chin began to tremble with fear, Joel lowered himself beside her and touched her shoulder comfortingly. Skaja wondered for a moment if they were friends.

"Anger is his biggest weakness in his defenses, as he often overlooks things in his fury," Nyana answered. "But physically, anger is also his strength. There are fewer soldiers who are loyal to him than you might think. He controls others using fear and threats as his tools, or by using blood oaths. Take away their fear, and you will gain a lot of allies. Kill him, and you might win the war."

"But how do I do that? We have little resources and fewer men."

Nyana gave a regretful shrug before the entire council room burst into arguments about their next move. Skaja rested her hands against the rough wood of the table, staring down at an indent in the corner. She blocked out all other sounds as she focused, and the arguing became a low hum in the back of her mind.

If they killed enough of Liam's men, the remaining might drop their weapons in surrender. But she also remembered that these were Heulwen soldiers. However many they killed would also be Calle's loss if they managed to get him on the throne. How could they accomplish their goal with as few casualties as possible?

Calle's contemplative murmur broke through her bubble of calm, and she recognized her own words on his tongue. "You stand a chance against another lousy fighter, but not against a valkyrie."

His head snapped up. He held up a hand, and a sudden hush fell over the room. "I know how we can win." His throat bobbed up and down as he swallowed. "I will recruit valkyries to our cause."

Inari's laughter startled her from where it emanated from the rafters up high. At his dangerous proposal, Skaja's heart dropped to her toes. And by the way Calle's expression steeled into defiance, she knew he felt it through their bond.

"No," she growled, her lip curled into a snarl. Her wings grew larger to match his defiance head on. "They will kill you. The moment you step foot on the island, you are a dead man."

But her warning went unheeded. "I've seen you slay a dozen men with nothing but your daggers in less than a minute *while* protecting me. What could a dozen valkyries do?"

She shook her head, wincing against the pounding in her temple. "You of all people will take your city by bloodshed? You will be attacking your own army, your own people."

Although she had no problem with it, she knew it would hurt Calle.

"If they are loyal to my monster of a brother, they are not my people. Besides, when they see we can win, when they see they have more to lose by fighting against us, I hope to sway their allegiance to me."

Inari laughed again from where she perched, one leg dangling precariously over the side of a rafter. She licked her lips, her gaze on Calle's hair. "My sisters will skewer you to a pole alive and dance around your twitching body until you die." A devilish grin. "I hope I get to do the skewering."

Several guards drew their weapons and moved forward, but Calle held them back with a raised hand. Skaja's wings ruffled in both annoyance and gratitude toward her valkyrie friend. Annoyance for setting her eyes on Calle, and gratitude for speaking the truth of the danger.

"My hair is off limits, Inari," he said.

Skaja stepped closer to him and glared at her friend. "You forget I have claimed him under my own protection. He cannot be harmed."

Inari swung her leg back and forth, back and forth. "But he will be in spite of the valkyrie code." She licked her lips again. "Bringing a man to the island...you will be severely punished, *and* he will die."

A murmur of arguing filled the room. Some people were in favor of the risk, but instead of sending Calle, they wanted to send someone else. Other people adamantly argued against the idea of sending their prince to his death. She tried to hide her horror when her father volunteered to go. A woman would have a better chance at recruiting valkyries, but even then, no one had enough authority to sanction such an attack except Nyana. The fae queen was not only injured, but she was too sweet and lacked the necessary spine. More than likely, the valkyries would take her in as their own and not allow her to leave.

Her heart, still at her toes, now dropped all the way to the pits of hell at the burning passion raging through Calle's blood. She felt every surge of defiance, every heated argument waiting on the tip of his tongue, every pounding beat of his heart that echoed in rhythm with hers.

"No." She glared at him.

He glared back. "Yes. It's the only way."

"It's *one* way. Not the only way."

Inari cleared her throat, and when everyone turned their attention to her, she shimmied down the wall and dropped deftly to her feet. The room at large took a collective step backward. Both Avonia and Typheal positioned themselves between her and Calle.

As if she didn't notice the sudden hostility in the room, Inari said, "King Liam is furious with the valkyries for the attack on the Pits, and even more furious about freeing the prince. His troops continue to attack the island." She looked Skaja in the eye, and her long ears drooped with sadness. "Catarina was killed in your absence."

Shock coursed through her, followed by a heaviness in her chest. The girl had only been fifteen, not even a fully fledged valkyrie yet.

Continuing, her friend said, "Paula is livid at King Liam. Wants him dead." She gestured between Skaja and Calle. "If you play your cards right, she might agree to help you. But only to avenge Catarina, is my guess."

Murmurs filled the room, followed by hope. "Then I will go by myself." Skaja's wings spread the slightest bit, ready for immediate flight.

"She's also afraid of Liam," Inari said, now leaning casually against the wall. "Never wanted to get on his bad side in the first place. She wouldn't attack without the assurance of our sisters' safety."

Our...

Not anymore. She wanted to stay with Calle.

Calle said, "What you mean is, she won't aid us unless the royal family vows to leave the valkyries alone. I need to go. There's no other choice."

She clenched her fists on top of the table and hung her head. He was right. Paula would never trust Skaja's word. But if the promise came directly from Calle's mouth...

She turned her head slightly to find him watching her, concern in his amber eyes. "You really think you can do this?" she asked softly, and the entire room fell into a quiet as deep as the Crowbeak watering hole as they waited for his answer.

"Making allies is what I know how to do best. Stop me or aid me, Skaja, the choice is yours alone. But I cannot do this without you."

He leveled her with an intense stare, an unspoken plea in his eyes.

True, if he could befriend a valkyrie such as herself, he could befriend anyone. But a few dozen valkyries? It was unheard of.

"You don't understand the risks." She held her hands to her heart when her chest ached at the thought of losing him.

"Yes, I do. You forget I was in the Pits when the valkyries attacked. It was a brutal massacre. I prefer not to get skewered if possible."

After gazing back at him for several long moments, she finally relented. He would not be swayed. He'd find a way to do this with or without her, and he'd be safer with her.

"Then pack up. We'll leave immediately."

The council decided to only send the two of them with Inari, as they didn't want to risk the valkyries feeling threatened by sending a small army to their doorstep. The idea of sending their prince into the heart of danger unnerved everyone in the room, but they agreed it was the best, and only, choice.

The meeting ended, and in the hallway, Skaja grabbed Calle's hand and pulled him behind the privacy of a pillar. She smashed her lips against his, attempting to speak without words, to portray how much he meant to her. He kissed her back with equal fervor. A small moan escaped her throat as his fingers trailed up her back and intimately stroked her wings. As difficult as it was, she broke the kiss and pushed him away enough to gaze into his eyes.

"Promise you'll be careful," she breathed, the kiss acting as a final goodbye in the instance that something might go wrong.

"I promise," he said quietly, placing a soft kiss on her hand. "Quite frankly, I'm more afraid to fly with Inari than I am about confronting an entire island of valkyries."

"She'll behave." *I hope.*

"Let's pray she doesn't push me to my death before we even arrive."

CHAPTER
31

Calle clutched onto the griffin for dear life. His knuckles turned white as he gripped the tough fur. Wind tugged and clawed and whipped through his hair. Tears streamed from his eyes as he attempted to keep them open against the bright afternoon light and relentless wind.

Houses, fields, and forests passed by beneath them. *Far* beneath them. They were little specks against a brown and green canvas, with an occasional splash of blue.

Two arms wrapped around his waist, followed by a long sniff into his hair. He shuddered and attempted to elbow Inari away, but his fear of slipping off the winged beast currently outweighed anything the frightening valkyrie could do to him. His attempt was feeble at best.

"I can't wait to skewer you!" Inari shouted over the wind, followed by a cackle. His skin crawled with discomfort. Skaja was friends with this madwoman? She needed better friends.

He risked a glance over his shoulder, only to find Skaja flying a little further behind. Her beautiful golden-white wings stretched out on either side of her, and the mere sight of her stole his breath away. Light rippled across her feathers like sparkling diamonds. The gold in her hair glittered like strands of sunlight.

And she didn't glance in his direction.

Instead, her head swiveled back and forth as if scanning the ground and skies for threats. Her wings glided strongly across the sky. Between his magic and Cian's herbs, her healed wings never faltered.

"Eyes ahead, lover boy," Inari said as she nudged his cheek so he gazed forward. The ground beneath them transitioned into ocean, and in the distance, he spotted an island.

"That's it?" he asked in awe. Bright green stared back at him from the island. Deep blue water crashed into white spray as if warning away any daring intruders.

"Is that admiration I detect?" Inari snorted before she placed a hand on top of his head and shoved him down into a crouching position. "We have lookouts who no doubt already know we're headed toward the island. Keep out of sight unless you want to be pierced by an arrow before we even touch the ground."

Despite the fear pounding through his blood, he couldn't help but smirk. "Careful. It almost sounds like you care."

She shoved his face into the griffin's fur and then stroked his hair with her fingers. "About you? No. But I care about my friend. I don't want to see her punished." She ground his face into the creature's spine as if to make her point. "Don't you even think about messing up your part."

He grimaced and massaged his forehead, though he continued to crouch. "What kind of punishment?"

Her shadow just in front of him revealed her shrug. "Paula is soft on Skaja, but she'll be really angry in spite of it. Saving a man's life is usually rewarded with the punishment of getting one's tongue cut out, and then banishment. But Skaja has done far more than that."

Dread rained down on him and drenched him in sticky trepidation. But instead of raindrops hitting his skin, he imagined it was blood. Skaja's blood.

"No one told me that," he whispered, eyes wide, but the valkyrie still heard him.

"Love does nasty things to a person, including giving their lives for the other. Skaja knows what awaits her. She's fully prepared to die for you. Hell only knows why."

"We have to turn back." He reached for the griffin's reins, but Inari smashed her elbow between his shoulder blades. Pain shot across his back. Black shadows seeped into the corners of his eyes. He felt himself slipping but managed to grasp onto a tuft of fur. His head spun, and to keep himself from slipping further, he rested his forehead on the creature's spine.

"We can't turn back now," she growled. "They know we're coming."

Squeezing his eyes shut against the pain still rippling across his back, he said, "Aren't you worried? Won't you be punished too?"

He turned his head slightly to watch as she steeled her expression, eyes toward the island. "Like I said—love does nasty things to a person."

Skaja flew beside them, eyebrows furrowed with concern as if she'd felt the fear in their bond. "How are you faring? Inari, are you playing nice?"

The valkyrie tightened her arms around his waist and laid her head on his back. He attempted to push her away, but squeezed his eyes shut when nausea churned in his gut. She certainly knew how to hit hard.

"Nice enough," she answered. When he cracked his eyes open, he noticed Inari's big, toothy grin. "I see why you like him. He smells nice."

"Stop smelling me." He elbowed her in the shoulder, which jostled the reins in her hands. The griffin jerked sideways, nearly throwing him right off its back. It screeched before glaring back at them.

Once Inari regained control, he gave Skaja a pleading look. "Leave me to go by myself. I can't allow you to get hurt."

Skaja bravely continued to fly by his side. "You won't even land before they shoot you through the heart. Not without my help."

"Please," he rasped, but only received a glare in return.

"No."

"Quiet," Inari growled, once again pushing his head down as they neared the island. "Remember when you didn't talk at all in the Pits? Let's go back to that, shall we?"

Calle held his breath and squeezed his eyes shut. Terror loomed over him like dark red clouds, ready to release its drops of blood. Trepidation teetered beneath him, and he knew one wrong shift of his body might expose him to his death.

"Skaja, block him now," Inari ordered, and he heard Skaja's wings cut through the sky in front of the griffin. A shadow passed over his eyelids, and he opened them slightly to find her feathers blocking him from view.

They descended lower, lower, lower until the griffin's feet touched the earth. The unexpected jarring impact flung him off the beast, and he crashed to the ground. Skaja quickly helped him up and spread her wings wide to hide him. Inari pushed him even further behind the griffin. Even one flying beast and two valkyries did nothing to make him feel safe on an island filled with women's hatred of men.

"Skaja, Inari, I see you have returned," a female voice said, freezing him to the spot. A small crack appeared between Inari and the griffin, and he dared to peek through. A fierce-looking woman stood at the front of a triangular formation with five others flanking her. Like Inari, she wore feathers in her short brown hair, but fur on her body. She wore little clothing, exposing her arms, legs, and stomach, as if she weren't afraid to get hurt.

Or as if she knew no one could touch her.

"Paula," Inari said with a nod of her head.

"Who did you bring with you?" the valkyrie leader asked.

Slowly, Skaja drew her daggers. Paula's jaw clenched as she stared at her young pupil, but she made no move for her weapons. "I know you are angry about how I lied to you, but I did it for good reasons. Where have you been? You've been gone for weeks."

Calle touched the hilt of his sword. His heart hammered inside him as if trying to quickly build a shelter from the inevitable. He wasn't ready for this. But he had no choice now.

Skaja answered, anger and hurt in her tone. "I met my mother. And my father."

Paula's entire body stilled. "Who took you there?"

"A man. A kind man. A man I have claimed, and perhaps the only one who can stop Liam's troops from attacking the island and killing more valkyries. I advise you to listen to what he has to say."

Both she and Inari stepped aside, and the moment Paula's eyes landed on him, she inhaled sharply and drew her sword. On instinct, he drew his as well and raised the weapon when the valkyrie leader rushed forward to attack, but Skaja jumped in front of him and blocked it with both daggers.

"What are you doing?" Paula shouted in her face. "He's a man!"

"He's Prince Calle! King Liam's brother."

Paula's eyes widened and she stepped backward, though she kept her sword raised. "Now it's your turn to lie. Prince Calle is dead."

He cleared his throat, as he wanted to do the talking without further implicating the woman he loved. "Have you not heard the rumors? Or listened to any of Liam's men you have killed? The king sent his troops here because he thought the valkyries captured me from the Pits."

Fire blazed in Paula's eyes as she snapped her head in Skaja's direction. She seemed to have put all the puzzle pieces together all too quickly. "Tell me all of this is a direct result of the blood oath you are forced to serve."

"It was at first." Skaja edged toward him until her fingers brushed his, and then they intertwined. Fear rolled in his stomach. Was she trying to goad them? "But Calle released me from my oath a short time ago."

Before giving Paula a chance to reply, he said, "Liam has not only made a fool of you, but he has wounded and killed your sisters. He needs to be overthrown, but I don't have enough men. I humbly ask for your help."

The woman's jaw ticked as if he hit a nerve, but she still threw her head back and laughed. The valkyries behind her laughed as well. "I would be doing Liam a favor by killing you, wouldn't I?"

Skaja dropped his hand and stepped in front of him again. "I won't allow it."

"No?" The valkyrie leader grinned as she looked from him to Skaja, and to the valkyries standing behind her. "Skaja, you have disappointed me. You've broken our sister code. You've saved a man. Brought him to our home. And you are willing to kill us to protect him."

Calle swallowed, and despite his brave front, his hands trembled.

Paula continued, "I have not forgotten your hand in this, Inari. Here's what will happen." She stuck the tip of her sword into the ground and leaned her weight against it. "I will aid you, Prince Calle. *If* you defeat the garguaran in the arena."

Skaja's face paled, and the sight of it caused burrs of dread to stick to the lining of his stomach.

But the valkyrie wasn't done speaking, "If you somehow manage to conquer the beast, I will grant you aid and spare your life and those you forbid us to kill. But if it kills you…" She turned her head toward Inari and Skaja. The fire of anger demolished the sadness in her eyes. "Inari, if he dies, your punishment will be to kill Skaja."

Now Inari's face paled, and as if her legs trembled, she caught herself against the griffin's harness.

"Do we have a deal?" Paula asked.

His hand trembled as he stuck it out to her. There was no going back now without horrible repercussions. "Deal."

Instead of shaking it, she spat at his feet and turned her back to him. "Drop your weapon. Place your hands behind your back."

He did as he was told, and the moment his hands touched his lower back, three valkyries seized him. His breaths came in short, ragged gasps as they trapped his hands with a rope and roughly tied a blindfold around his eyes. One of the valkyries kicked him behind the knee, and not able to catch himself, he stumbled forward and crashed face first against the dirt.

The sound of feet rushed toward him, but Paula barked, "Touch him at all, Skaja, and he will fight the garguaran with his eyes bleeding out."

A whimper escaped Skaja's throat, the only indication of her presence. Aside from the small sound, her heart beat in tandem with his. With fear, terror, concern, and...defeat.

She didn't think he could do this.

What, exactly, was he about to face?

He clambered pathetically to his feet in his temporary blindness, tripping a couple times on his way up. Someone grabbed the back of his shirt and shoved him forward. He stumbled but managed to stay on his feet this time.

The scent of pine and fresh river water suffocated him, as if every fiber of the island squeezed the breath from his lungs. Taunts and hisses followed him, but he didn't know whether they were human, fae, or something else entirely. His shoes scuffed against dirt, then grass, then rocks, until finally they gritted permanently into hard sand. Steel doors creaked open with a long whine, and with one final shove to his shoulder, he stumbled and crashed into a floor made of sand.

No one untied his hands. His eyes remained blindfolded.

The steel doors squealed shut with a slam.

"I decided not to blind you," Paula said, her voice now coming from somewhere above him, "only because Skaja refrained from touching you. But know this, Prince Calle. I will not fight beside a weakling. If you want our aid, you must be smart, resourceful, and a fine warrior. Skaja, come here. I will bind your hands to the railing. If he dies, you must watch it. If he falls, you mustn't try to help."

Skaja made no protest, but he felt her heart beating like the thrum of a rabbit being chased by a wolf. Or was that his heart? He hadn't had enough practice with the bond to tell for sure.

"I love you," Skaja said miserably.

Slowly, he picked himself up and tried to locate her despite the blindfold. He could have wept with joy at hearing those words from her lips. "I know."

A strangled sob escaped her throat, but otherwise she said nothing more.

Crash!

Something large and heavy hit what sounded like a metal door. Calle's breath quickened, and he desperately tried to free his hands but to no avail. He attempted to draw on his magic, but in his fear, it acted weak like a muscle he hadn't exercised in a while. The magic warmed the rope around his hands, but then it sputtered out and died just as quickly.

A cool shiver raced down his spine, telling him he was in the shade. If he could calm down enough or find direct sunlight, he might be able to free himself.

The earth shook with a mighty cry.

He felt like the rabbit now, blinded and cornered by an unseen beast.

Another metal door squealed on what he assumed was the other end of the sandy prison, but he didn't wait to find out what might come out of it. He started running the way he'd come, and his shoulder slammed into a wall.

Awkwardly, he rubbed up against the wall, feeling for something sharp. He hissed when a small object cut his collarbone. The creaking door grew louder, as did his desperation. Spinning around, he rubbed the rope that bound his wrists against the sharp object, assuming it was the hinge of the door.

The earth shook again as the beast roared, before it rumbled like a stampede of wild horses.

Right toward him.

He abandoned his vain efforts at freedom and dashed in another direction, sand flying up with each footfall.

Smash!

The creature hit the wall he'd deserted, and judging by the rumble following the crash, it was large. Very large.

Once again, the ground thundered with deafening footsteps, and the vibration rolling through the sand caused him to stumble. He wasn't going to last long against this creature. He had to think. And fast.

Again, he reached for his magic, but it shied away from him. His monumental fear scared it into the deepest, darkest pit within himself. Instead, he reached for Skaja through the bond. Her heart beat slower than his, if only barely. He latched on tight, hoping she would understand his need.

Something heavy smashed into him, and he cried out as his feet left the air for mere moments before he crashed on the sand, rolling, rolling, rolling until he hit a wall. *Thud.*

His head ached. His mind spun. Fire rolled through his shoulder.

He climbed to his feet through the pain and pumped his legs as fast as they would allow despite his hands tied awkwardly behind his back. Something warm and sticky dribbled down his side, and his clothing quickly became soaked.

That wasn't perspiration. It was blood. His own blood.

The garguaran roared, causing further dizziness, and he momentarily lost his sense of hearing, his ears ringing. He tripped over an object in the sand in his blindness, and his body shuddered with excruciating pain.

Bam!

What seemed like a large paw hit the ground right beside his head. A gust of hot, sticky breath hit him like a furnace, reeking of rot and blood.

His heart catapulted to the skies as he rolled to the side and to his feet, only for his head to brush the underside of...of...something *very, very* large.

No matter how hard he tried, he couldn't calm down. His magic refused to work.

He smashed his bound wrists against the creature, but to his horror, the blow bounced off like a harmless fly. The shock of the hit reverberated up his arms and into his skull. It stunned him enough to give the creature time to shift its body, and once again, something hit him and sent him flying across layers of sand. Shouts and jeers drowned his hearing, likely coming from what sounded like dozens of valkyries.

Desperation clung to him like the blood in his clothing. The moment he struggled to his feet, he reached out to Skaja again. *Please help me.*

Although they couldn't speak mind to mind like he was able to with Maisy, he felt Skaja tug back.

A sense of calm rushed into him as if he dipped himself into a cool lake. The rapid pulse in his blood calmed into a languid beat. For a single moment, the terror disappeared, the hopelessness vanished, and his magic crept out from its dark prison. He grabbed a hold of it, and it willingly burned through his body, concentrating at the base of his wrists. His skin grew hotter and hotter until the rope began to sizzle.

Snap!

The rope fell from his wrists, and he threw his blindfold off.

Only for the terror to threaten to return.

The garguaran wasn't a mere creature—it was a beast.

It was the size of a house with a large, round belly, head-sized scales for armor, and spikes all along its back. Its snout curved into a wicked growl, showing teeth sharper than the jagged spires towering from the Heulwen cathedral. Its long tail stretched across the sand, flicking back and forth with astounding strength.

The creature snapped its tail in his direction, but this time he ducked beneath the attack and ran toward it. Magic pooled in his hands, the shimmering gold forming a solid handle which stretched into the length of a sword.

He smashed the weapon against its hind leg. He stabbed the beast beneath its belly. His sword bounced off harmlessly. The plated scales were made of indestructible material. The armor was impenetrable.

As if annoyed at the small man poking and prodding at its belly, the garguaran huffed and stomped its feet in agitation. The ground rumbled beneath Calle. He struggled to stay upright, and when it started to lay down as if wanting to crush him, he jumped out from beneath it, dragging his sword along its side.

Not even a scratch.

The creature roared and snapped its sharp teeth at him, narrowly missing him.

And just like that, it leaped to its feet and pounced. Sand flew in all directions. In moments, Calle found himself on his back, pinned by the terrifying creature. His previous calm shattered as he struggled to free himself from its massive paw. His shallow breaths escaped in gasps. His heart beat frantically as his fingers dug through the sand to locate his sword.

The garguaran's teeth snapped downward as his fingers closed around the hilt of his weapon. He stabbed upward into its mouth and lodged the tip between two of its enormous teeth.

Its pained roar shook the skies.

While it gnashed its teeth and reared up on its hind legs, Calle scrambled to his feet and raced across the sand to the opposite side of what appeared to be a fighting arena until he stood in a patch of sunlight. Tall, fortified walls stretched high into the air, with spectator seats at the very top. He met Skaja's eye. Her wings trembled with terror. *For him.*

She didn't think he could survive this. He briefly wondered how many others before him hadn't. He wasn't sure he could survive either.

Unless…

His gaze snapped to the creature's mouth. It gnashed its teeth together as if trying to dislodge the sword, but only managed to drive it in deeper.

Now his own body trembled in fear as he considered what he must do.

He met Skaja's eye again and placed his hand against his heart, letting her know he loved her. He wasn't sure he could survive this. But he had to try. For Skaja. For his people. For himself. Many people would die if he weren't successful.

When the creature began to charge at him, he widened his stance. One by one, he threw balls of fire at the gigantic monster. The fire bounced harmlessly off its scales, but one of the flames entered its nostrils.

It screeched and thrashed its head from side to side, but it continued charging. The ground rumbled like an earthquake swallowing the island whole. He threw another ball of fire directly into the creature's mouth.

Right as it snapped its jaws around the entirety of his body.

And darkness engulfed him.

CHAPTER
32

Skaja screamed.

She tugged at the chains around her wrists, but no matter how hard she tried to break free, she remained bound. The metal dug into her skin, the hard edges cutting at her until blood ran down her fingers.

Another wailing scream escaped her as she kicked at her chains. Through the blur of her tears, she glanced down into the arena only to find Calle gone. The garguaran had eaten him.

"Please, no!" she sobbed. "Release me. I beg you!"

In her desperation to escape her chains, she flipped herself over the side of the railing and pulled as hard as she could, her feet braced against the wall. The metal cut deeper into her wrists, blood now dripping into the sand far below.

"Stop that, or you're going to lose both your hands." Paula and another valkyrie grabbed her and heaved her back over the railing, fighting against her screeching and flailing.

"Calle!" she screamed. She kicked Paula in the stomach and elbowed the other valkyrie in the jaw before several more pinned her against the railing to hold her steady.

Paula smashed Skaja's face against the cold metal, forcing her to stare at the garguaran below. Tears of defeat trailed down her cheeks, unfettered sobs escaping her throat. The beast paced back and forth, its limbs twitching as if from discomfort.

"You brought him here," the valkyrie leader said in a menacing tone, "now you must face the consequences. This gives me no pleasure, Skaja. You have been my right-hand woman for a long time. But rules must be upheld. Not even you are above reproach."

The beast twitched some more and let out a whine. It gnashed its teeth and swung its head.

"What was so wrong with aiding him?" she sobbed. "Now you both have lost."

"Whether or not the prince lived, we have won. If we aided him, we would have won. If he died, we would have won. It is not my fault he was a mediocre warrior."

Now the beast lay on its side, panting and whining.

Several tears fell over the brims of Skaja's eyes and splashed onto the railing. "You have taken everything from me, Paula. If you didn't feel as if you owed him anything, what about me?"

Paula's grip on her loosened slightly as if from surprise or guilt. "That's not fair."

"It is. The least you could have done was tell me the truth from the beginning. You never gave me a choice. I would have liked one."

"And what would you have chosen?"

She barely managed a one-shouldered shrug, and she winced against the pain of her restraints. "I don't know."

More tears escaped her eyes as her heart felt a tug of hopelessness. Of desperation. Of defeat.

Of panic.

Her eyes widened and she bolted upright, only for the valkyries to push her down again and hold her there. That wasn't her panic. That was Calle's. He was still alive.

And from the shared aching in her chest, she realized he couldn't breathe.

In a surge of hope, she calmed her own heart and channeled it through their bond. Calle latched on greedily like a man dying of thirst. Or suffocation, in this case. The garguaran's whines grew louder, which turned into pained roars. The beast kicked its legs against the sand, writhing and whining and gnashing its teeth.

Smoke escaped its nostrils and leaked from the gaps of its sharp teeth. By now, the other valkyries noticed the odd display and turned to watch with confusion.

As ribbons of smoke leaked from its snout, it kicked more ferociously against the sand. Skaja poured more calm through their bond, and in a shocking blink of an eye, an explosion from within the beast rocked the entire arena. Scales and flesh and teeth erupted outward and smashed into the arena walls, some pieces embedding into the metal like a sword into flesh.

Calle tumbled out of the creature's blown-up body, covered in blood, guts, and who knew what else. He landed on his hands and knees, gasped in a lungful of air, and expelled the contents of his stomach all over the bloodied sand.

The valkyries stared in shocked silence.

Overwhelming relief and gratitude gripped Skaja, and she couldn't help but sob in happiness rather than despair. He was alive. He'd defeated the garguaran. It remained to be seen whether Paula would extend her aid as promised, but she was simply grateful he was alive.

Calle pushed himself to his feet and swayed before he met Paula's eye in a look of defiance and triumph. Although he didn't glance Skaja's way, he placed his hand against his heart. She felt his love. Deeply. Truly. Passionately.

"I have defeated your beast," he called out. His face turned a bit green, but he managed not to vomit again. "Will I have your aid?"

Finally, Paula removed her hands from Skaja, her eyebrows furrowed as she unlocked her wrists from the chains. She itched to jump over the railing and fly to Calle, but she refrained.

But only barely.

"I am a woman of my word," Paula said, standing tall with her spine straight and her eyes blazing. "Give my valkyries a few hours to rest, and we will fly out just before dawn. You and I will speak more before our departure."

The words seemed to cause Paula physical pain, as she rubbed her temples and sighed before turning to her. "Skaja, you may take him to clean him up and provide him food and rest. But he must be blindfolded. He has seen enough of our island as it is."

"Of course," she breathed. "Thank you."

"Don't thank me. He has earned our aid." She rubbed her temples again. "And you."

Without another word, Paula left the arena with her entourage flanking her heels. Skaja wasted no time. She rushed down the stairs and unlocked the gates from the outside before she flew into Calle's arms and gripped him tight as if she might lose him at any moment. She cared little about the blood and guts that covered him. What mattered was he lived.

"Come on," she said as she found his discarded blindfold, tied it around his eyes, and tugged on his hand. "I don't think Paula will change her mind, but I don't want to test our luck."

She helped him bathe in the river, dress his wounds, and dress him with clothing left from men the valkyries had killed in the past. By the time she borrowed a griffin from the fields, climbed on behind Calle, and flew him to her home on the cliffside, darkness had fallen across the skies like an exhale of relief. Only when they were safely inside the circular abode did she pull the blindfold off and set it aside on a table.

****

"Where are we?" Calle murmured as he turned in a full circle, fatigue thick in his voice.

"My home. I live here alone, so no one should bother us. You are safe here."

He pulled aside a curtain to stare out, his gaze roaming across tall trees, towering lookouts, and sparkling ocean. She joined him beside the window in silence. Ever since the arena incident, he'd tried not to think about what had happened. About being eaten by a beast. About using his magic to blow it up from the inside. But now the terror of the ordeal crashed into him at full force.

He needed Skaja. To hold. To put his fears to rest. To feel her solid body against his to know that they were both alive.

Emotion clogged his throat, and he wrapped his arms around her and pulled her into an impassioned kiss. Tears leaked from her eyes. Her chin trembled, but she only latched onto him tighter.

"I thought I lost you," she said when they broke apart. Their foreheads rested together. They breathed the same air. Their hearts beat in perfect sync. "I have never been more devastated in my life."

"I know. I was in a panic, not only because I couldn't breathe, but because I thought they would execute you right then and there." He chuckled wryly. "At this point, I'm pretty much invincible. Nothing can kill me."

She glared at him. "That's not funny."

"It is a little."

Exhaustion buried him like mountains of little rocks, as well as the flare of pain in his shoulder. He pulled her onto the bed with him and tucked her safely inside his arms. "How are your wrists?"

"They'll manage."

He inhaled deeply, savoring her scent. "Every last drop of my magic is depleted. But in the morning, I can heal them."

She shook her head, and her body trembled against him. He kissed her cheek, her neck, her shoulder until the shaking subsided. "I'd rather you heal yourself," she answered, her voice wavering. "And I don't want you to fight tomorrow. Stay in the fortress where you'll be safe."

"Not a chance."

So suddenly, she spun to face him in the bed. Terror leaked from her eyes, and her wings trembled violently. "Calle Everdon, you will stay in the fortress, or I'll tie you up against your will. I can't lose you again. It was terrible enough the first time."

For a long few moments, he remained quiet, searching her eyes to find a barrage of emotions staring back at him. Through their bond, he felt her dread, and also the roots of her love for him growing deeper into fertile soil. He treasured her love like nothing he'd ever treasured before. She had never experienced the blossoming of love. He knew all too well the daily terror of the thought of losing the ones he loved. He could imagine the new realization for her would be quite shocking and nearly unbearable.

He took her hand and kissed the scabbed cuts on her wrist, and then he moved his lips to her palm, to her fingers.

"One day, we can live without this constant fear, Skaja," he whispered in the darkness. "But until tomorrow dawns, we have to push through it. I will not sit by like a coward while others fight in my stead."

"But I'm afraid."

"Me too." He ran his fingers through her soft hair, brought it to his lips, and kissed that too. "We'll get through one hard thing at a time. Together."

She nodded in acceptance and snuggled closer until her head rested beneath his chin. When he wrapped his arms around her, he relished the feeling of finally being the one to protect her. It wasn't in combat. It wasn't her life in his hands. But her heart.

And he would protect it for as long as he lived.

CHAPTER
33

Apparently, riding "just before dawn" meant several hours before. It was more likely they'd arrive "just before dawn" at this rate. Either the valkyries were eager to get this over with, or they were more eager for bloodshed than they let on.

Flying beside a couple dozen valkyries was one of the most exhilarating—and terrifying—things Calle had ever done. After an hour of flying, Inari finally pulled his blindfold off. The sight of armed valkyries riding on winged beasts with sharp teeth and menacing claws caused his blood to curdle.

He glanced over at Paula, who flew at the head of the group. She sat straight and focused on her griffin, commanding the skies like a queen. He resisted the urge to remind her to spare his soldiers. Although he feared that once in battle, the valkyries would blindly attack anyone in their way, he chose to put trust in Paula to command her sisters.

It was a terrible idea.

The griffins flew in a triangular formation, the shape perfectly balanced. Large wings beat quietly in the indigo sky. Feathers and fur rustled delicately in the breeze.

Calle's heart jumped as he stole a glance at Skaja, who flew near the end of the formation as if given a lower rank in the sisterhood after all her unvalkyrie-like blunders. She wore feathers in her braided hair. Her daggers lay in their sheaths at her shoulders. Intricate armor covered her torso and plated skirt. Bands of metal circled her upper arms and wrists, and her purple valkyrie tattoo stood out on her shoulder, which only added to her fierce appearance.

She was the most alluring woman he'd ever known.

The flight continued to pass in silence until his heart gave a start at the large silhouette in the distance. The Heulwen castle. It appeared like a little, dark gold speck, with smaller dark silver and golden specks surrounding it.

His heart beat with panic. "We left too early," he called to Paula, whose shoulder twitched when she definitely heard him, but ignored him, nonetheless. "I won't have my magic to aid me."

When the valkyrie leader continued to pay him no heed, he reached for the griffin's reins, but Inari moved them away. "Paula," he tried again, but she interrupted him.

"There is no mistake, princeling," Paula called to him, though she continued to stare forward. "I know many within Heulwen's borders are capable of magic, and I also know the sun gives you power. You are more at a disadvantage if you fight with the sun at your back. You are but one man. When your enemies are cut off from their supply as well, you are all on equal footing."

Calle rubbed his temples and took a deep breath of frustration at this newest obstacle. Paula was smarter than he'd given her credit for, but to fight without his magic? None at all? He was as dry as a well in the middle of a desert.

She continued, "My valkyries have all been trained to fight in the dark, which gives *us* the advantage."

He nodded. "Thank you. I will never forget this."

Although no reply came, her shoulder twitched in acknowledgement. Valkyries would be friends of Heulwen for at least as long as he lived.

As the silhouette drew nearer, Paula said, "Heulwen soldiers will *never* find their way to our home again. Do we understand each other?"

"You have my word."

"The word from a man means next to nothing, but I will accept it nonetheless."

Anticipation leaped through the breeze like a living, breathing creature. A spark of excitement and trepidation fueled him, but it came directly from Skaja. She was enjoying the promise of a good fight more than she would likely admit to his face.

"Get ready, sisters," Paula said, nodding to the flicker of fire on one of the walls. "They've spotted us. Remember, we fight for our home. We fight for our fallen sister, Catarina. But today, we do not fight to obliterate. Kill Prince Calle's enemies, and no one else."

Valkyrie war cries shook the skies, and if Calle hadn't been on this side of the roar, he might have soiled himself.

Arrows flew in their direction, and he flinched as one whizzed right past his face. But still, they flew fast and straight until the griffins landed on the nearest castle wall with a *crash*.

Griffin screeches snuffed out all other sounds, even the fearful cries of soldiers who dropped their weapons and ducked for cover. Several even fainted. The fight continued at the northern wall, but at a much smaller scale than before. His soldiers appeared exhausted and barely hanging on while Liam's soldiers switched out when they tired. Both men and women cheered at the arrival of the valkyries.

Inari turned the griffin to give the soldiers below a good view of Calle. He didn't hesitate. "This is your last chance!" he called over the din of screeching and terror. "Join me or get cut down by an army of valkyries. All previous trespasses will be forgiven. Otherwise, you will either surrender or die."

Some threw down their weapons and ran. Many others switched sides. Somewhere near the castle, someone released a frustrated cry full of rage and vengeance. He turned his head to find his brother outfitted in armor, surrounded by a wall of harpies and loyal soldiers. Among them was Avonia.

His heart skittered like ice shattering across stone. Those harpies were bound by their oaths. Trapped. They had no choice but to protect their sovereign king.

He gave one last request to the valkyries, "Kill none of the harpies. They have no choice but to protect Liam. Only stall them long enough for this to end."

Valkyries yipped in excitement moments before the griffins leaped from their perches. Calle's stomach dipped at the sudden drop, but he held tight with one hand clutching the griffin and the other drawing his sword.

The thunder of weapon against weapon boomed across the battlefield. Valkyries moved with terrifying speed and nimbleness. Calle's eyes found it difficult to keep up in the darkness, so where they moved, he moved. Which, in this case, he followed Inari as she jumped off her mount.

Panic pricked at his side when feathers and claws and tails flew over his head. He all too easily lost sight of Skaja.

He took a deep breath and followed behind Inari, striking and parrying and cutting down the enemy. Time dragged as his fatigued muscles and aching shoulder slowed him down. In the chaos, he fell too far behind and lost sight of Inari too, forcing him to forge his own path.

It's almost over, he encouraged himself and stumbled through the pain and exhaustion. *Just a little longer.*

Up ahead, valkyries engaged the harpies in combat. Weapon clashed against weapon. Shield against shield. They matched each other in strength, skill, and agility. If he didn't act now, someone was bound to get killed.

When a path broke to his brother, he raced through before the waves of soldiers crashed down on him. He didn't think. He acted.

Liam spun around in surprise and blocked his attack with his sword. The clash vibrated through his arms and rattled his skull. He clenched his teeth against the rocking tremor, forcing himself to move when his brother struck out again and again.

In his fatigued state, he struggled to keep up with Liam. His brother was faster, stronger, more ruthless and cunning, and Calle was without his magic.

"Not so brave now when the sun is down," Liam laughed as he lashed out with his foot. Calle moved too slow to dodge the attack as his brother's armored boot smashed into his ribs and sent him flying backward onto the cobblestone.

His back struck the rough ground, and a piercing pain shot through his injured shoulder. Without giving him a moment to recuperate, Liam charged with his sword. Calle barely managed to roll out of the way and staggered to his feet. Pain and fatigue pressed heavy on him, and he knew he would lose the fight if it dragged on for much longer. He needed to end this. Now.

He pooled his focus with every last bit of energy he possessed. He watched the way Liam moved, the way he attacked, the way he dodged. Every single spar with Skaja came to mind, and each piece of advice she'd given him.

He ducked beneath Liam's swing. He side-stepped a jab. And when his brother struck again, Calle watched and listened and anticipated.

In an agile move, he rolled beneath the girth of Liam's sword, sliced him across the back of his unarmored knees, and rotated onto his feet as Liam fell and crashed to the ground.

Calle pulled back his arm with the intent to stab Liam through the throat and end the battle.

But he paused.

The tip of his sword hovered over his brother's throat, and instead of seeing the cruel, menacing monarch who had unfairly subjected him to slavery for six long years...he saw his brother. The one who had climbed trees with him as a child. The one who had shown him how to ride a horse for the first time. The one who had teased him and read books with him at night when their parents had thought them to be asleep.

His grip on his sword slackened as the roar of rage faded in his ears.

In some strange, twisted way, he loved his brother. He forgave him for everything he'd done to him, for every second of agony and loneliness he'd suffered through.

He could not take the kingdom from Liam. Not like this. He would never be able to forgive himself.

In his hesitation, he hadn't noticed Liam reaching for his weapon until it was too late. The flash of silver caught the torchlight, and Calle cried out as he squeezed his eyes shut and flinched away.

Clang!

The sound crashed right next to his ear, and he opened his eyes to find Skaja's dagger crossed with Liam's sword. But one look at her wings had Liam smiling a twisted, evil smirk. Despite his bleeding legs, he staggered to his feet.

Calle froze. Not just because he couldn't kill his own brother, but because Skaja stared at Liam as if in his thrall.

Her arms shook, the blade of her dagger clattering against the metal of his weapon.

Liam's words sent a chill racing down his spine. "A blood oath runs deeper than you understand, Calle." His gaze never left Skaja's. "Scarlett Svera. My life is at risk. You must kill the man who threatens to end it."

Her entire body shook now, and he couldn't help but step back in shock as he glanced between the two of them.

"No," she rasped. Blood leaked out her nose, her mouth, and a trickle from her ears, as if the very defiance from Liam's order was killing her.

"Stop!" Calle shouted over the battle around him. He rushed forward to stop him, but Liam lifted his sword until it sat on Skaja's shoulder, right beside her neck. He didn't dare take another step, let alone move a muscle.

Liam turned his wicked grin in his direction. "You are a fool to have released her from her oath to you. Did you not even stop to consider she still has allegiance to *me*? If she keeps fighting me, she will die."

Not again. I beg you. Please spare her.

But the higher powers must have been laughing in his face because Liam moved his weapon closer until the blade cut into her skin the slightest bit. She didn't move. Perhaps she *couldn't* move.

"Please," he whispered, eyes wide.

With his continued smirk, Liam said, "What will kill her faster? Her defiance? Or my blade?"

Calle threw down his sword, even as his chest heaved with agony. The weapon clattered against the cobblestone with an air of finality. "You may take my life instead, Liam. That's what you've wanted all along."

"Call off your valkyries, and then I will give you a swift execution. If you don't give me any trouble, I will make sure Scarlett's head doesn't fill the same basket."

Skaja's body trembled even more violently than before as she fought his command. Her own blood soaked her clothing. Color drained from her face. Her eyes begged him to finish Liam no matter what happened to her.

In no life would he take that risk.

He started to raise his hand to give the signal for a ceasefire. But before he managed the feat, an arrow whizzed inches past his ear and embedded itself in Liam's forehead.

Shock slowed time as Liam fell backward, taking his weapon with him. The moment he hit the ground in a deafening crash of armor, silence followed. Harpies stopped fighting. Soldiers stared in confusion. And dawn drew back the curtains, allowing the sunlight to introduce the start of a new day.

Calle inhaled a breath of sunlight and snapped his attention to the one who had fired the arrow. Paula sat on top of her griffin, her expression grave as she lowered her now-empty bow.

People began moving again, murmuring words and sheathing weapons when no longer obligated to fight through Liam's blood oath. Calle rushed toward Skaja and cradled her face in his hands. He gently turned her head one way, and then the other. The bleeding had stopped, and the cut on her neck was shallow.

"Are you all right?" he whispered as he leaned slowly toward her until their foreheads rested together.

She nodded. "You didn't kill him."

He squeezed his eyes shut and shuddered. "No. I'm sorry. I should have."

"I'm glad you didn't."

But then she moved so quickly, he struggled to follow her movements as she stepped in front of him and stood in a defensive stance, both daggers drawn. The harpies who had rushed toward them stopped hesitantly at the sight of her. Liam lay lifeless on the ground, and with it, his hold on the harpies had died with him.

They answered to him now.

"Forgive us," one of them said as she dropped to her knee, followed by the others. They bowed their heads in submission. "We owe you a great debt. We are at your mercy, Your Highness."

Hurt and anger bled through his veins. These very same harpies had helped Liam send him to the Pits. Whether or not under oath, they had doomed him to great suffering for six miserable years.

But without it, he wouldn't have met Skaja. He wouldn't have changed what happened for the world.

"I will deal with the lot of you later," he said in as commanding of a tone as he could muster after the painful ordeal with the garguaran, a long ride to Heulwen, and very little sleep. "Except you, Avonia. Rise and come with me."

Avonia followed closely at his side, and Typheal quickly caught up from his position at the steps.

Calle gripped Skaja's hand tightly, pouring every flicker of love and gratitude through their bond until her knees nearly buckled and a sheen of moisture lined her eyes. But it was the only thing he could do before he released her and took charge like the king he was never supposed to be.

He commanded his soldiers to take the weapons from the losing side. The dungeon was going to be filled to the brim for a few days. Perhaps even a few weeks. At least until he gave everyone a fair trial. And when more sunlight bathed the battlefield in the warm caress of renewal, the world had bowed for a few moments to peace.

Finally, he approached Paula where she tended to her griffin and gave a bow of his own. "Thank you. I am in your debt."

The valkyrie leader shook her head and regarded him with a curious stare. "I was in Skaja's debt, and that debt has been repaid. I will hold you to your promise, princeling. I expect not to be bothered anymore."

"Like I said, you have my word."

Paula's mouth twitched in amusement moments before she mounted her griffin and raised her hand in the air. The beast leaped into the skies, and one by one, valkyries followed, leaving hardly a remnant of themselves behind other than the deaths they had dealt on the battlefield.

Slowly, Skaja approached with a look of regret in her eyes, and the look alone punched a hole through his stomach. Heartache quickly filled the hole as she pulled one of her daggers free from its holster. Her heartache echoed back at him when she gazed into his eyes for only seconds, but the goodbye in them shattered the control in his knees. They began shaking, but by some miracle, he remained standing.

Without a word, she tucked the dagger into his belt before flying after her sisters. His gaze followed her long after she rejoined them in the skies.

"Why is she leaving?" Typheal murmured, his gaze following his daughter as well, his expression stricken with grief. "She's supposed to stay."

Despite his aching heart, Calle smiled as he pulled the dagger from his belt and inspected it beneath the sunlight. "This is her way of saying she'll be back soon."

Surprisingly, Avonia laughed and shook her head bemusedly. "She really is awkward with men."

His smile grew wider. "And I love her for it."

She turned to him and squeezed his shoulder. "Thank you from the bottom of our hearts for bringing her home."

The heat in his heart softened to a sweet, loving warmth as he returned his gaze to the small specks in the sky. "She was the one who brought *me* home."

CHAPTER
34

A light wind whispered across Skaja's wings as she landed on the castle wall and crouched low in the shadows. Long stretches of clouds blocked out the moonlight, and she took advantage to creep along the wall on silent feet. One flicker of moonlight on her feathers would cause them to shimmer like large crystals of snow in the dead of night and give away her position.

Two guards walked along the parapet, the orange and yellow flames flickering from their torches as they strode in the opposite direction.

She pulled the hood of her cloak more securely around her head as she crouched low and followed the parapet around the castle until she spotted torchlight flickering within the castle walls. Her dagger warmed her hand, eager to reunite with its pair after three long months of being away.

The flashing firelight against the stone walls up ahead alerted her to someone's approach. Quickly, she ducked into a stairwell and descended slowly enough for her footsteps to make nary a sound.

Mere seconds rested between the two parties on this side of the wall, so she held her breath and glided across the courtyard, heaved herself onto a windowsill with the shutters open, and slipped inside the castle.

Only to find herself in a large, empty corridor.

Judging by the faint scent of lingering candlelight, someone had passed through recently.

The dagger in her hand grew warmer against her skin as she kept to the shadows. Months ago, she had memorized the layout of the castle, but her eyebrows still furrowed when she couldn't remember if the right hallway led to the dining quarters or the throne room.

So instead, she allowed the dagger to guide her.

Two courtiers dressed in fine clothing alerted her to their presence with their loud laughter and noisy footsteps. She tucked herself smaller between a table against the wall and drapes brushing the floor. They passed right on by, not noticing her in the shadows.

The hilt of her weapon grew even warmer, which signaled the close proximity to its pair. But when she glanced around the corner, she cursed her luck. Two harpies stood guard at one door, while another two harpies guarded a door just around the corner.

Calle must be inside.

Her blood stirred excitedly, with a hint of nervousness, but she forced it to calm when she had no doubt he could feel every emotion passing through their bond.

For a moment, she listened to their bond without alerting him to her presence. Weariness. Pain. Loneliness.

She frowned. He was not as happy as she had expected him to be now that he had gained the throne. Liam's death must have been hard on him, and she knew how much she had hurt him after leaving without a word.

Not wanting to dwell on it for long, she spotted a servant heading down another hallway and followed her as silently as possible. The woman slipped into what appeared to be a servants' passageway.

Naturally, Skaja followed.

But instead of stalking the woman through the narrow maze within the heart of the castle, she followed the dagger's silent instruction until she stopped in front of a door. It was unguarded.

Too easy? Or was this door usually unguarded?

As quietly as possible, she opened the door, slipped inside the room, and closed it behind her. The magnificence of the large room stole the breath from her lungs. Ceilings stretched high in an array of different shades of gold. Tapestries hung on the walls from floor to ceiling, depicting anything from gentle woodland scenery to the fury of battle. Pillars of gold lined the room. A table of gold and silver stretched across the area, and at the very head of the table buried in a pile of papers?

Her heart stuttered moments before it exploded with immense happiness.

Calle sat alone at the table, his appearance changed since she'd last seen him. Instead of shabby borrowed clothes, he wore fine clothing befitting a king. His dark blue tunic dipped low enough for her to catch a glimpse of the top of his chest, covered in a green-blue silky vest. His sleeves were rolled up to his elbows, and his brown pants were tucked into black boots, her dagger sheathed at his belt. He'd gained more muscle, but everything else remained the same. His auburn hair with plaits on either side of his face. His warm amber eyes. His sweet mouth ready for a smile at any moment.

However, it didn't smile. Instead, he lifted a hand to his heart and rubbed his chest as if an ache lived there.

And suddenly she realized he'd felt her joy moments before.

And she felt how much he missed her.

Impatience got the best of her as she glanced around the large room. No guards in sight. She crept up behind him on silent feet until she stood behind his chair. Her heart thrummed faster and faster, and if it beat any quicker, she feared it would give away her ruse and he'd turn around to find her.

"You should take more care," she murmured in his ear, causing him to shriek and jump a foot in the air. She grinned and continued, "Otherwise, a valkyrie could sneak in and assassinate you."

Now on her feet, their gazes locked, and she felt a range of emotions flood through their bond. Shock. Disbelief.

Happiness. Relief. Her own emotions reflected his as the amber in his eyes captivated her, and just the sight of him caused her heart to tumble with overbearing joy.

"Skaja," he gasped moments before his hands reached for her and pulled her into a tight embrace. Two harpies opened the door on the other side of the room, concerned expressions, but they quickly shut the door again to give them privacy.

She clutched onto the back of his shirt as if even the faintest of breezes could snatch him away. "By the towers of oblivion," she sobbed into his chest. "I missed you so much."

His body trembled against her, his tongue seeming to find difficulty forming words. Instead of a reply, he held her even tighter against him, his fingers pulling off the hood of her cloak and tangling in her hair.

"Why were you gone so long?" he finally asked, though his voice trembled in sync with his body.

She rested her head against his solid chest and listened to his heartbeat within. It beat in sync with hers, filled with love, hope, and immense relief.

"Valkyries are honorable. It's why we don't run even from our deaths." She pulled away, enough to look into his eyes but not enough to break free from the comfort of his arms. "I broke at least a dozen valkyrie rules. I returned for my punishment."

He stiffened against her, and slowly, his eyes widened as he looked her over. "What did they do to you?"

"Nothing I expected. My tongue is still intact. They didn't take my wings. And strangely enough, they didn't banish me.

I'm free to come and go as I please as long as I never bring another man to the island."

"Then what happened? What was your punishment?"

"Cleaning. It was dreadful. I reeked of garguaran guts for weeks, and then I nearly sneezed my brains out as I washed the towers. It took me months to finish it all."

A sigh escaped her as she finally broke away from him and sat on top of the table, her hands braced behind her, both legs crossed. New purple tattoos peeked out from beneath her long brown boots, and Calle's careful gaze didn't miss them.

He captured one of her boots in his hands and slowly slid it off her foot to reveal swirls of silvery purple ink covering the ribbons of scars on her legs. Heat blossomed on her skin as his hand slid from her ankle to the back of her knee.

"These tattoos are new," he croaked, reiterating the words she'd said to him upon first discovering the golden tattoos on his back.

"I was ashamed of my scars before because they showed my weakness. You have taught me to accept and honor them."

"Who gave them to you?"

She knew why he asked. They were Heulwen tattoos. "A friend of Cian's. A female elder who lives on the edge of the city. I fully expected black. But…this purple is beautiful."

"Yes, it is," he murmured. His finger traced the swirling pattern all the way back down to her ankle. And when he gently lowered her leg, he leaned closer until both palms lay flat on the table beside hers. He hovered over her, his lips a breath away from hers. "Marry me, Skaja."

Heat burst like a bubble inside her, which rippled outward to every inch of her body as if the smooth, glassy surface of her emotions were disturbed in the most beautiful way. His eyes blazed with a passionate intensity, a determination that told her he'd never give up if she refused him.

Overly aware of her bright red cheeks, she murmured, "There have only been a handful of times in my life where I imagined what it must be like for someone to propose to me, and most of those times were in the past three months. Not a single one of those fantasies included me sitting on a table with one boot on the floor."

Finally, his mouth twitched in amusement, but he didn't give an inch. Neither did she. "Our relationship has been strange from the start. Can't start putting it into a perfect box now."

She noticed one of his hands hovering the slightest bit off the table, and she couldn't help but grin when she realized he was preparing himself in case she tried to slap him.

"Would I become Queen?" she asked, trying hard to hide her trepidation. But she knew he sensed it in their bond.

"Yes."

"Would our children be Sun Fae or harpies?"

His throat bobbed up and down as he swallowed. "I don't know."

"Will my freedom be stripped away?"

Now, the very tips of his fingers brushed hers like a careful whisper. "Never."

Despite having had the last three months to prepare for this moment, she found it much more terrifying to take the leap than she expected. But she knew she would take a hundred leaps to be with Calle. No matter what responsibilities she must shoulder. No matter what she must give up. She knew what she wanted.

Her hands softly trailed up his arms, to his shoulders, until she ensnared him in her embrace. "I will take that leap with you, even if you are too heavy for me to carry."

A relieved exhale escaped his mouth moments before his lips captured hers. She returned his kiss with equal fervor as the distance of the past several months snapped them back together.

They broke the kiss to press their foreheads together. Sweet, warm happiness beat in sync between them, and she knew this was what she wanted for as long as she lived. Calle by her side. Always. No matter what.

"I want my dagger back," she said suddenly as she leaned back a few inches and held out her hand.

He didn't return it to her. "How else would you find me if we are separated?"

She laughed and slipped it out of his belt despite his reluctance. "I will always find you, with or without it."

"Then in that case..." He shrugged one shoulder. "I suppose I can part with it."

A wide smile broke out on his face, and the sight of it melted her to the core. This man had changed her so completely. She owed everything to him. Absolutely everything. And she refused to take a single moment for granted.

Gazing into his amber eyes, she whispered one last time, "Always."

ABOUT THE AUTHOR

Sydney Winward is a fantasy and paranormal romance author who dabbles in the occasional historical fiction. She loves building complex worlds filled with magic, strong characters, and emotional stories that can make you laugh and cry.

Sydney is the author of the Sunlight and Shadows Series and the best-selling Bloodborn Series, and when she's not writing, she's reading, thinking about stories, or going on adventures with her children. She lives in Utah with her husband and three amazing kids.

www.sydneywinward.com